BLACK MAGICK & ENVY

ROBERT SANBORN

BLACK MAGICK & ENVY

ROBERT SANBORN

YUCI
books

BY ROBERT SANBORN

League of the Moon

In Your Dreams

The Red Witch

Blood, Magic & Mercy

Black Magick & Envy

Soul of the Witch

This one is for my two Dads, Robert Sanborn Senior and Martin Crombie. Two very special guys who make up parts of the whole that is lil' ole me.

And also to my sister, Colleen. Keep up the fight! We love you!

Vinci Books

vinci-books.com

Published by Vinci Books Ltd in 2025

1

The publisher and the author have made every effort to obtain permissions
for any third party material used in this book and to comply with copyright
law. Any queries in this respect should be brought to the attention of the
publisher and any omissions will be corrected in future editions.
A CIP catalogue record for this book is available from the British Library.
Paperback ISBN: 9781036705459

"A heart at peace gives life to the body, but envy rots the bones."

— Proverbs 14:30

CHAPTER 1
JO IN THE SNOW

Snow. Already. It was only November ninth, and it had been sixty-five degrees the day before, but leave it to New England to serve up a semi-blizzard the next day.

Joanne closed the Cracked Cauldron coffee shop early. No sense keeping the place open when most everyone was hunkered down at home. In short order, she would regret that decision.

Normally, on a day like this, Henry would wait out front with her orange Jeep. Not tonight. Henry's dad hurt his back, so he'd packed up the Jeep and Delilah and headed for Portland, Maine. Jo insisted he take the four-wheel-drive for the trip. The storm started by the time he left, but once he crossed into New Hampshire it was supposed to pick up steam.

She closed the door, locked it, and pulled the collar of her navy peacoat up around her neck, then stepped into the storm.

"Not much of a storm *here*," she complained to the empty street.

Fat flakes seesawed toward the ground like feathers loosed from a giant Snow Owl. Jo turned her head toward the sky, stuck out her tongue, and caught one of them.

"Mmm," she cooed.

She loved the snow. Ever since she was a little girl, it never failed to enchant her. It didn't matter where she lived, what family she was currently a part of, or how bad the circumstances at the time were, snow equaled refuge.

Anything which helped evade the endless parade of pervert foster dads was a refuge. But there was something about being outside when it snowed that made things seem better.

Maybe it was the quiet peace of it. Snow shaved the rough edges from the harsh city sounds. As if God decided enough was enough, and it was time for some peace and quiet.

She felt cozy being bundled up as it fell all around—her own private little snow globe. Just her, the snow, and the crunch under her feet. It soothed her soul. When she was outside and the flakes fell slowly, like tonight, she would pick one out and follow it all the way to the ground. There was nothing to think about. Nothing to worry about. Just follow that one little, crystallized pillow of frozen water until it became one with the others. Rinse and repeat. The world disappeared for a while. That was good. Sometimes, there was *nothing* better.

From a very young age, Jo discovered making the world go away—if just for a little while—allowed you to come back to it. It wasn't always a place she *wanted* to come back to, but getting away from it—escaping into the snow—

always brought her back a little bit stronger, a little bit wiser, and a lot more centered. It helped her deal with the crazies.

At least, it did until she'd found booze and drugs. When that happened, at least in the beginning, it snowed *every day*.

She made her way through the hush to the end of Essex Street. A lonely plow scraped the quiet from the street in front of her, then turned the corner and gave it slowly back. With peace restored, Jo made her way toward the Salem Common. The sight of the wrought-iron gates brought her another level of comfort. Her heart hummed with satisfaction as she stepped through the entrance and into the empty park. It was just her, the snow, the soft yellow lamps dotting the Common, and blessed silence.

Puffy flakes floated across shafts of golden lamplight. They reminded her of potato chips, and she said, "Betcha can't eat just one!" She laughed at her own joke and it echoed from somewhere in the vast park.

That was odd. Not only was there nothing for her voice to echo *from* in the huge and empty park, but the echo sounded nothing like her own voice. What returned sounded deep, dangerous... and male.

Jo stood still, listening. Her cherished silence tainted by fear and unease. She strained to hear... something. Anything. What moments ago was a blissfully silent and peaceful walk in the park had turned sour. Echoes of Armand Moreland's warning from the last time they'd gotten together at Wanda's Wicca'd Emporium played on a loop in her mind.

"Watch your back," he'd said. "Keep your guard up."

He had warned them that the children of the void would come back for them. She felt the hair on her neck stand up. The park appeared empty, but she knew they were near.

Jo looked around, seeking a way to even the odds. A place

she could give herself a fighting chance. She spied the gazebo in the middle of the park and sprinted for it.

It was fifty yards away and to her right. The first of them sprang from the dark, as if pulled from the blackness between snowflakes. It stood directly in Jo's path to the gazebo. Another warning from Armand flashed through her mind, although it wasn't as much of a warning as it was permission to act. He'd told everyone in the League of the Moon to defend themselves, "By any means necessary."

Bad news for whoever this shit bag was, or *used* to be. Jo never broke stride. She ran full tilt toward the entity as it raised both hands in her direction. Anticipating a magical attack, she beat the creepy bastard to it. Green fire exploded from her upturned palm, knocking the hulking entity flat on its back. It struggled to regain its footing and slipped in the snow. It would never get a chance to make another mistake.

Jo still carried the enchanted hunting knife she'd claimed from the demon Chesrule. She whipped it from the pocket of her peacoat, slid to a stop next to the massive entity, and drove it straight through its neck. A blinding flash of light, a wail of pain and frustration, and the entity was gone—sent to the nothingness from which it came.

As if ignited by the loss, five more entities apparated in the spot where the first perished. The initial attack slowed her, but she was quickly back at full speed. She sprinted toward the gazebo, sensing her only chance to defeat the odds was claiming the higher ground. Her arms and legs pumped in furious rhythm. Vaporous breath trailed her, pistoning from her mouth like steam from a train. The knife glinted gold in the lamplight, keeping time with her breath. She took the stairs two at a time, making it to the top in less than two seconds. Once there, she stood in the middle, knife out, readied for battle.

The gazebo had two sets of stairs, six steps to a side, and were wide enough to accommodate multiple tourists. If her enemies were smart, they'd come at her from both sides. Jo knew hoping for them to come at her all at once, and from one side, was wishful thinking.

They seemed to read her mind, pulling up short. Three split from the group and rounded the gazebo, taking position on the opposite side. Jo stood calmly in the middle, twirling the knife slowly in her hand. She turned toward the group of three. Her green eyes bathed the gazebo in emerald light. With the knife in her left hand, she beckoned them with her right. "Come get some."

At first, the entities seemed tentative in the face of such boldness from the witch with the green eyes. Then, they found courage. The first screamed with rage and charged Joanne. Exactly what she wanted.

Of course, the one that broke from the pack first was the biggest, but also proved to be the dumbest. It charged head down, like a bull. Jo dodged its attack, brought the knife down as it passed, and watched as he burst into pieces and then disappeared in a flash of light.

One down.

The others learned quickly from the mistake of their gung-ho counterpart. Jo looked from the couple on her left to the pair at her right. They were coordinating. *Telepathically*. They moved as one, taking each step on either side of the gazebo at the same time. She knew if she let them onto the platform all at once, she was a goner.

The pair on her knife side would have to die first. It was simple math, when you came right down to it. If she attacked first from that side, she'd probably save herself about a half-second. In a fight like this, it was an eternity. From decision to execution, less than a second passed. Her aim was true. The knife cleaved the head of the blackened shape of what used to be a man—*and was God knew what* now, Jo thought—turning it to dust after a blinding flash of light. The entity beside it froze in fear, and the bolt of green Jo shot from her hands sent it hurtling toward oblivion before it knew what happened.

Three down.

Jo never turned to watch the remaining pair. She leapt from the gazebo, flew over the steps to the snow-covered grass, dropped, and rolled until she reached the knife, popping up with it thrust forward. The entities were on her fast.

As Jo raised the knife, the one in the lead swiped at her arm, knocking it from her grasp. It flew high in the air, then tumbled through the night. Golden light from the Common lamps winked off the bright steel as it landed, point first, on the lawn. Jo made a move for it, but the second entity flanked her and kicked the legs out from under her. Jo landed hard on her back, the wind knocked from her lungs. The dark mass who'd knocked the knife from her hand was on her in a flash, and the one who'd swept her legs now lay across them, pinning her at the knees.

The entity straddled her stomach and stilled her arms with its knees. It leaned forward, placing the black mass of its face directly on Joanne's. Its breath was ice cold, its lips colder. They clamped over Jo's, and as it drank her life force, everything that made her who she was flashed before her eyes.

Jo tried to scream, tried to fight, but could only watch,

helpless. Images of Henry and Delilah floated in midair, and were swallowed into the black mass pinning her down. They purred like lions at a kill, and it sickened her.

Memories, and the emotions attached to them, flowed from Joanne and into the children of the void. Tears fell from her eyes as the fullness of her soul was ripped from her body, and the essence of who she was drained into them, bit by bit.

Henry, Delilah, Wanda, Archie, Mercy. As their images hung in the air between her and the dark mass, Jo realized, to her horror, she was forgetting their names. Henry was now the handsome guy—familiar, but nothing more. What a cute child. What was her name? I know that tiny woman in the purple cloak, or do I? Who's that guy with the ponytail and the hat?

"Have you found it?" hissed the entity pinning her knees.

The dark mass on Jo's chest peeled its lips from her and hissed its reply. "Yesssss. They will be pleased."

Jo felt everything slipping away. All she was and all she'd been, in this life and others, and all she would ever be, was being devoured. There was nothing she could do to stop it. The children of the void had claimed the reward promised by the Red Witch.

Only one face remained with a name attached to it. But *that* was weird, because that face didn't hang in the air before her, like the hot guy, or the cute child, or the little woman in the purple cloak. It was *behind* the entity, hovering over it. Armand Moreland stood above them all, knife in hand, raised and ready.

What was his name again?

The well-dressed man slashed down brutally with the knife, killing the entity on her chest. Something flashed brightly in the air a few feet above her face. Before the entity pinning her legs could reach it, Armand Moreland opened his mouth and swallowed it down. Then the vampire whirled and executed the last of her enemies.

The darkness vanished. The pain of memories lost fled. Names she couldn't come up with moments earlier were back on her lips once again. Then everything went dark.

The next time Joanne opened her eyes, Armand Moreland was reaching a hand toward her. She took it, and he pulled her gently to her feet.

"What are you doing here, GQ?"

"I was about to ask you the same question, Joanne."

Jo was taken aback by his question. Not because it offended her, but because she couldn't remember how she'd gotten to the middle of the Salem Common.

Moreland watched as Jo turned in circles, a look of total confusion on her face.

"It will come back to you. Here, take my arm. Do you remember where you were headed?" asked Moreland.

Jo was still looking around, confused. "I think I was on my way to Mercy's house. At least that rings a bell. For what reason, I don't quite remember."

"Let's keep moving. We'll head to Miss Glass's. Maybe the walk will help. It will come to you. Just be patient."

Jo leaned her head on Moreland's shoulder. Moreland took this as a sign of trust, but also a sign that Jo hadn't quite gotten her memory all the way back. It had only been a month, and her distrust of him hadn't simply vanished. He knew this, but kept his silence. Once she realized fully who he was, and also why she was out here, her head would come off his shoulder soon enough.

They walked onward through the snow, and ever so

slightly, her head came from his shoulder. He was smiling on the outside but felt some regrets. He'd hoped they would become closer. That she would learn to trust him. But it had only been a little over three weeks since everything went down with the Red Witch, and he knew it would take her more time.

Time was something Armand Moreland had in great supply. At least, at the time, it seemed so.

"So, Mr. Moreland. What the hell just happened back there?"

"Ah, good. You're remembering. Well, first off, you were just attacked by no less than six entities from the void. They surrounded you on the gazebo in the middle of the park. You killed four of them straightaway, but the other two got a hold of you. They were claiming your soul. Something promised them by the Red Witch."

Jo pulled her arm free from his.

"Are you serious?"

Moreland raised his right hand. "God as my witness."

Fear ripped through Jo. "Why don't I remember any of it?"

"You will. It might take a day or two, but it will mostly come back to you."

Jo nodded, but a look of skepticism hung on her face.

"I believe you were on the way to Mercy Glass's apartment. At least, that's what you told me. Shall we continue on?"

"I think I can find it on my own, thanks."

"Humor me," said Moreland. "I love a snowy night. Keep me company for a bit."

Jo shrugged. "Suit yourself."

The phantom intimacy of moments ago vanished. The

true state of their relationship resumed. This saddened Moreland, but gave him something to strive for.

They walked on in uncomfortable silence. When they reached the edge of the Common, Jo sucked in a surprised breath.

"What is it?" asked Moreland.

Jo turned to him, shocked. "You just saved my life, didn't you?"

Moreland smiled.

CHAPTER 2

INTERLUDE WITH THE VAMPIRE

"I did," said Moreland. "But you handled yourself admirably. You took out four of them before I ever got close."

Jo wiped at her eyes. "I almost lost everything. I didn't listen to you. I thought nothing of just going out for a stroll by myself."

The rapid return of her memory and the sudden burst of emotion surprised him. He did his best to blunt it. "Flagellating yourself is pointless. We all have to look out for each other now. There's no other way."

Jo nodded, but it didn't make her feel any better. It was more than the realization she'd almost died, almost lost everything that made her a spiritual being inside and out. There was something... missing now. What it was, she couldn't say. Intuition tingled. It was the mental equivalent of running your tongue over the site of a tooth extraction, but forgetting when, or how, the dentist did the deed.

They walked on in silence until tires crunched the snow next to them.

"Kind of a shit night for a stroll, isn't it?" asked Byron Miller.

"Chief Miller! What brings you out on a lovely night like this?" asked Moreland.

"It goes with the territory. Everyone else gets to sit home and sip cocoa. I bring it with me and drive around town. It doesn't *really* suck, though. I just like to bitch."

Byron crawled the Explorer next to Moreland and Jo. She avoided his gaze, which struck him as strange. They'd hit it off since all the shit with the Red Witch had gone down.

"Jo? Everything all right? You don't seem like... you."

"Hi Byron. I'm okay. I just had a bad day at work."

Byron studied her, not buying a word but keeping his powder dry. Jo wasn't the kind of person you pressed for details when she didn't want to talk about something. He filed it away for later.

"Can I give you two a ride?" he asked.

Moreland deferred to Jo.

"I'm okay. Really, Byron. I'm on my way to Mercy's right now. Armand was headed that way and said he'd go with me."

Byron frowned.

Jo knew he didn't buy it, and didn't care.

"Okay. I'm on all night. If either of you need anything from me, just shoot me a text or call."

Jo and Moreland thanked him and watched as he eased the Explorer into the gently falling snow.

When Byron looked in the rear-view mirror, Jo and Moreland passed under a streetlight. Something in the way Jo was walking struck him as odd. As he drove on, he tossed it around in his mind. After a few minutes and a ton of frustration, he let it go. Sometimes thinking about something else entirely could shake an answer loose.

He was lost in thought, never realizing his subconscious mind was guiding him until he tapped the Explorer's brakes. When the SUV came to a stop, he was looking up at the gold lettering of Wanda's Wicca'd Emporium.

HENRY HAD JUST PUT Delilah in her crib. Now it was his dad's turn.

"Mom. Where are the clean sheets?" asked Henry.

"Where they've been for the last thirty years," Jeanne quipped.

Henry smiled. He should have known better. Not much changed in the Trank household. "You're right. What was I thinking? Okay Dad, you ready?"

"Ready as I'll ever b-b-be."

Dominik Trank was a stutterer. He had it mostly under control, but this was a stressful time for him. Stress brought out the stutters.

"Dad, it's not a big deal. Don't freak out over it. Okay?"

Dom nodded. The embarrassment he felt at having to be cared for was written all over his face.

Henry pretended not to notice. He bent at the waist, hoisted Dom on his shoulders, and carried his father up to his bedroom.

"You are one strong sonofabitch."

"Dom, language," yelled Jeanne.

"Dad, you know she has bionic hearing. "

Dom laughed. "You'd think I'd have figured it out by now.

Henry placed him in the chair next to the bed and proceeded to change his bedding.

"How long did they say you'd be out of commission?"

"Oh, about another month. It's mostly muscular. Still hurts like a mothe—"

Henry gave him a look.

Dom smiled. "You saved me that time."

"Someone's gotta save your ass."

"Henry," Jeanne yelled from downstairs, "I can hear you just as well as your father."

"Sorry, Mom."

Henry gave Dom an *'are you kidding me?'* look and whispered, "Her hearing's gotten *better* since I left home."

Dom nodded sadly. "Nothing escapes that woman."

Henry finished with the sheets, put the comforter on the bed, then hoisted Dom on his shoulders and laid him gently down.

"Well, at least you're not changing a diaper for me."

Henry gave him a deadpan expression. "I don't even want to contemplate that."

"That makes two of us."

"Speaking of diapers, I have to see if DeeDee needs a change. I'm gonna head downstairs now. You need anything else?"

"Nah, I'm good. Th-th-th-thanks, Henry."

Henry ignored the stutter. He leaned over and kissed Dom's forehead.

"Good night, Dad."

"G'night Henry."

When Henry got to the bottom of the stairs, Jeanne had the landline phone in her hand.

"Byron Miller is on the line."

Adrenaline shot through Henry's veins. Byron calling him here meant nothing good.

"Do you know what he wants?" asked Henry.

"He didn't say. We just talked about Penny and the grandkids. You'll find out soon enough."

Jeanne handed the phone to him, then gave him his privacy.

"Hi Byron. What's up?'

"Heya Henry. I was out on patrol tonight. Storm duty—"

"Has it let up at all?"

"Not really. But that'll change. Listen. I don't want you to worry, 'cause it's probably nothing."

"Okay..."

"I just left the Salem Common. Jo was out walking with Armand Moreland. I don't think anything is wrong, but she didn't seem herself."

"Okay..." Henry nibbled at his thumb. A habit he'd picked up from Joanne.

"She seemed kinda... off. Is everything alright with her these days. Anything bothering her?"

"Not that I know of. When I left her, right before the storm got bad in Salem, she was in a great mood. Said she was going to get together with Mercy and some of the witches from AA."

"She usually walk there with Moreland?"

"She might, I have no idea. Why?"

"I can't put my finger on it. She just seemed like something was bothering her. Like she wasn't present. I don't know. Maybe being around all you freakin' empaths has got me thinking like you guys now."

"You say that like it's a bad thing."

Byron laughed. "I would have told you it was, not too

15

long ago. I just wanted to give you a heads up. I don't think it's a big deal, just a feeling. Thought you'd like to know."

"Thanks Byron. I'll call her as soon as I hang up with you."

"Okay. Bye then."

Henry killed the connection then walked into the kitchen to put the phone back in its cradle.

"What was that all about?" asked Jeanne.

Henry shrugged. "Beats the hell outta me. Byron said Jo wasn't acting herself."

"Well, if Byron thought it was important enough to call about, it probably has some weight to it."

Henry nodded. "You're right. But that doesn't fill me with joy, if you know what I mean"

"Call her."

Henry pulled the cell from his back pocket. He tapped the number for Jo and she picked up after three rings.

"Hey Jo. What's going on down there?"

Jo sighed. "Did Byron call you?"

"He did."

She let out an exasperated sigh. "That man. I'm okay. There was just a little... incident tonight."

Henry sucked in a breath. "What happened?"

"It was nothing. Just a few of the void boys coming after me..."

He could hear the fear in her voice, and was scared beyond belief when she started to cry. Something that happened maybe once every leap year.

"Jo? What's the matter? Tell me."

There was silence for a few moments. Then, he heard her crying, but it was muted.

Armand Moreland came on the line. "Henry?"

"Armand? What's going on?"

"She doesn't want me to worry you, because you've got enough to worry about up there. I have decided to overrule her. I don't mind telling you I've stepped several feet away from her to tell you this."

Henry smiled, despite the seriousness of the situation. Jo didn't like others deciding how to defend her. And she sure as *shit* didn't like being told what to do. So he understood why Moreland put distance between them.

"Spill it, Armand. What happened?"

"I knew you were going out of town to take care of your father, so I decided to keep tabs on Joanne. I know she wouldn't appreciate me saying that, hence the distance between us now. It was a good thing I did. As much as she wouldn't want me to worry you about what happened, I feel it imperative that you know. She came close to death tonight, Henry. Six of the children of the void attacked her. She killed four of them before they finally overpowered her."

Henry's pulse raced. "What did they do to her?"

Moreland took his time before answering, then said, "They were in the process of extracting her soul from her body. Because I'm a vampire, I could *see* it. Whether she will admit it or not, that is a traumatizing event. She may not be herself for a little while. If there is any way you can come back here, I think it's a good idea. She needs you. And I think it best we all meet at Wanda's as soon as you get back."

"Where are you headed?'

"I'm escorting her to Mercy Glass's apartment on Witch Hill Road. I think she'll be safest in the company of witches."

"Okay. I'm leaving tomorrow morning. I'll have my cousin come here and take care of Dad."

"That sounds like a capital idea, Henry."

"And Armand?"

"Yes?"

"Thank you."

"You're welcome, my friend. See you soon."

When Henry hung up, Jeanne was standing in the kitchen entranceway, the landline phone in her hand.

"Mom, I have—"

"Leave right now, Henry. I already called your cousin. He agreed to come up and help with Dom. And don't worry about Delilah. I'll take care of her until you get back."

Henry shook his head. "You're amazing. You did all that while I was on the phone?"

Jeanne smiled. "Go take care of your wife, honey."

CHAPTER 3
WITCH, COP & CASKET

Instead of heading home in the storm, Wanda closed the Emporium early. She'd put on a pot of herbal tea shortly after. As she walked back from her safe room, steaming mug of tea in hand, she doused the lights. Wanda placed the mug on a shelf near the picture window overlooking the snowy street, then pulled the chair from behind the register and placed it next to the shelf.

She thought nothing so peaceful as watching snow fall from the safety and comfort of a warm room with the lights out. Contentment stole over her like a heated blanket, settling her nerves and calming her soul.

Wanda had the same ritual as Joanne. She would pick out a snowflake from the gently falling crowd, and then follow its journey earthward—a meditation in white.

The gentle cascade lulled her into a light doze, only to be startled awake by a soft rap at the front door. She leaned forward to glimpse the enclosed landing of the shop's entranceway. Byron Miller's police issue Ford Explorer idled at the curb, its exhaust trailing lazily upward. Byron, ever the vigilant public servant, faced the street. His eyes bounced from one storefront to the next. He turned only when Wanda finally opened the door and let him in.

"Byron! What are you doing here tonight, sweetie?"

"Hi Wanda. Just wanted to check on things. I went by your apartment earlier. Didn't see any lights. I figured you'd be here."

Wanda nodded, but his tone suggested more than a wellness check. She told him so.

"Nothing gets by you, does it?" asked Byron.

She smiled and shrugged. "Not really, honey. Now, what's on your mind?"

Byron ran his hand the length of his face. Wanda recognized the telltale sign he had something uncomfortable to discuss.

"I just saw Jo and Armand Moreland over at the Common. I got the feeling something was wrong with Jo. And—"

"She wouldn't tell you a thing, right?"

He looked surprised. "Right. See? This is what I'm talking about! How do you *know* stuff like that?"

"Well... you do that face rubbing thingy when you're nervous. Then you mentioned Jo. It's not magic or rocket science. What happened?"

"That's just it. She wouldn't tell me. And I think Moreland was scared to say anything. I was hoping you could find out."

Byron's concern for Jo touched her. Ever since the two had met, they'd hit it off. It was a father-daughter kind of thing with a healthy measure of ball busting thrown in. Wanda got a kick out of it. She was thrilled someone as good and decent as Byron felt like he did towards Joanne. God knew there'd been enough creeps in *that* role in Jo's life.

"Did you call Henry?" asked Wanda.

"Yep. Said he's coming back in the morning. I just thought you should know. Especially after what Armand said about those void fucksticks."

Wanda, much like everyone else, had let her guard down a little when it came to Armand's warning. It wasn't intentional, just a biproduct of lapsed time and diminishing urgency. She was silently kicking herself in the ass for that now.

"Don't beat yourself up over it, Wanda. None of us has been exactly on top of our game when it comes to Moreland's warning."

Now it was Wanda's turn to be surprised.

"What's that wife of yours been teaching you?" she asked, smiling.

Though dark in the shop, Wanda saw the shift in his aura. Pinkish-red embarrassment crept into his colors.

Byron shuffled his feet and looked at the floor. "Oh, you know. Some meditation stuff. And she does that Reiki thingamajiggie for me after work a couple times a week."

Wanda crossed her arms and smiled. An *'oh really?'* look lit her face.

"What?" asked Byron.

"Nothing, sweetie. It's just nice to see you've changed your tune on," Wanda made quote fingers, "all this mumbo-jumbo."

Byron shrugged. "Well, after these last couple months it's kinda hard to deny it. So, I figure I better protect myself any way I can. You know?"

"I do. It's nothing to be embarrassed about either,

sweetie. Most people don't take it seriously enough to change—or even *try* to change. But, whether they admit it or not, the spiritual side of life is real. It makes me a little bit sad, sometimes."

"What does?" asked Byron.

Wanda took a moment. "I don't want to get too philosophical... I think how much better the world would be, and how much happier *people* would be, if they'd just turn inward. Even for a little while. Everyone is in such a goddamned hurry! *'I need this. I have to have that.'* Reaching *outward* for peace. They never realize *why* they're chasing after the things they chase. You know what I mean?"

Byron shrugged. "Kinda."

"They're trying to fill a void." Wanda threw up her hands. "I'm guilty of it. *Everyone* is guilty of it, to a point. We all want our own pile of goodies, thinking that's what'll quiet the beast. That some hole in our lives will be filled once we get what we want. The irony is it *works* for a little while, too. You follow?"

Byron nodded. "I'm with ya."

"When I used to drink, that's what I was looking for. A way to fill the space inside that never seemed filled. It's a hole in the soul, if you will. A Higher Power-shaped hole. It's different for everyone. Some use drugs. Some use sex. Some just get off on seeing others suffer. That last group—I think they're the worst. Well, worst is a strong word. Most damaged is closer to the truth. They revel in the misery of others, mistaking the pleasure of causing pain as fulfillment. They're the most troublesome because, once that rush wears off, they're more miserable than ever. The stakes get raised. Now it's not just causing others some discomfort. Now it's pain. Suffering *sustains* them."

Byron said, "Seen plenty of that doing *this* job."

"I'll bet. My point is, these are the types of souls we're dealing with. These *'children of the void.'* They've lost their way—so far removed from the light they'll never find their way back. Whatever magic they were born with died when they were very young, or was snuffed out by others too damaged to help them become whole. It's sad, really."

"What are you getting at, Wanda?"

"We need to understand what's at stake. Knowing where these souls are coming from is how we protect ourselves. Did Armand tell you what he saw happen to Jo, Byron?"

Byron shook his head, "I told you, he didn't say a word. I think he was afraid Jo would tear him a new one. You think he's holding out?"

Wanda tilted a hand back and forth. "Holding out? No. You know how Jo is. I'm surprised she talks to Moreland at all. Surprised and happy though. That's major progress for Jo."

Byron knew a little bit about Joanne's past. Very little. As Chief of the Salem Police, he'd heard her name mentioned in connection with assaults on her foster parents, and rumors she was involved in breaking and entering; the latter never proven.

He knew little about the circumstances leading up to those crimes. He'd asked Penny about it, but she knew even less than he did. Asking Henry for that information was a non-starter. Byron knew Henry would never speak to him about Jo's past, and he wouldn't have much respect for him if he did. Ditto for Archie.

He'd abandoned the issue because he'd gotten to know and like Joanne. They'd already been through hell together in a few short months. There was a bond there. Nosing around in her past seemed wrong. But the investigator within wouldn't shut up. The bastard always wanted to know more than he was entitled to—and he usually won out. Though he didn't relish the idea of poking through Jo's past, he had a nagging suspicion it might become necessary. An intuitive feeling it might save her life. Where it came from he wasn't sure, but he had his suspicions.

The Byron of six months ago would have laughed his balls off at the Byron of today. The witches of League of the Moon had changed him. They'd opened up doors inside he would have never explored on his own. His fascination with matters spiritual and paranormal grew like wildfire. Penny was largely responsible for stoking those flames. The events leading up to the end of the Red Witch's life had provided an opening for her, and she'd grabbed it with both hands.

She'd started slow, sending him email links to YouTube videos for five minute meditations. At first, he'd resisted—deleting the videos the minute they'd landed in his Gmail account. Penny was persistent but not overbearing, patiently sending videos until the barrier Byron built finally sprung a leak. Once that happened, and Byron tasted the fruits of meditation, she handled him with kid gloves. A question here, a suggestion there. Gently leading him where he needed to go and then letting the magic happen. It worked.

Penny knew, now that the door was wedged ever-so-slightly open, the investigator in her husband couldn't resist the lure of the inward journey. The clues meditation laid bare for Byron about the workings of his own inner life were like lone candles scattered in dark woods—he'd be compelled to follow the trail.

The change in her husband thrilled her to no end, and

she'd nearly fainted when he'd asked her to give him Reiki treatments a few times a week.

"You're serious, aren't you?" she'd asked, trying to hide her surprise.

He'd shrugged, blushed a bit, then said, "I just figure it can't hurt, right?"

She'd been treating him three times a week since.

Penny was bursting at the seems to tell someone, *anyone*, about the almost miraculous change in her husband. The last thing she wanted to do, however, was embarrass him and spook him from this strange new land. She'd confided in Wanda. If anyone in the world was capable of keeping a confidence, it was the witch who'd kept Henry's secret for twenty six years.

Penny's revelations played on a loop behind Wanda's eyes. From that day to this, it colored every interaction she'd had with the Chief of the Salem Police, current conversation included.

"I don't know what happened to Jo. If Moreland was with her though, there can only be a couple of reasons," said Wanda.

"I'm all ears," said Byron.

"Either he showed up to stop something from happening, or he saw something happening and intervened on her behalf."

Byron put his hands on his hips and nibbled his bottom lip. Then, he closed his eyes and ran the conversation from the Common through his mind once more. The words weren't what mattered here—not much was said. It was that moment he'd glanced in the rear-view mirror. Jo had been tentative. Her shoulders were slumped, and her posture suggested a weird submissiveness. That wasn't her.

Something happened to Jo, that much was obvious. He had every intention of uncovering the truth, never realizing a few short moments from now that option would be off the table.

Wanda waved a hand across Byron's face. "Earth to the Chief. Are you in there?"

"Sorry. Just thinking about Jo and Moreland."

He told her about Jo's demeanor back at the Common.

"I only caught a brief glimpse of them in the rear-view. I could be wrong about it, of course. The rear window was smeared with wet snow—"

"What does your *gut* tell you, honey?" asked Wanda.

He smiled, "Tells me I'm headed over to Mercy's place."

Wanda gave him a smile that didn't quite reach her eyes.

"You don't think I should pursue it?" asked Byron.

"Huh?"

"The thing with Jo. You smiled when I said it, but you don't seem too thrilled with the idea."

Wanda held up both hands. "Oh no. By all means check it out."

Byron asked, "Something else on your mind?"

Wanda put her right elbow in her left hand and tugged at her lower lip. Her own telltale sign something bothered her.

Two can play the observation game, Byron thought.

She shook her head. "It's probably nothing. Have you met the owner of that new shop on the corner of Essex and Washington?"

"Not yet. One of the guys at the station said he's from outta state. Maine, I think. Name's Jagger Corey. Why?"

"Like I said, it's probably nothing. Just a funny feeling."

"Worried about competition?" Byron needled her.

Wanda smiled. "Hardly. The more the merrier, in my opinion. I'm probably just imagining shit, sweetie."

Byron shook his head. "You? Not likely. You see something out of the ordinary?"

"I watched him moving in the other day. Similar stuff to mine. Except for one thing. And he was doing his damnedest to hide it."

"What was it?" asked Byron.

"A casket."

CHAPTER 4
MOVES LIKE JAGGER

Jagger Corey peeked through the black drapes covering the second floor windows of his new storefront. The cop had been in the shop of the white witch for an awfully long time. It made him uncomfortable. He knew this was an irrational fear. Why would the police be concerned with him? He was just another witch opening another store in a city famous for witches and stores selling witchy things. A veritable needle in the haystack, if you will.

It wasn't the cop he feared. There was, as far as he could tell, nothing magical about the cop. Said cop, however, had powerful friends. You didn't need magical ability to see how powerful the white witch at the store down the block was. And you didn't have to be Sherlock freakin' Holmes to figure out she and the cop were connected. The guy was at the store at least three times a week.

He wondered if maybe the cop and the witch were riding the old broomstick together? It was possible. He laughed out loud picturing the cop, who stood well over six feet, and the witch, who couldn't be more than four-foot-ten, in the throes of—whatever. The image doubled him over with laughter. Then he thought about the casket, and the laughter ceased.

The witch had seen it.

On the day he'd moved into the new shop, he'd delayed moving the casket. No sense advertising *that* item. It would have to wait until the cover of darkness. When he thought about its contents, it made sense in more ways than one.

Essex street was dark and empty that night. Or so he'd thought. He and his partner had parked the moving van right up against the front door, minimizing the chances of observation and speculation. The open space between the van and the door was about a foot. Eighteen inches at the most. It was as close as they could get without damaging the brand-new, black and orange awning. Jagger found himself wishing they'd waited to put up that awning.

After the casket was stowed upstairs in his new shop, Jagger accompanied his partner back to the moving van. The man hopped behind the wheel. Jagger slapped the rear door twice and sent him on his way.

Just before he turned to go inside, he gave Essex Street a final once-over. That's when he saw it. A brief twinkle of light caught his eye. It came from the shop at the far corner of Essex Street. He focused like a laser on the spot, waiting to see if it happened again—watching breathlessly for any sign of movement. When nothing happened, he re-entered the building and dashed for the second floor. Breathing hard, he pulled a chair toward the window, sat, and inched the black drapes apart. It didn't take long. Something twinkled once more in the shop's window. This time, it moved slowly away and eased into the darkness. Someone was watching. What they'd *seen* was up for debate.

A few days and several inches of snow later, he watched from the same window; his suspicion growing.

But that's not completely true, he thought. *Is it?*

Suspicion be damned. He knew for a *fact* they were talking about him. Just like he knew, for a fact, the cop would knock on his door in the next few minutes. If pressed, he couldn't explain *why* he knew certain things. Only that the images came to him unbidden, crystallizing in his mind, and then materializing moments later in the real world.

There had always been a part of him that was good at guessing what came next. It was something akin to déjà vu on steroids. But this? Actually seeing events happen in his mind and then unfold almost exactly as expected? No, this was another level. Things here were different.

It was new. It scared him a little. He *loved* it.

The *reason* it was happening to him meant little, and he avoided dwelling on it. No sense worrying about something beyond your control.

"Never look a gift horse in the mouth," his mother had always said. He hated that phrase. Hated her, too. But the mean old bitch and her useless sayings were as much a part of him as this new power. For once, he agreed with her.

The new piece in his collection of magical artifacts was *also* a gift.

The casket arrived in the dead of night at his shop in Portland. No knock on the door. No advance warning of any kind. Just a loud thump from the loading dock out back. He'd been up late *that* night, too.

At the time, he'd been sorting receipts from the day's sales. It had been unusually busy for a Monday, and he was deep into it. The noise made him jump in his chair and the receipts flew from his hand. As they rained down like so much confetti, he held his hand over his heart and took a few deep breaths to calm his nerves.

Once settled, he donned a black silk top hat, threw a purple and orange-striped scarf around his neck, and tucked it into his shirt beneath a scraggly, brown beard that resembled a ferret on chemo.

Jagger took his first tentative steps toward the loading dock door, hiding the wiry frame of his body behind stacks of boxes along the way. He darted from one to the next, peeking around each and pushing a pair of round, wire-rimmed, ill-fitting glasses back up the ridge of a long, thin nose. A customer had once remarked he looked like Harry Potter if Harry had given up on magic and turned to heroin. Jagger sent a special curse her way after closing, smiling days later as he read her obituary.

At the loading dock door, he waited. Cloaked in darkness, Jagger crouched below the window in the door and held his breath. He rose slowly until his eyes crested the bottom of the window frame, listening for the tiniest sound and searching for the slightest hint of movement. After several moments, somewhat sure it was safe, he went into action.

With his left hand he undid the dead bolt, cringing as it snapped open. As he twisted the knob, he seized an aluminum baseball bat he kept next to the door with his right. Jagger yanked the door open, raised the bat in the air, and charged into the night, screaming at the top of his lungs. The war cry was cut short as his knees slammed into something hard. He tumbled forward and over the object in front of him. The aluminum bat flew from his grip and clanged across the cracked pavement of the parking lot, and he landed hard on both hands.

"Ow! Ow! Ow! Motherfu—"

He stopped mid-curse, the pain in both scraped and bleeding palms quickly became an afterthought. He tilted his head back and forth, frowning with confusion.

"What in the actual fuck?"

Moonlight reflected dully from a black, brushed-metal casket. Jagger shook his head back and forth a few times, as if doing so would shake an explanation free. Once convinced he hadn't lost his mind, he turned in a circle, looking for any sign of who might have left this monstrosity on his loading dock. The empty field surrounding the shop's property gave up no one. He took this as a signal he should move the thing inside right away.

The casket looked heavy, but when he grabbed hold of one of its silver handles and pulled, it moved easily. Whatever *was* inside didn't weigh much. At least, that's the way it *seemed*. Jagger pulled on the handle again. Again, the casket glided toward him. Something was off. It took a third pull on the handle before it finally hit him. There was no sound. Though the black behemoth rested on the cement loading dock, every time he pulled the handle and dragged it toward the door, there was no metal-on-concrete scratch. *It was silent!*

Jagger got down on his hands and knees to inspect the bottom of the casket. When he realized that wasn't enough, he lay flat on the ground, his right eye level with the bottom. He gasped in surprise when he saw the weeds sticking up out of cracks at the far end of the parking lot. The casket was floating about half an inch above the concrete!

From experience, Jagger knew the casket was bewitched, and the spell would be short lived. He sprang to his feet, kicked open the loading dock door, and pulled the black metal mystery silently inside. Then he closed and locked the door behind him. Out of an abundance of caution, he returned to the door and scanned the parking lot for the next few minutes. Moments later, satisfied no one had seen—or was watching—he turned to take in his mysterious prize.

Jagger clasped his hands behind his back, bent at the waist, and walked slowly around the casket, taking in every detail. Nothing struck him as remarkable, other than the damned thing was still *floating* above his shop floor. As if reading his thoughts, it thumped downward. A ring of dust puffed from the displaced air around its perimeter. When it settled, a black envelope with his name scrawled across the front in gold script appeared from thin air, resting at the casket's head. He smiled. Whoever had left the casket on his loading dock had a magical flare for the dramatic.

Jagger snatched the envelope up and tore it open. He unfolded the note and read...

The Red Witch is dead. Her demons are captured. It's time.
~ Gemini.

Salem was calling.

"About fucking time!" he'd whispered.

When he was pulled back to the present, he thought about the journey here. Irony of ironies, his family tree traced back to Salem.

Jagger was a descendent of Giles Corey.

Corey and his third wife, Martha, had been accused of witchcraft in 1692. Upon his arrest, Corey had refused to enter a plea of either guilty or not guilty. The sheriff at the time invoked a practice known as pressing, where they would place the subject refusing to enter a plea beneath heavy boards and then slowly add rocks and boulders until the weight *pressing* down forced a plea. Legend had it that when the sheriff asked Giles how he pled, Giles replied, "More rocks!"

His great-great-great times infinity grandfather had held out to the bitter end, becoming the only person in American history to have been pressed to death for refusing a plea. He'd never met the man. Never would. All the same, it made him proud. It was the only thing about anyone in his family tree of which he felt pride.

Giles Corey's pressing had taken place outside the courthouse where the punishment had been handed down. The area was later converted to a cemetery, and Giles Corey was eventually buried there. People to this day claimed they saw the apparition of Giles making his way across its grounds. Jagger had fond memories of the day the Red Witch made it possible to visit the site. She'd even brought some soil from his grave back over.

"Gramps definitely had some stones," he whispered, then cackled at his own wit.

Motion on the street below pulled his attention back to reality. The cop was coming, just as expected.

Jagger sat in the dark silence. Snow ticked lightly against the windows. When the knock came from the door below, he waited a bit before answering. Then, he rose from the chair, removed his top hat, mussed his hair, stripped down to his underwear, and grabbed his bathrobe from the peg on the wall. Better to appear roused from a deep sleep than fully dressed and on high alert. Anything to allay suspicion.

As he made his way down the steps and into his shop, he thought about Giles Corey. If pressed, haha, he would give this cop nothing.

CHAPTER 5
RIDERS ON THE STORM

H enry drove at a snail's pace. The storm had come as advertised after all, and for no good reason he cursed the Channel Five meteorologist.

"Just had to be right this time, huh asshole?"

The taunt made him feel better, but it failed to prevent the Jeep from sliding a bit here and there. Four-wheel-drive was great until the snow started coming down hard and heavy and wet, then turned to ice as the temperature fell off a cliff. The only vehicle appropriate for the shit was a tank, and even *that* was debatable.

The sign ahead was partially obscured by the driving snow, but as he got closer he saw the letters ETTS. He'd made it safely to the Massachusetts border. It had taken him roughly an hour to get there. At this pace it would be another hour and a half to two hours to make it all the way to Salem.

Before he finished the thought, he saw the blue and red strobe of emergency vehicles.

"What fresh hell is this?" he asked the Jeep.

Henry slowed to a crawl, then pulled up close to the officer waving him down with a flashlight and opened the window.

"The road's closed sir. We've got a jack-knifed tractor-trailer and about seventeen cars piled up behind it. You're gonna have to exit here and take the surface roads to wherever you're going. Sorry, buddy."

Henry thanked him, rolled up his window, and made for the exit ramp. He tapped the cell phone and opened Google Maps, then tapped the "Home" icon. When the map came up, the voice navigation told him there was a three hour delay on his current route. Every alternate road was a red streak almost the entire way toward Salem, and the estimated time of arrival read *3hrs, 47 mins* in bright red at the bottom of the screen.

"Fuck!"

Henry stabbed at the phone and changed the destination on his GPS to his parents house. The roads were clear heading back north; that wasn't much of a surprise. The strongest part of the storm seemed strangely contained mostly within Massachusetts, with just a slight spillover in Maine. He tried voice command to call his mother, but the call wouldn't go through. Jo's phone yielded the same result.

"Of course. When I need it *most*—"

Henry tried the two numbers again, then several others. All with the same result. After a time, he gave up and gave in.

"Time for an Audiobook." He took the Jeep's silence as agreement.

He opened up the app and selected "Brother Odd" by Dean Koontz. Chapter Four was where he'd left off last. In a twist of irony, the main character was stuck in a monastery in the middle of a snowstorm.

"Maine. Monastery. In the snow, what's the difference?" he asked Mr. Jeep. It wasn't lost on him that he'd started talking to Jo's car. Then he shrugged and told the Jeep, "Who gives a fuck? Right?" He slapped the wheel in frustration, then settled in to the story.

The timestamp at the bottom of the GPS read *44 mins* in green. It was the only positive development in a night of utter chaos. Had he known he wouldn't make it anywhere close to his parents' home, he might have parked the Jeep at the side of the road and camped out for the night.

JO AND MORELAND arrived at Mercy's doorstep on Witch Hill Road. She told him everything was okay and thanked him for the escort.

"If it's okay with you, I'd rather stay here until you're safely inside," said Moreland.

Jo said, "Suit yourself." A growing unease had gripped her since the events on the Common. Something she couldn't put her finger on. Something missing. Whether it had to do with Moreland or the after-effects of a spiritual attack, she wasn't sure.

The feeling she needed to be away from the vampire *himself* had also grown since then. Intuition screamed at her to get away. When Mercy finally answered the bell, Jo stepped around her and bolted inside.

Mercy jumped back as Jo rushed through the door, and then watched as Jo flew up the stairs and into the second floor apartment.

She turned to Moreland. "What's going on?"

"Nothing good. But I'll leave that for Joanne to tell you, if she so chooses." Moreland tipped his cap. "Goodnight, Miss Glass."

Mercy stood in the open doorway and followed Armand Moreland's progress down her snowy walkway and into the night. As the vampire turned the corner, Mercy could have sworn she saw something strange surrounding him. It confused the hell out of her.

Vampires were the living dead. Dark, mysterious, and soulless. At least, that's what she'd always heard. In her current incarnation of twenty-five years, she'd met exactly two vampires—Armand Moreland and Xavier Saulis. In all the time she'd spent with them, which she had to admit to herself wasn't much, she'd never seen a hint of what she'd just seen.

Armand Moreland had an aura.

She wasn't one hundred percent positive vampires *didn't* have auras, but she intended to find out. And if it wasn't an aura... then what the hell was it?

Mercy turned back inside, closed the door, and bolted it. She shivered and rubbed her arms. The cold had nothing to do with it.

BYRON HAD SEEN some strange looking dudes in his time, but this guy took the cake. The red, terry-cloth bathrobe hung loosely down over Jagger Corey's broad and bony shoulders. It was cinched tightly around the man's narrow waist, forming a V shape from the shoulders down. The rest of the robe covered him to mid-shin, revealing spindly, hairless legs. His ankles stuck out obscenely from backless black slippers.

Byron bit the inside of his lip. Laughing in this guy's face would definitely get things off on the wrong foot.

"Good evening, officer. Is there something wrong?" asked Jagger, rubbing his eyes.

"No, sir. Just making sure everything is okay. I know you're new to the neighborhood and just thought I'd check in on you. Consider it a courtesy call. Storms like this tend to knock the power out. How are you fixed for emergency supplies?"

Courtesy call my ass, Jagger thought. He said, "Well, that is most considerate officer—"

"Miller. Chief of the Salem police."

"Chief Miller, thank you. I'm from Maine, so I'm well stocked and prepared for nights such as this."

"Maine, eh? Whereabouts in Maine?"

Jagger suspected the cop was well aware he'd moved to Salem from Portland, but he had to make it look good. He smiled wide, "I hail from Portland, Officer Miller. My shop was on the outskirts of town. Jagger's Magical Treasures. Ever hear of it?"

"Can't say I have, Mr.—"

"Corey. Jagger Corey."

Byron tilted his head, "Why does that name ring a bell?"

"Well, the lead singer of the Rolling Stones comes to mind. Then there's that song by Maroon 5—"

"No. I mean your last name. I know that name means something in Salem, but—"

"I'm a descendent of Giles Corey."

Byron intentionally gave Jagger a blank stare. He knew exactly who Giles Corey was, but he wanted to see how the man reacted. It was exactly what he'd hoped for; Jagger Corey was insulted. A resentful man was easy to trip up.

Jagger asked, "Surely living in Salem you've heard the name Giles Corey? The man who was pressed to death for refusing to enter a plea when accused of witchcraft?"

Byron nodded slowly. "I remember something about that. Didn't realize it was a witchcraft thing, though. Thought he was just some common criminal or something."

That one hit home. Though he could barely make out his face, Byron knew the insult struck a nerve. It was always the subtle things—tells, if you will.

Narrowing eyelids.

A slight twitch of the lips.

Tiny changes in posture.

All things he looked for to know he'd rocked a suspect's world. Even if just a little bit.

Jagger knew the cop was goading him. No doubt about it. He forced a smile back onto his lips, took a long, deep breath, and relaxed his shoulders.

Time to give this cop a taste of his own medicine.

"Well, that's an understandable oversight, Officer Miller," Jagger said. "It's a time honored tradition for the authorities to falsely accuse someone. Especially in the town of Salem. You could almost say it's a tradition handed down through generations."

Byron smiled. "I'm wondering about something, Mister Corey—"

"Jagger. Call me Jagger. No need for formalities here, Chief Miller."

Byron smiled. "Okay, *Jagger*. I was about to ask if you're following in the footsteps of your dear departed great, great —whatever—grandfather's footsteps."

Jagger tilted his head. "I'm not sure I follow, Chief Miller."

"Well, you said it yourself. "It's a *time honored tradition* for law enforcement to falsely accuse someone of something. Is there something you feel you're being falsely accused of?"

Jagger didn't like the direction this was heading. The cop was obviously trying to paint him into a corner. Though he'd known Miller was on his way to the shop, and he was pretty sure the white witch was the reason, he was unprepared for the direction the conversation had taken.

Since reacquiring his ability to see events before they happened, he'd played with it a lot. Nothing major; he would see something in his mind, then it would happen in real life. He'd tested it out in the weeks leading up to the move to Salem, but had never taken it this far.

Until now, it was usually something simple. The image of a customer browsing his store would come to him, seemingly out of the blue. He saw every last detail about them: the clothing, the hair color, even what their voice sounded like as he cashed them out. Then he would sit back, wait, and *voila!* It would all go down as he'd foreseen. But, up to this moment, it was always a passive event.

Now, engaged in a mental tug-of-war with the Chief of the Salem Police, he came to realize something about this all-too-real encounter; what took place once the bullets flew was another kettle of fish altogether. He'd been overconfident in his abilities, and had underestimated the cop. Time to regroup and live to fight another day.

Pucker up, buttercup, Jagger thought. *Time to kiss some ass and save your own.*

"I'm sorry, Chief Miller. Apparently I've hit a sore spot. I didn't mean to offend you by lumping you in with all law enforcement. Just as, I'm sure, you didn't mean to lump me in with Giles. Generalizations can be the scourge of polite conversation. So, my apologies."

This guy is good, Byron thought. He said, "No offense taken, Mister Corey. But the question still stands."

"What question?" asked Jagger.

"Is there something you feel you're being falsely accused of? Or, more to the point, is there something you're hiding that you don't want me to find out about. Something long and black. Maybe it has some shiny silver handles on the side of it?"

Jagger knew *that* question was coming. It surprised him how quickly the chief had gotten to it, though. And he knew to hesitate would instantly imply guilt of some kind.

"My casket display?" asked Jagger. He put forward his best *Is that what all this silliness is about?* face.

Byron's mouth dropped open just the slightest bit. He hoped the dark and the storm hid it from Corey, but doubted it. Whatever momentum he'd built against this guy had just gone out the window.

"Um, yeah," said Byron, trying to save face. "It's a bit odd."

"Not really. Remember, Chief Miller, the name of the store is *Jagger's Magical Treasures*. I have lots of *odd* displays."

Byron felt like Tom Cruise in "A Few Good Men" right before he asked Colonel Nathan R. Jessup if he'd ordered the code red. In a nutshell—a fool. And he knew the scrawny fucker *knew it*, too.

Jagger smiled, "I have nothing to hide, Chief Miller. Why don't you come in and see for yourself?"

Byron was already off balance by Jagger's ready and almost eager admission of possessing the casket. The last thing in the world he'd expected was an invitation to see it.

Part of him *wanted* to accept this creepy bastard's invitation. Another part screamed at him to turn around right now. He knew Wanda was watching from the darkness of her store. He knew if he didn't come out in a reasonable amount of time, she'd get suspicious and call in Raul Martinez to investigate. As he stepped over the threshold and into the darkness of Jagger's store, a man roughly the size and build of Byron closed the door quietly behind the chief.

There was a blinding flash of light, and then the darkness swallowed Byron.

CHAPTER 6
THE SCAR & THE SHIFTER

Mercy stepped into the warmth of the candlelit living room. Much like the safe room in Wanda's Wicca'd Emporium, beanbag chairs ringed its outer edges. A black rug with a gold pentacle rested at its center. There were five beanbags in total, and Mercy took a seat across from Jo in the only empty chair. Smoke hung lazily in the air, glowing gold with candlelight and carrying the scent of Dragon's Blood like a peaceful and silent messenger.

Jo met Mercy's eyes with only a fleeting glance and then cast her own quickly downward, studying the pentacle as if it contained answers to questions the events of the last hour raised in her mind.

The room remained silent for some time.

Mercy caught Jasmine Miso's eyes, and Jazz raised her left hand a fraction of an inch, palm out, indicating to Mercy they should wait until Jo was ready to talk. Mercy gave her a slight nod, closed her eyes, took a deep breath, then let it out

44

slowly. The other two women in the circle of five followed her lead.

The entire vibration of the room changed. Everyone felt it as the tension drained from Jo's shoulders and slowly rolled through the rest of her body. When Mercy opened her eyes again, Jo's brilliant green eyes were staring back at her. Mercy gave her a sympathetic smile, and asked, "Are you okay, Jo?"

"I think so. It's been a really fucked up night."

Do you wanna talk about it, honey?" asked Jazz.

Jo started chewing on her left thumbnail. Both Jazz and Mercy knew her well enough to know whatever she was about to say, it was going to be some heavy shit. When Jo teared up, they realized just how heavy it was; she wasn't exactly the crying type.

Jazz rose from her beanbag chair, walked over to Joanne, and sat cross-legged in front of her. She held out a hand and Jo took it into hers.

"We're here for you, Jo. It's what this circle is all about, sweetie." Jazz squeezed her hand. "Tell us what's up. Don't hold back. If you have to cry, then you fucking cry. There's no judgment here. Okay?'

When Jo smiled at Jazz, tears spilled down her cheeks. Mercy got up and left the room, returning with a box of Kleenex. She held it out for Jo, and the green-eyed witch accepted it with a grateful smile. Jo wiped away the tears, and then told Mercy, Jazz, Fermina, and Luci everything she could recall from the attack on the Salem Common. When she finished, she took a deep breath and let it out. "That's everything."

"Everything you *remember*," said Jazz. "But you said you started to feel nervous around Moreland, right?"

Jo nodded. "Yeah. It was weird though. I mean, you know what I thought about the guy when he sent the letter and all that."

Mercy and Jazz nodded in unison. Moreland was on Jo's shit list from the moment he'd sent the letter reprimanding the League of the Moon for her use of "overt magical power" on the streets of Salem. Wanda, Jo, and Mercy had all given him a ration of shit for the letter, and Moreland had ultimately admitted he was wrong to have sent it. From then on, he had more than made up for it by helping the League of the Moon find and kill the Red Witch.

In the time since, he'd become close with all of them. Armand Moreland now considered the witches of the League his family. His actions in saving Jo tonight proved him true to his words. So when Jo started to feel she needed to get away from him, it sent her into an emotional tailspin. She'd felt confused, scared, and disloyal. All at the same time. It was more than she could process. Piled on top of watching her emotional and spiritual insides being torn from her by a pack of spiritual hyenas, it was no wonder she was in the state she was.

Jo continued. "I just can't put my finger on why I *needed* to get away from him. The longer we walked, the worse it got." As she talked, she rubbed the back of her neck.

"You said you started to forget things. Names, feelings, memories. How long was it before all that came back to you?" asked Mercy.

"It seemed to come back quickly. But I really can't say, timewise, how long it took. Why?"

Mercy tilted her head back and forth, "Maybe it took longer than you think? I don't know. Maybe there's a blank spot in there somewhere. I know it's not the same thing, exactly, but when I had my near death experience, it took a few weeks before I remembered there'd been someone up there with me on that ledge at the quarry. I was convinced I'd done something monumentally stupid all on my own. It wasn't until later I realized Zachary Villitz "helped" me along."

Jo closed her eyes, trying to bring forth anything from memory she could, post-attack. Nothing came. She was rubbing her neck again. The area between the back left side of her neck and her shoulder blade felt sore and itchy.

Jazz noticed her discomfort. "Are you hurt, Jo?"

"I guess. All of a sudden my neck hurts like hell. And it's itchy as fuck."

Jazz got up from her spot in front of Jo, stepped around her, and kneeled behind the spot Jo was still rubbing.

"Lift your hand, Jo. I want to take a look," said Jazz.

Jo did, and Jazz peeled the shirt down from her shoulder.

"Did you cut yourself in the not-too-distant past?" asked Jazz.

Jo said, "Nope. Why?"

"Well, there's something back here alright, but it doesn't look recent. It's scarred over. Like it happened a month ago," said Jazz. "You remember anything like that?"

Mercy and the others had gotten up from their beanbag chairs and joined Jazz behind Jo. As Jo considered Jazz's question, the others drew in a collective gasp.

"What? What's the matter?" asked Jo, her voice rising a nervous octave.

"Umm," said Mercy. "The scar just shrank a little. As we were watching it."

Jo popped to her feet and dashed toward the bathroom.

She flipped the switch and ran to the mirror over the sink. "Do you have a make-up mirror, Mercy?"

Mercy was one step ahead. She pulled a leather bag from the sink's storage space, unzipped it, and held it so it captured Jo's back and faced the mirror above the sink.

Jazz, Fermina, and Luci stood wide-eyed behind Mercy and Jo, their mouths forming three perfect O's of surprise and awe. All five stood in stunned silence as a six-inch long, oblong scar shrank before their eyes with increasing rapidity. It folded in on itself over the next minute, and when it got to the smallest visible point, it flashed emerald green, released a puff of green-tinged smoke, and disappeared. The skin on Jo's upper left shoulder was once again smooth and unblemished.

"Okay. What the fuck just happened?" asked Jo.

COBWEBS. Dirt. Candles aglow. Mildewed stone walls. The rattle of chains. These were the things Byron awoke to. One by one they registered through a cloudy veil of pain in his head. He tried to move, yanking at the shackles holding him in place, and succeeded only in bringing a fresh bolt of agony rocketing from the back of his head to the front. The room went grey and stars filled his field of vision. It took everything he had to remain conscious. When he opened his eyes again, Jagger Corey stood in front of him, a glass of water in one hand, and something cupped in the other.

"You should have minded your own business, Chief Miller," said Jagger.

Byron gave him his best, ball-shriveling stare. It satisfied him when Jagger took a step back.

"Giving me mean looks won't get you anywhere," Jagger whined. "I brought you something for your pain. Eljin is a good servant, but he tends to be a bit... *enthusiastic* about pleasing me. So, my apologies for the state of your cranium. I brought you some Tylenol for the pain."

Byron said nothing.

Jagger nodded toward Byron's shackled right hand. "I'm going to have to feed them to you, obviously." Then he smiled, and said, "You'd be doing yourself a favor if you behave whilst I attempt to place the capsules in your mouth. Eljin is waiting at the top of the stairs. If he so much as hears a whimper from me, he'll be back for another bout of "enthusiastic" service. Neither of us wants that, I think."

Byron remained silent.

Jagger took a cautious step forward, waited, then took another. He made his way slowly toward Byron, glass of water in one hand, cupped Tylenol in the other. The water in the glass seesawed back and forth. Jagger's hands were shaking slightly. Byron took some satisfaction from it. Jagger was to Byron's left now, steering clear of the chief's snow boots.

That was when Byron first noticed he wasn't wearing his uniform anymore. The square pattern of his long underwear disappeared into the boots running halfway up his calf. He bit the inside of his lip in anger.

"Where the fuck is my uniform?" he growled.

Jagger had been leaning in to feed the pills to Byron. He straightened up quickly, like he'd been poked in the ass with a sharp stick.

"Not your concern at the moment, Chief Miller. I assure you, when all this is over, you'll have it back."

"When all this is over, you're going to be in a fucking jail cell, *Jagger*."

The glass in his hand stilled. Byron noticed his face change. Though the man was a beanpole, and nothing about his physical presence threatened in the slightest, Byron suddenly felt scared.

"Watch your tone with me, cop. I am a patient man, but I have my limits."

Like a phantom, Eljin appeared over Jagger's left shoulder. When he stepped out from behind him and into the light, Byron held back a scream.

As SWOLLEN snowflakes tumbled softly from the sky, Wanda held vigil from the safety, warmth, and darkness of the Emporium's picture window. Fifteen minutes earlier, she'd watched as Byron went into the shop at the end of the block. The Explorer sat half-on, half-off the sidewalk in front of Jagger's shop, idling exhaust slowly into the night sky. She tried focusing on the steam to calm her nerves. It wasn't working.

"Breathe, Wanda," she reminded herself. "Byron's a big boy. He can take care of himself."

She finally released the breath she'd been holding. Byron exited the store, looked her way, and waved. She watched as he put the cruiser in gear and drove around the corner and out of sight.

It wasn't what she'd expected. She'd assumed he would return and give her the dirt on Jagger. When she thought about it further, his taking off and not returning right away actually made a lot more sense. If Jagger had seen him leave and then head directly to her shop, he'd be immediately suspicious. And if there *was* anything—off—about Jagger's store or the man himself, Byron probably wanted to work it out on his own first. It was just his way.

Though she was burning with curiosity, Wanda resisted calling Byron and pumping him for information. Later, she would regret that decision.

ELJIN SAW the white witch in the store's window. Though tight, the cops uniform fit well enough. Byron's parka hid whatever bulges might give him away. He waved to the witch exactly as he'd observed the Chief of the Salem Police do many times, then climbed into the Explorer. A cursory glance in the rear-view mirror calmed any fears she might have caught on. Eljin turned the corner and drove into the night.

CHAPTER 7
FUTURE PRESENT

"I'll be fine, Arch. It's just a little snow," protested Annie.

"I know. I know. I'm just making sure you get off to a good start. I'm old-fashioned that way. Humor me. Okay?"

Annie rolled her eyes, pulled on her hood, and zipped up. Archie did the same, then opened and held the door.

Archie walked Annie, his receptionist, through the stormy parking lot and right up to her SUV. They'd been a team for more years than Archie could remember, and on days like these, he made a point of insuring she got safely home. Annie always gave him a hard time about it, going as far as calling him *Captain Patriarchy* when he did stuff like this, but she didn't really mean it. Archie was old-school, and Annie *liked* old-school. She also supremely enjoyed busting Archie's balls. *It's the best of both worlds*, she thought. It made her smile.

"What's so funny?" asked Archie.

"You're funny, Arch. You're walking me to a four-by-four

52

tank so I can drive three miles home, yet you risk your life in that rear-wheel-drive fossil. You don't see the humor in that? Why don't you let me drive you home and you can pick it up later?"

Archie had gotten most of the snow removed from her windows when he turned around to defend his VW Microbus's honor. "Fossil? Most would use the term 'classic.'"

Annie arched an eyebrow. "Classic? If you say so."

Archie smiled, "I appreciate your concern, Annie. Misplaced and uninformed as it is. But I'm not going home tonight. I have too much work left over and I'll most likely be bunking out on the sofa in my office."

She grabbed the *Oh shit!* handle on the driver's side of the Toyota 4Runner, hoisted herself into the seat, and said, "Don't work too hard tonight, then. I don't need your sorry ass working me into a layoff."

"Wouldn't dream of it," said Archie. "Be careful. See ya soon."

The moment he stepped into his office was the moment the power to the building went out. Archie cursed, then pulled his cell from the back pocket of his jeans and tapped the flashlight app. He went to a cabinet in the corner of his office and pulled a box of candles from it, then set about filling the empty sconces scattered about the room. With that done, he took a deep breath, let it out, and made his way over to the only window in his office.

Archie watched the snowfall in quiet, candlelit solitude. There was much work to be done tonight, and he fought off the twinge of guilt he felt for the white lie he'd told to Annie. The part about work *was* true, of course. But the nature of that work was best kept to himself. Annie was trustworthy, and a dear friend. Jagger Corey was a maniac. The fewer who knew about him, the better. Even the *mention* of the man's name drew the unsuspecting into his psychotic orbit. He thought he'd seen the last of him. But the bastard was back.

Jagger Corey was unstable, to put it mildly. Add that to his power as a dark witch; the possibilities were dark, frightening, and endless. Being partly responsible for unleashing the man's inner demons—with a healthy dose of prodding from his ex-psycho girlfriend Mondra, The Red Witch—only added to the urgency of the work that lay ahead. The fewer who knew, however, the better.

"How do I always put myself in these ridiculous situations?"

Archie crossed the room to the leather couch, kicked off his boots, then stood on stocking feet atop the cushions. A large, gold crucifix hung above the couch. To visitors, it appeared exactly as it was, though maybe slightly larger than normal. If one were to examine it closer, they might notice it wasn't flush to the wall. Where the arms joined the cross-section there was a pressure-sensitive button.

Archie made sure to press the middle with his left index finger. It was his own quirky superstition. When opening this secret cache, he always used his left hand—the magic hand. In centuries past, left-handedness had been associated with evil. Some went so far as to call it 'a mark of the devil.' During the mania of the witch hunts in both Europe and America, left-handedness was used to identify potential witches. Archie was a student of history as well as parapsychology. He considered the use of his left hand for tasks such as these a homage to those slain in ignorance, and a proper 'fuck you' to those who'd done the slaying.

The crucifix separated at its middle, exposing an opening

two-feet wide, three-feet long, and two-feet deep. Archie reached in with his left hand and brought out a small, rectangular cardboard box covered by a fine layer of dust. He tapped the edge of the crucifix and it slid silently closed, then locked with a hollow, metallic snap.

He brought the box to his desk, plopped down in his chair, and placed it in front of him. Candlelight played over its dusty surface, and he stared at it for a long time. Part of him dreaded going back to those sessions with Jagger. The things he'd uncovered about the boy—he was fifteen at the time—were disturbing, to put it mildly. To put not-too-fine a point on it, Jagger was seriously fucked up.

Another part—one he would never acknowledge existed to the outside world—had *craved* digging into the boy's psyche. He'd found it fascinating, back then, to uncover the roots of Jagger's demented and tortured personality.

In those days, a little younger and a lot less wise, Archie had thought of it as research. Simply delving into another human being's life and scientifically examining it as one would examine slides of some strange bacteria through a microscope. In his zeal to study his specimen, however, he'd neglected the subject's humanity. Jagger Corey had needed more than examination back then, he'd needed serious help.

Mind. Body. Soul. Magic. Archie had ignored all of these in the pursuit of raw data.

Dance, monkey. Dance.

It filled him with shame. He wanted to blame Mondra for his own shortcomings when it came to Jagger, but he knew the truth.

Archie peeled his eyes from the box. They settled on a framed picture of Henry, Joanne, and Delilah, but he didn't *see* them. Instead, his own face, bathed in soft yellow light, stared back, and he had trouble meeting his own gaze.

He turned away, sighed, and pulled from the box a tape marked *Jagger 1. September 10, 2004. Age 15.*

The battery-powered cassette player sat silently on the desk before him, daring him to press play.

Archie took a deep breath, held it, then let it out in a rush.

He whispered, "Challenge accepted."

～

HENRY WAS CRUISING north at a whopping fifteen miles-per-hour. The meteorologist in Boston had let him down, now his Maine counterpart had been added to Henry's growing list of least-favorite humans.

"How hard can it fucking be?" Henry asked his new friend the Jeep. "Read the map, make the call. Is there *really* more to it than that?"

There probably was, but he wasn't in a forgiving mood. The storm was supposed to be weakening in Portland, but the evidence falling across his windshield put the lie to that. Four-wheel-drive or not, he was sliding all over the place.

It was coming down so heavy and thick, he almost didn't see the overturned, red Toyota Camry—a car identical to his own back in Salem—in time. At the last second, he swerved to avoid running head-on into the Camry's side... and almost pulled it off. The Jeep slid sideways, clipping the back bumper of the Toyota and spinning it around. The momentum spun the Camry on its roof. The car's front end whipped around, then slapped the backside of the Jeep, sending it, and Henry, sliding across the one-lane divided highway.

"Oh shit!"

He'd always heard when you were skidding in the snow, you needed to turn the wheel into the skid. It didn't help. Fresh panic bloomed in his chest, and he turned the wheel back and forth in a frantic effort to gain control of the Jeep. The wheel spun in his hands as if the road were coated with Vaseline, and the Jeep hurtled toward the side of the road. The only thing separating Henry from a twenty foot drop was a length of chain suspended between two, three-foot-high metal posts. The Jeep's ultra-bright headlights set the chain to glinting. Beyond those glints—darkness.

"That is one sad fucking excuse for a guardrail!"

No argument from the Jeep.

As the front wheels caught and then rolled over the chain, Henry closed his eyes and prepared his body for the fall and crash. It never came. Instead, there was a wrenching, metal-on-metal sound. The four-by-four came to a violent stop, and Henry lurched forward. His neck whiplashed as the seat belt clamped down, sparing him a nasty knot on the head from the steering wheel by a fraction of an inch.

The cab of the Jeep was silent, save for the whipping sound of wind and the creek of metal as the truck balanced on the edge of darkness. Henry feared any sudden move might send it over, so he proceeded with exaggerated slowness. He took hold of the gear shift, and gently shifted from drive to neutral, then took a deep breath and let it out slowly.

"Okay. Now, foot on the brake. Off the gas. Reverse. Let the brake out easy..."

The Jeep jerked backward. Metal scraped against dirt,

rock, grass, and snow. Henry goosed the gas pedal and heard the rear wheels first bite, then spin. Hope surged in his chest as the Jeep bounced an inch or two backward and toward the road. Excitement lit him as dreams of a narrow escape played on the silver screen of his imagination. Then, as fate often does, it pulled the plug on the projector. Spinning tires and friction turned the snow and dirt into a muddy mess, and the Jeep bogged down and settled in. The angle of the truck was too severe, and the underside rested on the edge of the abyss. It was stuck, but at least stable. This failed to fill his heart with joy.

"Fuck!"

He resisted the urge to pound out his frustration on the steering wheel. Instead, he forced himself to calm down long enough to exit. When he got outside, he kicked at the ground, used language of a type Jo would have been proud of, and then plopped down in the snow, spent.

"Feel better now, shithead?" he asked himself.

Wind and snow mocked him.

Henry heaved himself from the ground and was about to turn toward the Jeep when something caught his eye. To his left, about ten or fifteen feet away, a yellow metal sign with red lettering swung from a chain. It clanged against one of two poles. Each pole was about two feet taller than the ones comprising the useless guardrail. The sign was obviously meant to chain off the path leading into the woods. Henry bent to read it. In faded red letters pocked with rust, it read PRIVATE PROPERTY, NO TRESPASSING. The other half of the chain clanged against the opposite post. Though the chain was weathered, the severed link was shiny, and the cut precise—as if recently sheared with a bolt cutter.

Henry was about to shrug it off when a light, far down

the path and beyond the reach of the Jeeps headlights, flashed briefly. He wasn't sure he trusted his eyes, rubbed at them with the heels of his gloves, and stared into the darkness. It glowed briefly again, then disappeared. He wasn't about to go into the forest in the middle of a snowstorm, so he jogged back to the Jeep to retrieve his cell phone. Sticking the tip of his gloved finger into his mouth, he pulled it free from his hand to better work the phone. In tiny white letters at the top of the screen, it read 'No Service,' right next to zero bars at the top left.

Looking to the sky, he asked, "What next?"

When he brought his eyes back toward earth, the red Camry provided the only answer he needed. Someone drove that car. No one was in it now. He looked from the Camry, to the trail, and then back to the Camry. The choice was clear.

Henry went to the back of the Jeep and flung the tailgate open. A flashlight was Velcroed above the wheel well and a duffel bag filled with survival supplies was Bungee-corded just beneath it. He grabbed both items, slammed the tailgate closed, then shut off the Jeep and pocketed the keys.

Whoever had been in the red car either knew there was help at the end of that trail, or was wandering the woods dazed and confused. Either way, he had to help.

Henry took a deep breath then made for the trail. In all the excitement and frustration, he failed to notice one very important fact; there were no footprints in the snow on the trail, and no footprints leading away from the Camry.

CHAPTER 8
DISCONNECT

Chief Byron Miller was pissed off. Not in the way one might think, however. He wasn't mad at Jagger Corey. Well, he *was*, but he was furious with himself.

"Miller? How in the hell did you let yourself get locked in some psycho's goddamned cellar?" he whispered. He *knew* better! Every ounce of intuition had screamed at him not to step over the lunatic's threshold, but he did it anyway. Prideful. Stupid.

"Cocky idiot!" he spat.

He was pretty freakin' certain the skinny little creep was batshit crazy. *And* with a giant—and scarily silent—partner-in-crime to boot. Whoever *Eljin* was, he was most likely riding around the streets of Salem in Byron's Explorer doing God knew what. What scared him most though, was Eljin's new face.

Byron awakened to a cold feeling on the back left side of his neck. There was just enough slack in the shackle's chain to feel the hairline back there. His fingers brushed across a small divot of missing hair. In the time between, Jagger must have concocted something from the missing lock of hair and then had his lapdog drink it down. When Byron had recovered consciousness, and Jagger was about to feed him the Tylenol, Eljin appeared at his master's side.

The hulking man stepped briefly into the light, and Byron almost lost his shit. Eljin was already transforming. It wasn't a perfect likeness, not by a longshot, but he could have passed for Byron's slightly larger brother. From a distance, Byron realized, they'd be indistinguishable.

He sighed, understanding Wanda would see Eljin leaving Jagger's storefront and assume it was him. The nut was either trying to buy time by fooling Wanda, or worse, he had some kind of plan that involved using the chief's likeness. None of it was good news.

Dread filled him when he realized not only was he trapped and helpless down here, but Jagger probably knew Wanda was responsible for Byron's appearance at his shop's front door. There was no telling what the psycho might do— and no way to stop it from happening.

It was when things seemed to be at their lowest he remembered something that sparked an ember of hope. Penny! Maybe she'd been doing her astral travel thing! A guy could hope, right?

Byron discovered the hard way his wife was a witch. When the dust settled and the Red Witch was on the run, Byron and Penny sat down and discussed the revelations of that evening. Penny, it turned out, had the ability (and the cunning) to keep tabs on her husband as he did his cop thing. Riding shotgun, in effect, and keeping him safe.

In all the years he'd been on the force, he'd always chalked up his survival in some of the most dangerous situations to finely honed instincts sharpened by years of dedicated service. He'd gone so far as to label this uncanny ability to see danger coming his "Cop's Intuition." For sure, a certain amount of it *was* just that. But the lion's share belonged to his wife. The witch.

For the longest time, even after he'd seen what she could do, he had a hard time believing it. He wasn't sure of the exact time or date he'd given in, finally admitting there was *something* to all this magical mumbo-jumbo, but he suspected it wasn't long after seeing Raul Martinez saved from possession by the demon Inanis. When Raul had returned to the land of the living, and Byron had watched and then confronted the thing possessing Raul, the last barrier was crossed. Denial just wasn't an option anymore.

From that day forward, he'd reluctantly embraced the things Penny had hidden from him.

It was a slow process. One does not go from skeptic to believer in the blink of an eye. Thankfully, Penny understood this and brought him along in baby steps. When Byron would get home from his shift, they would turn off the TV and retire to the upstairs guest bedroom.

Penny'd lit Dragon's Blood, laid out beanbags for both of them, and played a short, guided meditation video from YouTube on her iPhone. It took several sessions before Byron finally sat still for the entire five minute sessions. When he'd accomplished that, it still took several more sessions before he could still his mind enough to feel any effects from them. Gradually, it began to work.

It was subtle, at first. Byron noticed little changes here and there. Things that used to rattle him on the job didn't seem to have the same effect. Patience for some of the stupid mistakes his underlings made *used* to be in short supply, but suddenly seemed abundant and easier to come by. It even helped with his cigar habit. The cigars were his way of coping with the stress of the job. He'd go through four or five of them per shift. Now, he'd come home with two or three still in the box.

The changes were gradual; for Byron, they were profound.

He closed his eyes, calmed his mind, and thought about his wife.

"WHERE ARE YOU GOING?" asked Jazz.

"Where do you think? To find Moreland. That son of a bitch has some explaining to do," said Joanne.

"Before you go, Jo—"

"We, Mercy. Before *we* go," said Jo. "I want you guys to come with me. Safety in numbers and all that happy horse-shit. You all okay with that?" she asked.

"Damn straight we are," said Jazz.

Jo shot her an appreciative smile.

"I'm good with that, too," said Mercy. "There's just one tiny little problem."

The four witches gave her the floor, expectant looks all around.

"Transportation. We don't have a ride. Jazz, no disrespect, but the Civic won't fit all of us and it's almost useless in the snow."

Jazz was nodding and pulling out her cell phone before Mercy could finish. She tapped the phone's face and held it out like a slice of pizza. The speaker was on and all five witches listened as it rang.

"Jazz. I was just thinking about you! Where should I pick all of you up?"

Jazz was grinning from ear to ear. "Hi Penny. Still sharp as a tack, I see. You heard me before I even placed this call, didn't you?"

"I got skillz, sweetie."

"Yes you do. We're at Mercy's. The usual crowd. Can you fit all of us in your truck?"

"The happy bus? You bet. With room to spare. I've been waiting for a night just like this to test it out. I'm on my way now. Where we going first?"

"It's less of a where thing and more of a who thing. You pickin' up what I'm puttin' down?" asked Jazz.

"Yep," answered Penny.

"And Penny?" asked Jazz.

"Yeah?"

"Start thinking about a certain vampire-priest. We need to have a talk with him. Like yesterday," said Jazz.

"Gotcha. Driving and thinking. See you in ten."

Jazz hung up.

Penny tried to think about Moreland, but couldn't get her husband out of her mind.

SHE *HAD* TO CALL SOMEONE. Wanda was going crazy not knowing what Byron found out about Jagger. It had been at least half an hour—plenty of time, as she saw it, for Byron to toss around his thoughts and theories about the curious man and his shop at the end of Essex Street.

"Fuck it." She threw caution, and a potential tongue-lashing from Byron, to the wind.

Wanda hit the button on the side of her phone and brought up her contacts. She scrolled to Byron's name and was about to hit send when three sharp raps on her front door made her jump. The phone tumbled from her hand and fell directly into her half-filled cup of herbal tea. It landed face up and at an angle. Wanda watched as the screen first blinked, then strobed, and finally went dark.

"Oh, for fuck's sake!" she said, throwing both hands in the air.

She stared at the dead phone for a few moments longer, unable to accept it—much like a child when the top of her ice cream falls from the cone and lands in the dirt—somehow, someway, the universe will take it back. But the universe played for keeps. Be it a dead phone or a lost vanilla with chocolate sprinkles, the universe didn't discriminate.

When she finally looked up, a bolt of fear shot through her. A man stood at her front door, his top-hatted silhouette framed by LED-lit, gently falling snow.

Wanda rose from her stool behind the counter on legs made leaden by fear. The last person she expected to darken her door, especially on a night like this, was the newest resident of Essex Street. Being alone amplified her fear. And now her phone was useless. She was on her own.

The universe, just to prove it had a boundless sense of humor, decided now would be a great time to add to the fun. Jagger Corey's silhouette dissolved right before her eyes, and everything went dark. At first, she thought she'd died. Wanda screamed, then ran her hands up and down her body in the dark, confirming she was, indeed, still part of this world. As she inventoried every part of her physical being, a soft, yellow glow stole over her. When she looked up, Jagger remained in the door's frame. A lone candle glowed beneath his scraggly beard, it flickered in the soft wind of Wanda's Wicca'd Emporium's sheltered entranceway.

Jagger Corey smiled.

CHAPTER 9
SOMETHING OLD, SOMETHING NEW

H enry followed the intermittent flashes of light. Whoever was ahead kept a steady pace, ignoring his calls. With the wind whipping and the snow falling at an ever-increasing rate, he wasn't surprised the stranger couldn't hear him. After a time, he abandoned shouting and simply followed.

Where in the hell is this person going?

Being from Portland, well, for most of his life, anyway, Henry knew the city fairly well. At least, he'd always thought he did. The road he'd just left behind was one he'd driven hundreds of times. Probably a thousand. But he didn't recall ever seeing this vast, open field from the comfort of whatever vehicle he'd owned at the time. This didn't surprise him too much; most of the time he'd been cranking something by AC/DC, or Van Halen, or Metallica—too lost in enjoying the drive and the tunes to give a rat's ass about the surrounding scenery. *That* kinda shit was for geezers who went for drives to look at colored leaves.

Still, the whole situation felt wrong. He felt he was missing... something. A big something. When he finally figured it out, he slapped himself hard on the forehead.

"Idiot! Where are the footprints?"

He stopped in the middle of the field, turning in a circle and shining his flashlight across the snow covered ground in every direction. His own footprints directly behind him were, of course, well defined, though the further back he shined the light, their definition faded.

It was snowing pretty hard at the moment, and the wind had picked up considerably. It *was* possible this person's footprints had been erased along the way; they'd had a huge head start. If it was a smallish man or woman, the chances of obliterated footsteps were excellent. It couldn't be ruled out.

How in the hell could I have missed that?

It was the unanswerable question, and one which mattered little in the moment. Henry took a deep breath, then trudged on. His quarry was even further ahead since stopping to puzzle out the mystery of the footprints.

In the next few steps, the wind cranked into a sudden fury, as if angry with him for delaying his pursuit and wasting valuable time. Snow blew sideways, scraping across his cheeks and stinging them like a million tiny snow bees loosed by Boreas, the Greek god of the north wind, as punishment.

The bitter gale blew so hard he struggled lifting his head long enough to watch where he was going, and his progress slowed to a crawl. Reduced to stealing a brief glance forward here and there, he never noticed the low, fieldstone wall semi-buried by the growing drifts. Both knees hit the top of the wall at the same time, and Henry barked out in surprise. As he tumbled head over heels down the small hill on the wall's far side, he unleashed a stream of obscenities Jo would have cheered.

When he reached the bottom of the hill, he slid another few feet before he finally came to rest, face-up and on his back. That was when the winter night decided it really wanted to screw with his mind. Henry blinked several times, unsure of what he was seeing—and feeling. Where only moments before he could barely see two feet ahead in the gathering blizzard, he was now staring into a crystal clear sky filled with pinpricks of bright starlight. The wind was stilled. It was as if the fieldstone wall were the dividing line between alternate universes. Portland's version of Narnia.

"A wardrobe would have hurt a fuckload less than a stone wall!" he raged at the night sky.

Henry rolled onto his stomach, then pushed up from the ground, careful not to let his tender knees bump against the cold, hard earth. He shook the snow from his clothes and watched it fall and scatter across the grey and cracked asphalt beneath his feet. The night sky wasn't the *only* thing different on this side of the wall. Weeds shriveled by harsh winter air did their best to stand tall after struggling through the man-made barrier of the parking lot, but hung slanted in defeat. Henry traced their ragged path across the lot until his eyes fell on an object that didn't quite belong. A metallic-red aluminum baseball bat glowed softly in the starlight—a lone soldier in the middle of the weed-filled battlefield. The knob at its bottom faced him, and the barrel pointed directly forward, drawing his eyes onward and across the rest of the parking lot. The silhouette of a two-story, dilapidated structure loomed a mere thirty yards ahead.

Henry made his way to the bat, picked it up in stride, and

twirled it in his left hand. On the second twirl, he stopped. The knob had two letters on its bottom in permanent black ink; letters he instantly recognized because he'd put them on the bat himself years ago. HT. The bat had been stolen during a game. He couldn't remember the exact game, but it was towards the end of his high school playing career.

How the hell did it end up here? he wondered. A mystery for another time.

He stepped up onto the small loading dock and approached a set of black metal doors with small, wire-lined windows set head-high in each. Cupping a hand over his eyes, he leaned forward and peeked through the left door's window. The place was mostly empty, save for a few cardboard boxes barely visible in the dim starlight and scattered in haphazard piles across the dusty floor. It looked like someone had recently moved out, and hadn't given a thought to the building's future tenants.

Like they'd been in a hurry.

He tried the doors, but they were locked tight.

"Time to try the front," he told the parking lot. The Jeep could not be reached for comment.

As he strode along the side of the building, a growing sense of déjà vu crept over him. He couldn't recall ever coming to this building, or ever seeing anything like it in all his days in Portland. In what seemed a lifetime ago, he would have scoffed at these feelings. Over the past year and a few months, he'd learned to take them to heart. They'd saved his life and the lives of those he loved on more than one occasion. So instead of skepticism, he was switched to red alert.

Calm. Deliberate. Watchful.

He rounded the corner of the house. Instead of stepping

directly onto the front porch, Henry continued across the patchy lawn and into the middle of the moonlit street. When he turned to face the front of the house, he was grateful he'd heeded intuition. The porch was pitch black. Where starlight *should* have shown, shadows reigned. It was *unnaturally* dark. The only thing visible, because it rested above the porch and was haphazardly nailed to the shingles on the roof, was a sign. It tried desperately to appear professional, but instead looked like something from an eighth-grade art class. In chipped and peeling paint, the establishment's name was painted in yellow, sloppy cursive on a red background.

Henry read the sign aloud. "Jagger's Magical Treasures."

ARCHIE REWOUND the tape to the beginning. He'd listened to the first five minutes over and over, trying to understand exactly what was going on. In the year this conversation was recorded, the equipment he'd used had been state of the art... in 1993. Now, most of it belonged in a museum. The constant rewinding and fast forwarding was about to send him over the edge. The sound quality was tinny, but, thank God, crystal clear.

Digital recording was a thing then, of course, but the school's pencil pushers told him the tape recorder worked just fine, and then summarily denied him the funds for better equipment.

Cheap pricks, he thought.

He lamented that only three short years later, the iPhone would be invented.

Oh how we take for granted just how wonderful modern technology really is!

Archie took a deep breath, let it out, and begged the gods for patience. He pressed play on the ancient tape deck, fanned his transcription notes back to the beginning, then read as he listened...

Archie – "Dr. Archibald Love, interviewing Jagger Corey, September 10, 2004. Good morning Jagger, it's nice to finally meet you."

Jagger – "If you say so, doc."

Archie – "I do. Now, Doctor Hammond from Salem State Hospital has referred you to me because he thinks I can help you remember how you ended up in Salem. I want to state right up front that you are under no obligation to do this. I—"

Jagger – "Do what, exactly? No one has explained a fucking thing to me about what's going on. All I know is I woke up on the Common and the police accosted me, threw me in a cell, and charged me with public intoxication. I don't even drink! That big shithead of a cop tried telling me it was for my own good. He—"

Archie – "Lieutenant Miller is a fine officer. If he said it was for your own good, he meant it. I've known him personally for many years, and he just happens to be my brother-in-law. You're actually lucky it wasn't O'Malley who picked you up, he—"

Jagger – "So is that how things work over here? Your big shithead of a brother-in-law cop picks them up and makes sure you acquire your next payday? A family business?"

Archie – "No. That's not how it works. You were transferred to Danvers. Doctor Hammond makes the recommendation based on your case file, and then you are assigned someone. That happened to be me. Now, shall we continue?"

Archie could hear the rustle of Jagger's leather coat as he shrugged. The tape may have been recorded many years ago, but the fidelity was adequate. It helped crystallize the memory in his mind. He abandoned the transcript, closed his eyes, and let the tape take him back in time.

Archie – "You say you woke up on the Salem Common, and you've no recollection of how you got there. I'm curious, Jagger, what is the last clear memory you have before that night?"

Again, Archie could clearly make out the rustle of Jagger's leather jacket as he shrugged.

Jagger – "I was out walking in the woods in Portland. I couldn't tell you exactly where, but it was dark. I like the dark."

Archie – "Were you with a friend? Girlfriend?"

Jagger – "I'm not exactly Mr. Popularity in Portland."

Archie – "I take that to mean you were alone?"

Jagger – "Take it however you want."

It was years ago, but Archie felt the frustration building as if it were happening in the moment.

Archie – "Did you have a *reason* to be out in the woods alone?"

Jagger – "I don't need a *reason* to be out there alone. I like it out there. I can do the things I was born to do, and no one bothers me."

Archie - "What do you mean when you say 'the things you were born to do?'"

It was then Archie saw the change in Jagger. Up to that point, he'd been putting on the tough, *I don't give a shit about anything*, teenager facade. Jagger straightened his back, the smirk disappeared from his face, and the tone of his voice changed. The transformation was unnerving, and a chill ran down Archie's spine—one that had a tail about fifteen years long. It had been like talking to a completely different person. Someone older. Wiser. Dangerous.

Jagger – "Come now, professor, we both know what I'm referring to here. Do I have to *spell* it out for you?"

Archie swallowed down a nervous lump, both on the tape, and in the privacy of his candlelit office. Echoes of dread bounced off the walls of time, connecting past and present.

Archie – "I'd be grateful if you could clarify it for me, Jagger."

He winced hearing the stammer in his own voice. And remembered the dark smile on the young man's face. It chilled him for the second time.

Jagger – "Magic, Dr. Love. I practice magic in the forest."

Archie – "What kind of magic, Jagger?"

Though he knew what came next, he was still surprised. Archie fought the urge to stop the tape, then reminded himself this darkness was now back in his life. Less than two miles away.

Jagger – "The only kind that matters to *her*, professor. The kind that requires *sacrifice!*"

In the dark silence of his office, the old tape machine popped to a stop. It might as well have been a shotgun going off. Archie jumped in his chair and almost fell over backwards.

CHAPTER 10

DEBT SPELLED OUT

P enny pulled up in front of Mercy's apartment on Witch Hill Road, smiling at the sight of five witches bouncing up and down trying to keep warm in the cold. When she pulled to a stop, Jo grabbed shotgun, Fermina and Luci climbed into the back row seating, and Mercy and Jazz took the middle row behind Penny and Jo.

"Where to first?" Penny asked. She was looking at Jo, but Mercy answered.

"I think the best place to start would be the statue of Samantha, since that's how they get into the Council of the Realms."

Jo smiled at Penny. "What she said."

Penny gunned the 4Runner's gas. It slid a little, caught, and they were on their way. Less than five minutes later, they piled out and stood in a circle around the statue of Samantha from the TV show "Bewitched."

"So what do we do now?" asked Penny.

"I would say ring the bell, or knock on the door. But—" Jo smiled and shrugged. Mercy's idea of starting here seemed a good one at first. Getting in? That was something else.

"Jazz? Can you tell if he's been here?" asked Penny.

Jazz walked around the statue, searching high and low for a sign Moreland, or *any* vampire, had left trace evidence of their arrival or departure. She shook her head, "I don't see or smell anything."

"They have a smell?" asked Penny.

Jazz, Jo, and Mercy nodded in unison.

"Roses, sometimes," said Jo.

"Fresh earth," Mercy added.

"They can also carry the scent of their last victim," said Jazz. She was answering Penny's question, but looking directly at Joanne.

Jo tilted her head to the side. "What are you thinking, Jazz?" asked Jo.

"I'm thinking you need to go sit in the car for a couple of minutes, honey. Let me check something out."

Jo shot her a puzzled look, but did as Jazz asked.

"I need the rest of you to do me a favor. We're gonna surround the statue. But it's gotta be a precise alignment."

Each of them gave Jazz a look similar to the one Jo had.

"I need to set us up at five exact points. We're going to form a human pentacle around Samantha. Then I can do something that might give us an idea where ole Jeevesy might have gotten to. I'm not sure it'll work, but I'm going on a hunch. It can't hurt, right?"

No one argued.

Jazz stood at the point where Samantha's head was, then faced it. She directed Fermina to her left, Luci to her right, Mercy to her left but further away, then Penny took position opposite Mercy. Once done, she told the four witches to walk diagonally away from her, exactly seven steps each.

The pentacle points were aligned, now it must become manifest.

The streets of Salem were empty. None of the shops were open, and the power had gone out in most of the town. If there was ever a time to do something like this in public, it was now. What Jazz was about to do would make Joanne's attack of Zachary Villitz look like a walk in the park. If Armand Moreland had known, he would have had a coronary—or whatever passed as one for a vampire.

Jazz closed her eyes and began the incantation:

"Earth. Air. Fire. Water. Spirit. We call on you tonight. We seek the blood of Moreland, show us in the light."

For a few moments, all was quiet. Snow fell all around, ticking lightly on their winter coats. Then the first hint the spell was working appeared. Sparks of gold began to flow between the five witches. It was faint, with pinpricks of light popping, then dashing and vanishing like faeries playing paparazzi. A few moments passed, and the sparse flashes grew more regular, then much brighter. Sparks swirled, and brilliant colors glowed in the energized vortex.

Jo watched with fascination from the passenger seat of the 4Runner. She saw the outline of the pentacle form, and her jaw dropped in awe as it became a solid glowing circle with the five pointed star in its middle. The outer ring pulsed with the colors of the rainbow, while the inner ring remained a dazzling shade of gold. When she pulled her eyes from it, Jazz stared directly at her. It was then Jo realized the scar on her shoulder was starting to hurt. Nothing bad, just a dull throb. As the spell continued, the throb turned into an ache, and then bloomed full and painful. In a matter of seconds, her shoulder felt like someone was sticking a branding iron directly into the skin. As if the wound were opening again of its own accord. It was more than she could bear, and she passed out.

When she came around, she was looking at the lights of Penny's dashboard. She turned her head to the right, and Penny stared down at her, smiling.

"Welcome back!"

Jo said, "Saint Peter? If these are the Pearly Gates, I want my money back."

Penny laughed. "I think I'd make a great Saint Peter, bitch!"

Jo laughed, then tried to sit up. Pain flared in her shoulder, and she stifled a scream.

"Let me help you," said Penny. She put a hand behind Jo's back, and Jazz leaned over the backseat and offered her another.

When Jo was upright, she asked, "Okay, what the fuck was that all about?"

"Well," said Jazz, "we found out a couple of things. First, Jeevesy isn't home, but he's been here since he left Mercy's. The trail is still fresh."

"You're calling him Jeevesy again. That's not a good sign," said Jo.

Jazz said, "Until I know he's not up to some fishy shit, he's back to being Jeevesy."

Jo was immediately wary, "Why? What else is going on."

"Have you remembered any more of what happened

78

during the attack in the park? Or, more specifically, after the attack?" asked Jazz.

"I told you all I know. I wish I could remember more, but it's still a blank. You said it took you a while after your NDE to remember shit, right Mercy?"

Mercy nodded.

Jo turned back to Jazz. "What did you find out?"

Jazz took a deep breath. "Now, I don't know this for certain, but I'm about as sure of this as I can possibly be. If I had to guess, Jo... I think Moreland had to do more than just fight off those void creeps to save your life. I think you were closer to death than you realize."

Jo stared at her, but said nothing. She had a sneaking suspicion she knew *exactly* where Jazz was going with this.

Jazz continued. "The reason I had you come back to the truck was so I could separate the smells I was getting. The minute we got to Samantha's statue, I could smell Moreland. But his scent is on you, too. I noticed it at Mercy's, and then all the way over here in the truck. It grew stronger as we got closer. I asked you to come in here because I needed to be sure. And now I'm sure."

"Sure of what?" asked Jo.

"He saved your life by giving you his blood. I can smell it all over you. That wound on your shoulder? There's a reason it healed so fast. Vampire blood heals things like *that*." Jazz snapped her fingers. "Quick! Miraculous! There's nothing else like it on earth. It's one more reason they keep their distance from the living. If the modern world knew of the healing properties of their blood, they'd hunt them down mercilessly. They kinda got it goin' on."

Jo was blown away. It was a lot to absorb. She closed her eyes and searched her memory, but still couldn't recall anything beyond the point where she saw her most precious thoughts and memories being ripped from her soul. All she had were more questions. "So, if Armand did this, and saved my life, why would I be compelled to get away from him? I'm not shittin' you here, I wanted to be away from him as fast as I could."

Jazz nodded and said, "I have a theory on that too. But you might not like it."

Jo shrugged. "Whether I like it or not, does that change anything?"

"Nope. Not one bit."

"Then hit me with it. I'm a big girl."

Jazz blew out a long breath. "Another side effect of being healed with vampire blood... is attachment."

Jo rolled her hand. "Okay..."

"When I say attachment, I'm not talking about your friendship moving to another level just because he saved your life. I'm talking seriously deep shit here, Jo."

"Such as?"

"Such as sexual—"

Jo burst out laughing.

For the first time she could ever remember, Jazz looked mad at her. There were few people that could scare Jo into silence. Jazz was one of them. She didn't fear Jazz striking out at her, that wasn't even an option. Once you were a friend of Jazz's you were a friend for life; it was just how Jazz rolled. But if you didn't take her seriously when she was being serious, she'd let you know it. Now was one of those times. Jo knew it was out of love, and also out of a deep concern for what could happen. Dealing with the ins and outs of vampire behavior was, for Jazz, the *most* serious business. Her history with them was long, and she knew the kind of power tactics they pulled. Vampires didn't throw their blood around just for kicks. If they used it to heal someone, they usually expected something back. And, most times, the terms were non-negotiable. You did what they wanted or you paid a price.

Jo's face colored red with embarrassment. "Sorry. It just seemed absurd to me."

Jazz's face softened. And then she began to laugh. The other four witches joined in, and the tension gripping the interior of the 4Runner melted away.

"I know why you were laughing, honey. It just took me off guard because I'm so worried for you. But that image you had in your head was pretty hilarious!"

"What image?" asked Mercy.

"Don't you dare tell her!" said Joanne through a huge grin.

Jazz laughed then held up both hands, "All I can say, without giving it away, is Jeevesy might be walking funny after Jo got done with him. Use your imagination."

No one had a problem figuring it out, and they giggled their asses off for a good while.

When they settled and caught their breath, Jazz continued.

"Like I was about to say, it's usually a favor of a sexual nature. And trust me when I tell you, it don't matter what the vampire looks like. You will *want* to do what he asks. Once that blood is a part of you, it can make a ham sandwich look like filet fucking mignon."

Jo said nothing. The others paid Jazz rapt attention. She had the floor.

"Sex, however, isn't the only thing. And in this case, I seriously doubt that's it at all. I don't get that kinda vibe from Armand. If anything, he looks on you as part of his family now. He looks at all of us that way, I'm pretty sure. He's said so himself a bunch'a times. Now, Jo, you said you were dying to get away from him. To me, that seems strange."

"How so?" asked Jo.

"Well, in my experience, it's usually the opposite. The attachment... or desire to be with a vampire after that blood is in you, is almost irresistible. Either you have an iron will, or something else is going on here. At the very least, you wouldn't be fighting so hard to leave his company. So I don't think that's it. I think it was coming from Moreland. For whatever reason, he was shielding you from himself."

Jo's eyes went wide. "For what reason?" Then she remembered what Jazz had warned. "You said there were other kinds of attachment. What are they?"

Jazz shrugged. "It really could be anything. He might want a favor from you, or ask you to do something for him. Part of his shielding you from himself might have been to keep that a secret for now. You know, call in that favor when he might need it most? Nothing would surprise me. And you need to be ready for anything."

"I'm ready," said Jo.

Jazz locked eyes with her. "Don't bet on it."

CHAPTER 11
SIGNS AND THREATS

"**W**hat can I help you with, Mister Corey?" asked Wanda. She struggled to keep her voice steady. *Never show weakness,* she thought.

"It's not what you can help me with, Miss Heinze, it's what I can help *you* with," said Jagger. His voice was muffled by the door's glass, but she heard him just fine. The *I-know-something-you-don't-know* tone was unmistakable, even through the barrier. It chilled her.

"And what's that?" asked Wanda.

Jagger looked from his left to his right, then said, "It's very cold out here, Miss Heinze. Or should I call you Wanda?"

"Miss Heinze will do." Wanda saw anger flash across Jagger's face.

Screw you, pal, she thought.

"Well, Miss Heinze, it would be much better if I could come in and talk to you. I communicate far better when my teeth aren't chattering ceaselessly." His smile grew bigger. Wanda's creeped-out factor grew larger.

83

"I'm not in the habit of letting strangers into my shop, Mister Corey."

Jagger tilted his head. "Then how do you make a living?"

Smartass. "I meant after closing, Mister Corey. And usually not in a power outage, either. You need to go home."

The smile dropped from Jagger's face. He leaned closer to the door's window. The candle in his hand flickered, its wavy light making him look demonic. "I know why you sent the cop." Jagger kicked the bottom of the door hard, rattling it in its frame. In something close to a growl, he said, "Open. The. Fucking. Door."

Wanda backed deeper into the shop. Her initial impression of Jagger Corey had been way off. As she'd watched him moving in, from the safety of her shop these last few days, she'd thought him eccentric—almost comical. The way he dressed—with the top hat and the orange and purple scarf sticking out from the top of his tailcoat—had amused and even charmed her. And the way his clothes hung on his slight frame enhanced the effect. The scraggly beard and constantly perplexed expression rounded it out. Jagger Corey was as inoffensive a character as she'd ever seen in a town so diverse it could be the dictionary definition of the word.

All kinds lived in Salem, and that's what made it so special. Salem was not defined by race, creed, color, religion, nationality—it was defined by beliefs. Period. No one was excluded, and everyone was welcome. The city, to the outside world, was known as The Witch City, and with good reason. The grand irony was how welcoming the once unjustly persecuted, for which the town was nicknamed, accepted everyone. That was just how witches rolled. Wanda was no exception—until now.

There was something very wrong about Jagger Corey. He didn't *belong* in Salem, but she couldn't put her finger on exactly *why*. Part of her felt guilty for thinking this, but another part sensed something really... off. Like *X-Files* off. It had nothing to do with the last few minutes, either. Jagger Corey seemed *out of place*.

In the silence following his outburst, Wanda watched as he fumed in the doorway, his chest heaving and his breath chugging out in vaporous bursts. The last thing in the world she was about to do was let him through her door.

Then, he took away her choice.

"I know what you're thinking, witch. You're thinking you'll just wait me out until your cop friend comes back. I'll grant you—it is a sound strategy."

It was *exactly* what Wanda was thinking. That Jagger had figured it out filled her with dread at what came next.

"This is not something that's going to happen. That big, dumb cop is currently occupying space in my basement."

Any glimmer of hope she held for a rescue from Byron died on the heels of those words.

"That wasn't your cop boyfriend leaving my shop earlier, just in case you were wondering. Granted, he looked a lot like him. But that's one of my best tricks! The man you saw leaving is an associate of mine. His name is Eljin Black. Eljin has a talent for forms, Miss Heinze. With a little prodding— and when I say little, I mean very little; Mister Black is quite enthusiastic about his duties—and a sampling of the subject du jour... that means subject of the day, in case you were wondering—"

"I know what it means, ass hat." Scared as she was, his cockiness irked her.

Jagger cleared his throat. Despite the interruption, he

was enjoying himself now. "Very well. As I was saying, with a little prodding, and a sample from the subject, Mister Black can become whoever I wish him to become. He is currently the acting Chief of the Salem Police. So, it's in your best interest to let me in. We have much to discuss."

Wanda didn't move. She was afraid for Byron. Her phone was toast. But nothing in the world could force her to open the door for Jagger Corey. That's what she believed. Then, Jagger spoke.

"I'm not a stupid man, Miss Heinze. I know, as much as you're probably worried about the fate of your cop friend, it will not compel you to open this door. But there's something else, and I can't *wait* to tell you."

The glee in his voice both scared her to death, and pissed her off to no end. Wanda waited, if only to gain some measure of control over the situation.

"I've got all night, Miss Heinze. *But you don't.*" He sang the last three words as a child would sing *na na na, na na, naaaa.*

Wanda thought, *fucking psycho!* But she said, "Tell me."

"I thought you'd never ask! The *new* Chief Miller is currently on his way over to Salem University. Once he arrives, I've directed him to park outside the campus. He will remain outside until I instruct him otherwise. He will park at the far end of the lot where a certain snow-covered, VW microbus is currently the only vehicle in said parking lot. Candlelight illuminates a single window in that area of the campus. Doctor Archibald Love is busily working away in his office. On what? I can only guess. But I suspect I'd guess correctly. Are you with me so far, Wanda?"

She bristled at the use of her first name. Then, Wanda hung her head. "Yes."

"Now. Open the door, please."

Dazed, Wanda shuffled toward the front door of Wanda's Wicca'd Emporium—and let some crazy inside.

❧

THE LAST THING in the world Henry wanted to do was step on that porch. Standing in the middle of the road, his breath trailing into the night and his shadow sharply defined by unusually bright moonlight, he tried to figure out a way around it. Upon further inspection of Jagger's Magical Treasures however, he'd come up empty.

There were bars on all the windows of the first floor. The windows to the basement were non-existent because there *was* no basement; the building rested on a stone slab. The lone means of entry, other than braving the living darkness of the porch, was a small window just beneath the peak of the roof. It was more plywood than window. Most of the panes were smashed out, and the plywood board was hung from the inside. Which, when he thought about it, was a good thing. He could much more easily kick the board *in* than pull it loose had it been hung on the outside—like most normal people would have boarded up a window.

"Now all I need is a way up there," he said. This talking to himself thing was starting to become a habit, and he wondered if it meant something.

"Yeah, it means something, dummy. You're nervous and alone," he told himself, then shrugged, "Fuck it. Who cares?"

With that settled, he searched for a way up to the roof covering *The Porch of Doom*.

A repeat trip around Jagger's shack yielded nothing

qualifying as a makeshift ladder. He looked around for another business or house; there was nothing in the immediate area.

"What kind of fucking idiot builds a business in the middle of nowhere?"

Well, he thought, *kinda explains the condition of the place.*

"I must be getting calmer. I didn't talk to myself that time—I said, ironically."

He was on the verge of giving up. The porch was still a no go; everything in his being told him crossing its border would not do wondrous things for his health. The whole ground floor was barred up like a house of correction. And the basement that *should* have been a basement was not.

He studied the building, the bat firmly gripped in his left hand and tapping his right palm with its barrel. It was something he'd always done from Little League baseball and right up through his years playing for Portland High. Back then, it calmed him and helped him think as he waited for his turn at bat. It was having the same effect now. All those years, he'd been meditating without knowing it. In the calm, as the metronomic thud of the bat against his right palm soothed him, inspiration struck.

Henry stepped back onto the road, looking both ways for traffic he was positive wouldn't show, and made his way to the other side. On the shoulder were enough rocks of a decent size—roughly that of a baseball; some larger, some smaller—to get the job done. He grabbed about a half dozen for each pocket. As he crossed the road, his jacket drooped with the weight of the rocks, and he smiled when he saw the new shape of his shadow.

"I look like Grimace from McDonald's!" The last syllable of McDonald's echoed from the hills behind him.

He stopped in the middle of the road, dumped the rocks on the moonlit asphalt, and prepared to relive his glory days.

"Well, it's gonna be interesting to see how he gets out of this one, Jerry!" said Henry in his best impression of Boston Red Sox TV announcer Dave O'brien.

"This hasn't been his best year, to put it lightly," answered Henry in a somewhat poorer imitation of color commentator Jerry Remy. "I'll be shocked if he makes it out of this one, but even a blind squirrel finds a nut every now and then."

Henry could hear O'brien laughing. Remy did that to you.

Henry stooped and plucked the largest rock from the pile. Turning sideways, he placed his right foot on the yellow line dividing the road, using it as a stand-in for a pitching rubber. He cradled the rock in both hands, holding it chest high. *Breathe*, he told himself, as he sank into the pitching routine he'd used in high school.

"Here's the wind-up! And the pitch!"

Henry let it fly. The ragged looking support beam for the rickety sign took a direct hit. Splinters flew, and the left side of the sign sagged and slid forward. It hung over the edge of the front porch. He held his breath, watching the darkness below for any sign of life, positive something would reach out from it and snatch the sign away. When nothing stirred, he let out the breath he'd been holding, reached for another stone, and assumed the position.

Rock number two took out the opposite support, and the sign broke free. There was a louder than expected wood-on-metal scraping sound as the sign slid across the gutter. Though it appeared to be a haphazard, hastily assembled mess, the sign was much larger and heavier than Henry first realized. It snagged the gutter—most likely a leftover nail from one of the supports—and swung inward toward the forbidding darkness of the porch. It landed on the railing, face-first and flat and with a loud wooden slap, then seesawed between the darkness and the light. When the score was settled, most of the sign landed exactly where he feared. Only the top third was visible above the porch railing.

"Shit!"

There wasn't much choice. He'd have to brave that unknowable darkness and yank the sign to safety. There was no other way to get to the second floor.

"Oh gravity, thou art a heartless bitch," said Henry, quoting Doctor Sheldon Cooper from *The Big Bang Theory* TV show.

He hung his head and headed for *The Porch of Doom*.

As he drew closer he assumed his eyes would adjust, lightening the darkness. Instead, the porch seemed to grow darker. The air around it became colder. Henry slowed himself, looking left and right, preparing for the unexpected. He was close now, the sign less than five feet away.

Another step. Four feet. Colder.

One more. Three feet. Freezing.

Two.

One.

Then, the whispering started.

CHAPTER 12
TALE OF THE TAPE

Archie wasn't sure he could continue with the Jagger Corey tapes. The first one unnerved him. They got worse from here. Every word on each tape would be a constant reminder of how things could have been different. How he could have changed this young man's life if only he'd been paying more attention to the obvious cries for help. Jagger was a disturbed young man, and as with most, attention—positive or negative—was what they craved. He'd definitely given him attention, but not the kind he'd needed.

Maybe something on the tapes might point him in the right direction. *Something missed?*

It was possible.

"Stay on your toes, you old fool," he whispered.

Archie laid tape one on his desk, snapped up tape two from the dusty box, shoved it into the recorder, and pressed play before he could change his mind.

As if I have a choice, he thought.

Archie – "Dr. Archibald Love, interviewing Jagger Corey, September 17, 2004. Happy Friday, Jagger."

Jagger – "Every day's better than the next, Doc. Can't wait to leave here and head back to my scenic cell at Salem State Mental Hospital."

Archie – "It's not forever, Jagger. Just until we can get things sorted out for you. Find your parents and return you home. What's so funny?"

He saw Jagger's face on the backs of his eyelids, smirking. It was an *I know something you don't know* kind of smirk. Archie remembered biting his tongue.

Jagger – "You keep saying you're gonna help return me to my parents. But I've got a news flash for you, professor. You'll never find them. At least, not in this world."

Goosebumps sprung on Archie's forearms, and a chill ran down his spine. It mirrored his reaction from fifteen years earlier.

Archie – "What do you mean by that, Jagger? Are you telling me—"

Jagger's laugh made the tinny speaker on the tape player vibrate.

Jagger – "What? You think I killed them?"

Archie – "Did you?"

Another bout of laughter tore through the speaker, then abruptly stopped. In Archie's mind's eye, he witnessed the sudden and complete change Jagger went through in that long ago moment. It was like a switch had been flipped, turning off one part of his ego, then switching on another.

Archie, back then, always kept a note pad on his lap for sessions like these. In his own shorthand, he'd written: *2 in 1? Or maybe more?* He suspected Jagger might have Split Personality Disorder.

When next he spoke, the older, wiser version was in control.

Jagger – "I didn't kill my parents, professor. But I won't lie to you—the thought has crossed my mind. More than once. I won't do it, of course. The repercussions would be disastrous, on a number of—"

Jagger had stopped at this point, Archie remembered. Then leaned forward and said...

Jagger – "—levels."

With the last word, Jagger had wiggled his eyebrows at Archie.

Archie – "What does that mean, exactly? 'Repercussions on a number of levels?' I'm not sure I know how to interpret that."

Jagger had sat back in his chair then, Archie remembered. The look on his face had been one of calm smugness. He'd wanted to smack the little bastard.

Jagger – "You know, prof—could I call you Archie?"

Archie – "Let's keep it formal for now, Jagger. Professor is fine. Or Doctor, if you prefer."

Jagger – "I prefer Archie, since you've taken to calling me by *my* first name. It only seems fair, I think."

Archie – "All the same, Jagger. Let's keep things as they are. There are certain dynamics in psychology. Maybe down the road, that'll change. For now, let's keep things status quo."

The calm smugness dropped for the briefest of moments, in its place was a flash of red-hot hatred. So fleeting was it, Archie had almost missed it. But he didn't. And he let Jagger know it.

Archie – "You seem displeased with me, Jagger. And I don't think it's because I refuse to let you call me by my first name.

Jagger – "You're *just* like him."

Archie – "Just like who?"

Jagger – "My father. You even resemble him."

Archie – "I'm sorry that upsets you, Jagger. Would you like to talk about him?"

Jagger had barked out a laugh.

Jagger – "So now this is therapy?"

Archie – "If you'd like to call it that, we can. I do *that* too. I'm just interested in helping you so you can get back to your life, Jagger."

Jagger – "Is that so? Because from where I'm sitting, *Archie*, your eyes say one thing, but the rest of you wants something else."

Archie – "Really? Enlighten me, then."

Jagger – "First, let me ask you something."

In the here and now, Archie wanted to shake some sense into his past self. Instead of taking the reigns and directing Jagger to answer his question, he'd allowed himself to be led from the path. It was the beginning of the end.

Archie – "Ask away."

Jagger – "If I told you I can predict the future, would you believe me?"

Archie – "It would depend, I guess."

Jagger – "Depend? I tell you I can predict the future and the best you can come up with is 'It would depend?'"

Archie – "If you tell me something like Annie, my receptionist, is going to walk through the door in the next five minutes, there's a good chance you'll be right. I'd hardly call that predicting the future—more like playing the odds. So, when I say it would depend, it means you'd have to predict something which couldn't possibly occur through a likely scenario. It would have to be random and unrelated. Something not easily guessed through whatever your current circumstances might be."

Jagger – "You insult me, *Archie*. You think I would stoop so low as to try a cheap parlor gag? I'm going to tell you something that's *going to happen*. Possibly today. But I want to make it interesting. If I'm right, you have to sign the papers to release me. If I'm wrong, I'll continue on with this fucking foolishness until you deem it finished. Deal?"

Archie – "You're mandated by the state to visit with me at least four separate times, Jagger. I can't release you before then. The best I can do is sign your release form early. So, I can at least guarantee October first will be your last mandatory appearance in this office."

Through closed eyes, Archie replayed the scene in his mind. Jagger didn't seem bothered one way or the other about the conditions of the offer. This should have been a warning sign. Jagger hadn't given a shit about leaving treatment early, he'd just wanted Archie to play his game.

"You goddamned fool," he whispered to himself in the shameful solitude of his office. "He played you like a fiddle."

Jagger – "I guess that will have to do, Archie. So, for the record, we're in agreement. If I correctly predict an event I'd have no earthly idea was going to happen, you'll sign the papers releasing me, as stipulated, on time. Not a moment past the time I'm mandated to see you?"

Archie – "Yes. It's not going to happen, but fair is fair. I'll submit the paperwork the moment said prediction is proven correct. But I have to ask, when will I be receiving your grand prognostication?"

Jagger – "How about now?"

Archie – "Come again?"

Jagger – "I can predict something, right here, right now. But first, do you have the appropriate paperwork?"

Archie – "For your release?"

Jagger – "No, for the title to your car. Of course for my release, you imbecile."

Archie – "There's no need for that, Jagger."

Archie listened to 2004 Archie rifle through his desk, then heard the shuffle of paperwork. The Archie in the here and now, eyes closed, shook his head in disbelief.

"Talk about unprofessional!" he said to the empty office.

The only rational excuse that made him feel better about the whole thing was chalking it up to curiosity. At that point in his life, he'd been enthralled with the field of parapsychology. The possibility—however remote—of Jagger predicting the future was too tempting to pass up. He'd chased the fat, juicy worm wriggling on the hook and clamped down hard. All Jagger was doing was reeling him in.

Archie – "Here it is. Would you like to read it over?"

Jagger – "That won't be necessary, professor. I already know you've produced the correct form. I even know you have to flip to page three. I'll then initial on that page, you'll flip to page seven, I'll sign in the bottom left corner, and you'll sign the witness statement in the right hand corner. This will happen within the next five to seven minutes. Right after your receptionist... Annie? That was her name, correct?"

Archie – "Yes, but I already stated, predicting Annie—"

Jagger – "I know, professor. Simply predicting *Annie* will walk through that door will not suffice. We've covered that ground. It's not who will come through that door, and when. Even I'll admit, that would be *far* too easy. It's what she's going to *say*. Now, care to taste the future, *Archie?*"

He could hear the springs creaking across time and tape as he leaned back in his old chair.

Archie – "Proceed."

It was then Archie heard the soft rattle of jewelry through the tape machine's speaker. In the years since, he'd forgotten about it. The devastating accuracy of Jagger's prediction had washed it from his mind completely. Now, in the darkness of his office, and with the clarity afforded by the separation of time and space, he saw Jagger take hold of something at the end of a silver chain.

Archie fought to calm himself, then focused his mind's eye on the scene. He saw Jagger reach into the left breast pocket of his topcoat. He'd never noticed it before, but the silver chain hanging around Jagger's neck had always *been tucked into that pocket. It was an odd thing to do, but Jagger was the definition of odd, so Archie'd never thought twice about it.*

With his eyes still closed, Archie reached out and hit pause on the recorder. He ran the moment in slow motion in his mind, watching as Jagger reached with his right hand toward that pocket. The movement was subtle, as the boy almost always crossed his arms—a classic defensive posture—when conversing with Archie. With the deftness of a stage magician, Jagger had produced a gleaming obsidian gemstone. It was set in a polished silver claw, the points of which terminated halfway up its front— as if the creature to whom the claw belonged was presenting it to Archie as a gift.

Archie let the memory drift forward and saw that just before Jagger's dark prediction, there'd been the faintest glint from the obsidian stone—a brief flash of red light—there and gone. He thanked his lucky stars he hadn't blinked at the wrong time back then, because the memory would have been lost forever.

With a right hand feeling as heavy as lead, Archie pushed play on the recorder.

Jagger – "I'm sorry in advance to have to tell you this, professor. I'm not one that enjoys being the bearer of bad news. Annie is about to tell you your Aunt Jenny has passed. Have no fear though. She died peacefully in her sleep. Your sister just discovered her."

Archie – "Jagger. This is not even remotely funny. If you think I'm going to just sit here—"

Archie clamped his eyes shut even tighter, as if doing so would erase the past. Nothing changed. He heard the frosted glass of his office door rattle as Annie kicked it open from the bottom. She'd told Archie about half a million times to get the door fixed, and to this day he'd never done so. On *that* day, back in 2004, she'd let it slide. His heart had risen in his throat and threatened to strangle him as Annie breathed truth into Jagger's dark words.

"I'm so sorry, Arch," said Annie. The frosted glass rattled softly as Annie left his office and closed the door behind her.

In the present, Archie blew out the breath he'd been holding, then wiped at both eyes with the backs of his hands. "Son of a bitch."

There was silence for almost a full minute as the tape ran. Then...

Jagger – "I believe you have some papers to sign. Archie."

CHAPTER 13
ROOMS AND WITCHES

Armand Moreland was doing the best he could under the circumstances. It wasn't easy. It took everything he had to put up a wall between himself and Joanne. By the time they'd reached Mercy's apartment, the protective barrier he'd placed between them wore thin. Had they remained together for another minute or two, the consequences would have been disastrous. As it stood now, things were back on track. Well, as much as they could be.

The attack tonight on the Salem Common was something he'd anticipated, just not so soon. If he hadn't prepared, the green-eyed witch's soul might have been splintered and shared between those jackals from the void. They would have devoured her, and any prospect of future incarnations for Joanne would have depended on hunting down each one of them, and then extracting each piece of her soul to bring it back together. The torment she'd suffer was something he didn't want to contemplate. He'd known they'd been ordered to retrieve something and leave the witch intact, but in a frenzy things sometimes got out of hand.

Jo had done an amazing job of eliminating the first four. By the time the last two entities pinned her, Moreland had covered half the distance. In short order however, they'd gashed her shoulder to rapidly weaken her physical body. The snow was covered in blood. The adrenaline pumping through Jo's system, and the struggle she'd put up once they had her down, caused a dangerous amount of blood loss. The decision whether to heal her right then, or risk the time it would take an ambulance to reach her, was not an easy one. Then he recalled his *own* history, and what Henry would endure if he failed to act. When it came down to *that*, the decision was easy.

To keep her from dying, he had to use his own blood. Armand had known full well the consequences. Once Joanne was away from him for a time, the memories of the attack would come flooding back, and the pull she'd feel—the sense of *obligation*—would overwhelm her. She would feel duty-bound to please him.

Less scrupulous vampires used such debts to take advantage of a situation like this. They would find *any* excuse to use their blood to manipulate their victims. Most times, it was for sexual favors. Others had used the power of their blood to exact revenge, forcing their unwitting victims to lie, cheat, steal, or even commit murder as a form of payment. Armand Moreland had joined the Council of the Realms long ago to prevent such things from happening. And, for the most part, he'd succeeded—well, in this corner of the world, anyway.

There had been few times, in the hundreds of years since he'd become a vampire, where he'd had to use his blood in such a way. Ironically, one of those times had been on these very grounds.

The Salem Common, it seemed, was more than just a beautiful, wide-open space to stroll around in the middle of Salem. It was also a massive energy vortex. From time immemorial, it had been a place where the supernatural chose to apparate. Portals opened and closed in the huge space on a regular basis. Joanne, as well as her coven mates, knew about the portals—so, he figured, Jo should have known to stay away from the Common, at least when she was alone.

But she hadn't. And he wondered why.

The logical explanation? She'd been drawn there. The more he tossed the idea around in his head, the more he believed it to be the case.

Henry and Joanne lived on Lafayette Street. He'd visited them at their apartment shortly after the business with the Red Witch had ended. The Cracked Cauldron wasn't located too far from Wanda's shop, and the walk from that part of town shouldn't have taken her toward the Common. Yet she'd taken a detour. In a snowstorm, no less.

Armand Moreland dwelled on the mystery of Joanne's trip to the Common as he continued his search. He quietly pulled open another dresser drawer in the former bedroom of Mondra Tibbets. Though she was gone, Armand was certain the events of the night somehow involved her. He'd *had* the feeling ever since he'd left Joanne with Mercy and Jazz, though he wasn't completely sure why.

"Always trust your gut," he whispered.

He lifted and pulled the drawer from its tracks, then flipped it upside-down and dumped its contents on the bed. Armand sifted through the items: hairbrush, a tin of peppermint Altoids, condoms, Magnum condoms, KY Jelly, hand-cuffs, fur-covered handcuffs, leather whip, a vibrator with the title "Gazzminator" plastered along its impressive length, and last, but by no means least, a pornographic DVD titled "Hairy Porter and the Sorcerer's Bone."

Armand shook his head. "Is there nothing sacred?"

The thought of putting everything back in the drawer made him wrinkle his nose a little, and he wished he could magically produce a pair of sterile latex gloves. He was about to replace the contents when he noticed a small space between the back of the overturned drawer and the bottom panel.

Producing a pen from his suit coat pocket, he wedged it into the tiny opening, then tapped the top of the pen with the palm of his left hand. The panel budged little, so he tapped until the opening was wide enough to slip a finger through. Once he'd accomplished that, he wiggled the rest of his fingers through, then pulled up hard on the panel. It cracked in half. He tossed the pieces aside.

A single item sat in the revealed hiding spot. The black velvet bag had no markings on it. He removed it from the bottom of the drawer with his right hand, then gently rested it in his left palm. There was some heft to it, and whatever it was seemed solid. It didn't feel like salt, or some kind of spell powder—something he'd seen this type of bag used for in the past.

Armand bounced it lightly in his hand. Satisfied he had a rough idea of what it was, he placed it on the dresser, then pulled the sash at its top. He tipped it over and emptied it. The dark stone tumbled out of the bag with a loud clack against the hardwood of the dresser. The silver chain attached hissed out behind it and curled around the obsidian piece like a snake surrounding its prey.

Armand knew better than to touch the piece with his hand; it might be bewitched. Instead, he pulled the pocket square from his suit coat, unfurled it, and dropped it over the stone and chain. That done, he laid his left hand flat over the handkerchief, then made a fist and grabbed up everything at once. When he turned it over and unclenched, he was staring at a dark stone clutched in a claw of silver.

HENRY STOOD JUST two feet from the sign. He stopped, held his breath, and listened. For the longest time, the whispers stepped all over each other, and it reminded him of a crowd in the lobby of a funeral home during a wake. If you concentrated, you could pick out snippets of conversation. Like the verbal equivalent of a "Whack-a-Mole" carnival game, you'd get lucky and hit one here and there. No matter how hard you tried, you never could get all of them.

"It's him..."

"...the one..."

"...will never make it back..."

"...must not find it..."

"...smells just like him..."

He wasn't sure what to make of the things he was hearing, and at the present moment, the whispering whatever-the-fucks were the least of his concerns. The sign was the only thing that mattered right now. Getting inside Jagger's Magical Treasures suddenly seemed the most important thing in his entire life. Intuition screamed to get his ass in gear and get inside. And if there was one thing he'd learned from the last thirteen months, intuition—in the world of magic—was as reliable as the sunrise. There were clouds now and then, but you still knew behind them, the sun shone bright and true.

The sign hung over the railing, daring him to take hold. He threw caution to the wind, shot out both arms—before he could change his mind—and seized the edge of the sign. Henry yanked it with all his might, and it came over the railing of the porch easily at first. It was three quarters free when a rusty nail snagged the top of the railing. Splinters dug into fingers and palms, his momentum propelled him backwards, and his arms pinwheeled as he fought a losing battle with gravity and his ass met grass.

"Shit! Oh, that fucking hurts!" said Henry, shaking his hands in pain.

He sat on the poor excuse for a lawn for the next few minutes, pulling splinters from both hands. When he finished, he stood and made his way back to the sign. It was still leaning against the porch, but most of it was on the right side of the darkness. With hands pocked and bleeding from splinters, he ignored the whispers and snatched the sign from the railing. This time splinter-free.

His pride? That was another story.

He pulled the sign to the middle of the lawn, stood it on end, then pushed from underneath until it stood as vertical as possible without tipping over. It looked to be about two or two and a half feet taller than his own six-foot-two frame. Probably just high enough to lean it against the roof.

Before he lost his nerve—*splinters be damned*—he grabbed the sign, rushed to the side of the porch, and leaned it where the gutter had collapsed from neglect. It rested at a steep angle, but he only needed it to vault himself upward.

For the amount of trouble it had caused him already, the jump for the roof was almost without incident. Almost. Three quarters of his limbs were on the roof now, only his left leg dangled. Just as he tried to swing that leg up, he felt something cold grasp his ankle. It felt *a lot* like a hand.

"What the fuck is that!?" screamed Henry at such a high pitch he imagined Jo laughing, and saying, *'Don't be such a pussy!'*

The tug had been minimal, only enough to slow him a fraction, but it *was* there. When he pulled free and finally got all of himself onto the roof, a chorus of faint laughter floated up from the porch. Goosebumps covered him.

Henry lay on his back for a while, gazing up at the crystal-clear starry sky, wondering how a raging blizzard could turn into a night so calm. Well, at least *weather-wise* it was calm. Driving on the highway, he'd seen rainstorms where the asphalt was dry as a bone, and then bang!—a curtain of rain just appeared.

"I guess something like that with snow is *possible*," he told the night sky. In his heart, he knew that was bullshit. You just don't go from a raging blizzard, fall over a wall, and then Poof!—no more snow. It made zero sense.

Then there were the clouds. Or lack thereof. The few he saw, as he watched the night sky, seemed to be moving across it unnaturally fast. It was like a YouTube video with the speed setting fixed at 1.5x speed—fast enough to notice the difference but not so fast you couldn't make out what was going on.

The last thing he thought about, as he pushed himself up from the battered roof, was how he'd ended up out here in the first place. Where was the person he'd been following? Whoever it was, they'd had a huge head start. Even with the distance between them, Henry had assumed they must be hurt, and that he'd catch up eventually. The condition of the crashed red Camry made it unlikely the survivor had walked away unharmed. It wasn't impossible, just unlikely.

Too many questions, too few answers.

"Time to change that," he told the boarded-up window as he kicked it in.

Henry stepped over the window sill, then lowered himself into the room. Taking no chances, he stood next to the window and gave his eyes time to adjust to the darkness. It didn't take long. The moon was bright tonight, casting silver light far into the room. When his eyes adjusted, he sucked in a shocked breath.

"What in the actual fuck?" he asked Jagger's bedroom.

On the dusty dresser, against the wall opposite the freshly kicked in window, a picture was fastened to a large, oval mirror with yellowed scotch tape. Even from across the room, and even with the poor lighting, Henry had no trouble identifying the beautiful brunette with the brilliant green eyes who'd captured his heart and soul from the moment he'd first looked into them.

"Jo."

CHAPTER 14
UNCHAINED

To Byron, it seemed he'd been down in this skinny lunatic's basement for days. In reality, it was less than an hour. For whatever reason the guy had let Byron keep his watch. *Probably*, Byron thought, *because it's an old-timer's watch*. If it had been one of those fancy Apple watches, there's no way he wouldn't have taken it. Timex had been something back in the day, but it wasn't gonna save anyone with a text, email, or GPS locator.

Not one to sit idly around and wait to be saved, the chief used his time to work on escape. The chains were thick, new, and bolted solidly to the walls. There was nothing available to cut through them; that would have been too easy. Jagger was an asshole, not an idiot. The walls, however, held promise.

Most of the foundations he'd seen in the older structures in Salem were resting on granite foundations. Granite was tough. This place was no exception. But the place was old—older than most buildings on the block. Chains bolted into granite weren't going to give, no matter how hard he pulled at them. And he wasn't about to waste precious energy on a fool's errand.

Byron followed the path of the chain leading away from his right arm, estimating its length at four feet. It attached to a plate roughly three square inches and bolted into a solid granite block.

Not good.

The chain leading away from his left arm was a bit longer—about six feet. The plate holding it to the wall was, however, not completely bolted in granite. Two bolts were in the block, and two bolts were fastened to the mortar *between* the blocks. Mortar that—as evidenced by a small puddle forming on the basement floor—had seen better days. If water was getting through in the form of melting snow, the mortar was probably weakened.

Very good.

It was the thinnest of thin chances, but excitement sparked him.

Now, how to work the damned thing loose?

"What would Indy do?"

He started whisper-singing the theme to Indiana Jones, and cracking the chains just like Indy cracked his whip.

"Dun da dun daaaaaah, dun da daaaaaaaaaah. Dun da dun daaaaaaah, dun da duuunnn duuunnn daaaaaaaah!"

The chain obeyed in the form of a wave. At the end of each wave, the last link rattled in the loop attached to the plate. For a time, the only result was the monotonous rattle of metal on metal. Several minutes passed before the first chips of mortar popped loose and ticked across the basement floor. With the majority of the plate resting above the granite block, the chain's weight bent it forward, straining the lower bolts.

"That's it! Come on you bitch!" whisper-whooped Byron.

It took another ten-plus minutes before he finally worked the plate loose. As tiring as it was, he had the presence of mind to keep the plate from crashing to the floor. When the last wave of the chain worked it loose, he yanked hard. The plate flew straight at him, hitting him in the chest. Before it could rattle on the floor he stuck out his left leg, then sandwiched the plate between his thigh and left hand. He placed it quietly on the floor, then listened for movement from above.

Five minutes passed, and there was no sign Jagger or the big fucker had heard anything. Now came the hard part.

How in the flying fuck do I get the other chain loose?

Byron sat cross-legged on the floor, wiped sweat from his forehead, then closed his eyes and took a deep and cleansing breath. He felt the calm wash over him.

Since he'd begun meditating on a regular basis with his wife, the time it took him to reach a state of peace had dwindled. It was almost an automatic response. One of the huge benefits was how much it sharpened his thinking. When anxiety was removed from the equation, the results amazed him. In that state, he analyzed the situation.

The first thing that came to mind was how hot he was. Working the chain had built up a sweat, and that was to be expected. But he was sweating *buckets*. That seemed odd. Most of the construction in this part of Salem was old. This building was one of the oldest. It stood to reason the heating source might *also* be old. Once he'd finished with the chain, he'd expected to be freezing his ass off as the sweat cooled. Nothing changed. Sweat still poured off of him, and the basement seemed to have grown even warmer.

He scanned the dark for a heat source, and noticed an orange glow on the floor to his right. It was less than a foot away and came from just around the short wall to which the chain's plate was bolted.

Byron gathered the chain attached to his left wrist, then the plate. He stood and carried them to the end of the wall. When he stuck his head around the corner, he saw there was another two feet of granite. The orange glow beyond the span was much brighter. Stretching as far as the chain allowed, he found what he prayed would be there.

A coal burning stove! He did the calculations in his head. Steel, he remembered from college physics, melted at roughly 2200 to 2500 degrees Fahrenheit. Byron prayed it was the kind of stove he suspected, then saw the huge white bags stacked in the corner opposite the stove. Anthracite! It was what he needed.

"You just hit the lottery, you lucky fuck!" he whispered.

Anthracite coal burned at temperatures between 2500 to 3500 degrees Fahrenheit. If he could reach it, he could weaken the chain enough to snap it. It would have to be a sufficient amount to surround the chain. A handful wouldn't do.

A handful of that shit and I'm not gonna have a hand, anyway.

Byron scanned the room with the stove until he found what he needed. The handle of a shovel was just visible above the stack of bags. It was at least six feet away, but he figured he had just enough chain to at least knock the shovel over. He could work out the rest from there.

Byron let about two feet of chain play out towards the floor, keeping the plate at the end. Rocking his hand forward and backward, he got the plate pitching in a pendulum motion, then timed it so his left arm matched the chain's backswing. He let it fly, and missed. It took him four tries before he struck the handle of the shovel the right way. The momentum of the plate caused the chain to wrap around the handle at the top of the shovel. The instant he saw it happen, he yanked the chain for all he was worth, and the shovel flew directly at him. The business end of the coal shovel whacked him in the left shin.

Pain never felt so delicious.

Now came the hardest part—getting enough coal onto the shovel.

With one hand.

Chained to a wall.

Sweating bullets.

Without spilling it.

Piece of cake, he thought. He laughed out loud.

Byron picked up the shovel with his left hand, looped it through the handle, and then grasped the shaft overhand so the handle rested on his forearm. Gripped in this fashion, it was the surest way to avoid spillage. He thanked whoever ran this shitshow known as the Universe the door to the coal stove remained open. Thinking about the fragile-looking man he'd met at the door a little over an hour ago, the wide open stove door didn't surprise him. Jagger Corey didn't seem the coal shoveling type.

The chief smiled as he imagined shoving a lump of super heated coal up Mr. Top Hat's ass.

"How's that for a magic trick, asshole?"

After that, Byron got down to business. He leaned forward, his right arm extended as far as the chain allowed. The shovel trembled and teetered as he reached it into the mouth of the stove. It sank into the blazing orange coals with a satisfying, gritty, metal-on-coal scrape, and he let it rest for a minute as he gathered strength—and nerve.

One shot was all he was going to get. When the first pile of hot coal was withdrawn from the stove, the result would be a flattening of the pile. There wouldn't be enough left above the lip of the stove for another pass.

He gave himself a few extra seconds to marshal his strength, then lifted. The shovel came out with a smooth scrape against the bottom lip of the stove. Once it cleared, Byron had a brief moment of panic as the weight of the load caused the shovel to dip, and a glowing coal fell to the floor. But *that* turned out to be a blessing. It made him realize that instead of trying to bear the weight of the shovel and its load, he could let the basement floor do the work. He lowered the shovel to the floor, then dragged it around the corner and over to the chain still binding his right arm to the wall.

After that, it was a simple matter of lowering his arm enough to rest a small part of the chain along the floor. Then, he tipped the coal from the shovel and over the chain. He knew it would take several minutes before the structural integrity of the chain degraded. Once it did, he grabbed the links at the point furthest from the heated ones, and pulled until the hot-orange, melted-taffy metal came apart.

Byron smiled, but not out of self-satisfaction. When the super heated chain links separated, the metal stretched, becoming thinner. Once cooled, the ends formed two wicked looking spikes that, as luck would have it, were fused to the last link of the chain still shackled to his right arm. He had himself *quite* the nice weapon. Time for the basement stairs.

When he got to the top, he could barely see anything. Since he was out cold when they'd brought him down into

Jagger's Magical Dungeon, he had no idea how many steps lead to the first floor. His head was down, counting stairs, when he slammed, nose first, into the door at the top.

"Mother—" he started to yell, then stopped himself. He was pretty sure the place was empty. There hadn't been a peep or a footstep since Jagger and Bigfoot had left the basement—but why risk it?

The door. It was probably locked. *Why wouldn't it be?* He took a deep breath, then prayed to whoever he used to *not* believe in. When the knob turned easily in his hand, and the door clicked open, he thanked them.

Byron stepped into the darkness, ready for anything.

CHAPTER 15
EYE SEE

"Where do you think he went?" asked Penny.

"Who? Armand?" asked Jazz.

"No. Santa Claus. Yes, Armand."

Jazz shrugged. "Your guess is as good as mine. Depends on why he wanted so badly to get away from Jo."

At that moment, Jazz's iPhone chirped from the depths of her satchel. She fished it out and read the screen. "Speak of the devil," she said. "Jeevesy?"

Jazz's eyes narrowed and she pressed the phone to her ear, effectively cutting off any chance the vampire's words would be overheard. She remained silent for the entire call, then tapped the phone's screen to end it.

"What was that all about?" asked Jo.

"I can't tell you. *Any* of you. Penny? Could you drop me at my shop? There's something I have to do. And it has to be alone."

Jo persisted. "What did he want, Jazz?"

"Honey, if I could tell you, I would. But right now, I can't.

I need you to trust me. Remember what I told you earlier? All that stuff about feeling obligated?"

Jo nodded.

Jazz said, "Without telling you why I have to go alone. You need to understand it has to do with *exactly that*. You know I love you. Which is why I'm going alone. I need you to trust me on this one. I've been dealing with the vampires in this town longer than anyone else. So when I tell you I need to go alone, I mean it. Will you trust me?" asked Jazz.

Jo didn't answer right away. It was against her nature to let others handle her problems, an unfortunate byproduct of being an unwilling participant in the Foster Care system. You relied on yourself to survive, and you relied on yourself for protection. You trusted no one—especially guys. Double that when it came to vampire guys, though Moreland was the first vampire she'd ever encountered. New guy, new rules. C'est la vie. But something in the way Jazz was looking at her made her stand down for the second time tonight.

If this had been two years ago, she would have told Jazz where to go, and who to do it with. But this was the present, and she had a daughter she adored and a husband she loved madly. The choice was out of her hands. When it came right down to it, her own actions had set the ball in motion tonight, anyway.

What the hell was I thinking walking the Common alone? she chastised herself, then wondered just how she'd ended up in the first place. When she'd closed the door to the Cracked Cauldron, her plans were to go straight to Mercy's place. Something caused her to change her mind, but she couldn't quite recall what it was. There were too many blank spots in her memory tonight, and it was beginning to scare her. It made giving in to Jazz's wishes a hell of a lot easier.

She nodded at Jazz. "I don't like it, but ok."

The ride over to Jazz's shop was quiet. Everyone in the 4Runner seemed lost in their own thoughts. Penny saw the bright purple door to Jazz's shop as she rounded the corner. It stuck out like a sore thumb in the middle of a town that currently resembled a black and white movie from the 1940's. She pulled to the curb and put the truck in park.

"I'll call you as soon as I can, you guys," said Jazz.

"Okay. We're heading back to Mercy's," said Penny. "We'll be waiting on your call."

Jazz smiled, then closed the passenger-side door. She crossed the sidewalk and waited under the matching purple awning until Penny's truck turned the corner and was out of sight. Once the 4Runner was safely out of range, she reached into her satchel, grabbed her keys, and turned to unlock the door—then froze.

"Good evening, Miss Johnson," said Armand Moreland. He smiled from the open doorway.

"How did you get in my shop?" asked Jazz.

Moreland looked offended. "What kind of vampire would I be if I couldn't get past your security system?"

Jazz pulled the satchel open, dropped the keys into it, and put her hands on both hips. "Oh, I don't know. An honest one, maybe?"

Moreland ignored the jab, and invited her into her own shop. She held his eyes as she walked past him. "This better be good."

"*Good* is a relative term, Jazz. If I were to give this recent development a name, it would be... fortunate."

He closed the door on the storm.

Jazz plopped her bag on the counter next to the cash register, then inhaled the ghost of Jasmine—of course—

116

incense she regularly burned during the day in her shop. When she turned around, Armand Moreland's hand was extended, the pendant rested in the same tissue he'd used to scoop it up.

"Where did you get that?" asked Jazz.

Moreland's mouth widened in surprise. "You've seen this before?"

"Not that particular one, but one just like it."

"Where?" asked Moreland.

"Around Jo's neck. Where it still is."

"I'm curious. Who is with Joanne right now?"

"Penny just brought them back to Mercy's place. I don't think Penny is staying, but she's got Mercy and the twins over there."

"Twins?" asked Moreland.

"Two girls named Fermina and Luci. They've been coming to the meeting for the last few months."

Jo PAWED ABSENTLY at the pendant around her neck. She thought it was one of the coolest things Henry had ever gotten her, and she smiled at the memory.

"It's good to see you smiling tonight," said Mercy. "You haven't done it a lot." She pointed at Jo's pendant. "Is that the reason?"

Jo looked down at the obsidian orb resting in its silver claw. "Yeah. Henry ambushed me. I don't know how he did it, but it was tucked in the register under a stack of twenties with a note. Our one year wedding anniversary was a week ago on the second. I thought the bastard forgot it. I wasn't going to say anything, you know, since Dom got hurt.

Figured he had more important things on his mind. But it still kind of bummed me out."

Jo gave Mercy a *'sue me, I'm human'* shrug.

"I get it," said Mercy. "When did you say you found it?"

"That's the funny thing. I found it right before I closed the shop tonight. I was so excited I put it on right then! I haven't had the chance to call him and thank him. Maybe I'll wait till he gets back from Maine and just jump his bones. You know, thank him properly."

She gave Mercy a wicked grin. Mercy failed to return the smile.

At first, Jo thought Mercy might be feeling guilty about her forced romantic encounter with Henry when she'd been under the spell of her mother, the Red Witch. Jo had made it quite clear there were no hard feelings about it. She knew full well Mercy and Henry had zero chance of resisting the powerful spell. Especially when there had been a flicker of truthful attraction between the two to begin with. Jo was never jealous, however. It could just as easily have gone the other way. She knew Mercy found *her* attractive, too. It was nothing Mercy ever said, just an observation. A fleeting glance here and there. A touch of red coloring Mercy's cheeks when she feared Jo had caught her looking. She *had*, of course, caught her looking, but Mercy was hardly the first woman to be attracted to Jo. And would not be the last.

But this look was different. There was fear in it.

"What's the matter, honey?" asked Jo.

Mercy called Fermina and Luci over. "Do you guys see what I see?" Mercy pointed at the pendant cradled in Jo's hand.

"Oh, my God," they whispered together.

"What is it?" asked Jo. They were starting to freak her out.

Mercy put a finger to her lips, hopped up from the beanbag chair, and beckoned Jo to follow her. They went into the kitchen together, and Mercy opened a drawer next to the stove. She mimed removing the necklace and placing it in the drawer. Jo got the hint. Then she took Jo by the hand and guided her back into the living room. They sat back down, opposite Fermina and Luci.

"What's going on?" whispered Jo. She wasn't sure *why* she was whispering, but it felt right.

"Just so I'm sure I'm not losing my shit," Mercy whispered back, "we all need to tell Jo what we saw at the same time. Sound good?"

Fermina and Luci nodded in agreement.

Goosebumps broke out on Jo's arms when she saw the fear on their faces.

Mercy raised a fist, then silently counted one, two, three.

They whispered together. "An eye."

CHAPTER 16
BE KIND, REWIND

Tape three. Archie shuddered at the thought. The memories dredged up from tape two of his sessions with Jagger Corey had scraped the mental scabs buried deep in his psyche, and the wounds bled anew. He didn't want to go any further. Who wanted to be reminded of their failures?

Archie considered taking the tapes out into the parking lot, pouring lighter fluid on them, and burning them to a crisp. Exorcism by fire. But he knew it was too late now. Even if he barbecued all of them, the genie was out of the bottle. The remaining memories would come. It would take *longer* for the memories to return if he torched the tapes, but he'd only be putting off the inevitable. The truth had a way of bubbling to the surface. He remembered something Joanne had said to him once; "You can bury the truth Arch, but you bury it alive."

He smiled at the memory. His daughter-in-law was fierce, loving, loyal, and brutally honest. Taking his cue from her, he popped the tape in the player and got on with the business of re-examining Jagger Corey.

Archie – "How are you today, Jagger?"

Jagger – "Doing good, doc."

Archie closed his eyes and listened. Transported once more back to those days, the memory as vivid as if happening in the here and now. Jagger looked triumphant, a smirk plastered on his face.

Archie – "You seem to be in quite the mood today, Jagger. Care to share?"

It was at this point the change happened, sooner than usual. The smirk remained, but the alternate personality emerged. The thinker. The one Jagger called on to guide the other—or others; Archie wasn't sure there weren't more.

Jagger – "Well, professor, I'm ecstatic this is my last session. Wouldn't you be, if you were in my shoes?"

Archie – "I think you're mistaken, Jagger. You have one more left after today. Have you forgotten?"

Jagger – "To quote the Dark Lord of the Sith, Darth Vader, 'I am altering the deal. Pray I don't alter it any further.'"

He'd nailed the James Earl Jones voice. You had to give him that.

Archie – "Really? And how do you intend to do that? You realize you'll be arrested once again if you don't show up. I don't want that to happen, Jagger, and I don't think you do either."

In his mind's eye, Archie watched the smirk grow into a grin. Then Jagger laughed. It was a grating, unpleasant cackle. The kind of laugh only those who laugh little can pull off, because they lack the base natural resource underlying true laughter: Joy.

Jagger, Archie had realized back on that day, and again in the here and now, had little experience with joy. Or love. Or compassion. If he ever had, it was fleeting and short-lived and undoubtedly involved inflicting pain on another being.

Jagger – "I'm taking my leave of you, da— Archie. Where I'm going, you can *try* to arrest me. But let's just say... you'd be out of your jurisdiction. And that's putting it mildly."

Archie's eyes flew open. He pitched forward in his seat and stopped the tape. He rewound it and played the last line from Jagger again. And then again. On the third replay, it came to him.

"Oh. My. God."

~

HENRY STARED at the image of his wife taped to the dresser mirror. He rubbed his eyes several times, hoping against hope he was having a dream or some type of hallucination. The image remained. He remembered the moment captured in the picture. It was the day they'd left the hospital with Delilah. Jo's hair was pulled back tight in a ponytail, and she was looking up at him, smiling with love and contentedness. Only, he'd been cropped out of the picture. Delilah had too.

"What in the actual fuck?" he whispered to the darkened room.

Getting his mind around seeing a picture of his wife in the room of a complete stranger was one thing. Add to that how he'd come to be in this room in the first place, and it made absolutely zero sense.

The only reason he'd even ended up in this place was because of the overturned Camry. Even *that* had happened only because the highway accident had caused him to change course. *Shit*, he thought, *none of this happens if Dad hadn't hurt his hip*.

That thought stopped him cold. How, exactly, had Dad hurt his hip? It hadn't been Dom's fault, according to Henry's mom. He tried to recall what she'd told him over the phone right before she'd asked him to come up and help out with his father. Closing his eyes, he replayed the conversation in his mind ...

"Hello?"

"Hi Henry, how are you, sweetheart?"

"Doing good, Mom. What's up?"

"There's been an accident. Before you get nervous, everyone is fine. Your father hurt his hip and he's going to be out of commission for a bit. I wouldn't ask—"

"What do you need me to do?" asked Henry. "I'm there."

"Well, we might need you to stay up here for a couple of weeks. He can't put any weight *at all* on the hip until it starts to heal. I'm not what I used to be, Henry. I already tried to move him around and nearly threw my back out. Your cousin Billy has been helping out but he can't be here as much as we need, not with newborn triplets. I should sue that goddamned contractor!"

"Mom, not a problem. I'll be up there tomorrow. I'll bring Delilah with me."

"Oh! I can't wait to see my little sweetie!"

Henry smiled. His mom was gaga over Delilah.

"So who's this contractor, and what did he do?"

Jeanne blew out a disgusted breath, and Henry'd thought, *here we go*. "Some skinny weirdo your father hired. Guy came right off the street, said he happened to notice the gutters on the front of the house were damaged. Must have happened during that monsoon we had about a week ago.

The guy offered to fix them right on the spot. You know your father and saving money. The guy quoted him some ridiculously low offer. You get what you pay for, I guess. Had a car like yours with a ladder strapped across the roof and everything. Kinda weird he didn't have a truck or a van. Anyway, the stupid bastard left the ladder right in front of the front door, just lying across the steps. Dom never saw it and went ass over tea kettle. I screamed a blue streak at the guy. Told him to take his shit and screw. When this is all over, he's gonna be one sorry fucker!"

Henry had smiled on the other end, knowing exactly how mad his mother was by her choice of colorful language. Jeanne Trank swore about as frequently as a lunar eclipse.

The memory faded. The mystery deepened. The agenda, however, became crystal clear.

He'd been set up. Someone needed him to be... here. In this place. And away from Salem. *Away from Jo.*

Henry was finally able to move from his spot in front of the kicked out window. Each step he took toward the dresser felt like wading through molasses. The answers, he knew, were there. He was terrified by what might be revealed.

He bumped into the dresser, not remembering how he'd mustered up the courage to cross the room. He'd been lost in thought, his mind conjuring up nightmare scenarios based on scant facts. The picture of Jo filled his field of vision once more, closer now, and the frightening possibilities scattered from his mind like confetti in the wind. He snatched the picture from the mirror, leaving four ragged corners trapped in yellowed Scotch Tape, and a clear square of mirror surrounded by dust covering the remainder of the mirror's surface—all evidence of a lengthy obsession.

Moments after Henry touched the photo, it vibrated in

his hand. His vision went cloudy, and the room changed. In the blink of an eye, the space was bathed in bright sunlight, though it still remained a cluttered mess. In the vision, the picture of Jo was where it had been—taped to the mirror—and a wave of disgust rolled through him as his hand moved of its own accord, and a finger traced the line of Jo's chin.

Henry realized he wasn't in control of his own body, and the actions of whoever's vision this was—Jagger, from the name on the sign outside, he guessed—would dictate his every move. Instinct screamed at him to figure out a way to escape the vision; intuition told him to ride it out. He chose the latter, and let the vision take him.

"We're coming for you, beautiful," said Jagger. "You belong with us, not him."

This struck Henry as odd, since he saw no one else in the room. He was hoping to get a good look at the creep, but he'd only caught a fleeting glimpse as Jagger whipped around and headed for the bedroom door. Out of the corner of Jagger's eye, Henry thought he'd seen a beard, a top hat... and maybe a scarf that was a mix of dark and light colors. Whoever this guy was, something about him seemed oddly familiar. The man he assumed was Jagger opened the door to the room. The memory ended.

Henry's vision went black for a brief instant. In the darkness of Jagger's bedroom, he staggered and almost lost his balance. Then, a new vision formed behind his eyes. A figure stood before him, blurry and out of focus, at first. She was talking to him. No, shouting. Her words were garbled, like listening to someone talk while submerged in water. When the vision cleared, and the words began to make sense, Henry was looking once again through the eyes of Jagger.

The woman's greasy blonde hair hung straight down, as

if pulled by some force. Over her shoulder, Henry saw a light with a string attached. The bare bulb swung slowly back and forth, and he realized he was looking up from the floor at the angry woman. The swinging light bathed her features in alternating patterns of dark and light, and he never could quite see her face in totality. Pain wracked the right side of his face, and he smelled and tasted blood.

"I'm sorry!" he heard Jagger say. "It won't happen again."

"You're goddamned right it won't happen again! Do you realize how much trouble you've brought down on us, you little shit?"

He heard Jagger sob.

The woman yanked Jagger by the hair into a sitting position, then reached behind herself and swiped something from the table. She thrust a newspaper in his face. Her hand shook with rage, and Henry had trouble reading the headline.

"Take it!"

He saw Jagger reach for the paper with trembling hands. The masthead of the local paper read *Pourtlande Press Herald*. Someone had misspelled Portland on that day, *and probably didn't have a job by that evening*, Henry thought. After a time, Jagger's hands steadied, and Henry saw the headline.

Rituals suspected in disappearance of local pets. Bones found in woods.

What the hell? Henry thought. *Was this kid getting his ass kicked for hurting animals?* If that was the case, then the tiny bit of sympathy he'd felt for Jagger had just gone out the window.

The scene went dark, and the vertigo-like feeling stole

over Henry once more. At least this time he was a little more prepared for it.

When it cleared, he found himself—or, more correctly, Jagger—in the middle of the woods at night. A fire burned at the center of a stone pit, and a cauldron hung suspended from two stakes at either side with a warped metal rod resting across their tops. Henry watched as Jagger dropped ingredients into the cauldron, and then on the fire heating it. Sparks flew. Embers twisted upward and into the night while fire hugged the cauldron's sides. Jagger's breathing was relaxed and calm as he went about his business; the practiced calm born from experience.

How would I know he's experienced at this?

Henry realized something was different with *this* vision; he was hearing Jagger's thoughts. Feeling his feelings. Somehow, being trapped inside this body was having a strange effect on him, as if he was becoming part of the kid. It didn't feel good. Henry wanted out. Wanted it so badly he could have screamed. But there was nothing he could do. He wasn't entirely sure how he'd gotten here in the first place.

A vague image of a picture in his hand swam to the surface, then something to do with a beautiful, green-eyed brunette. Maybe she was in the picture? He couldn't remember for sure.

Joanne! How could he forget his wife's name? Or that her picture had been taped to some psycho's mirror? What the hell was happening to him?

Music began to play, and he wasn't sure where it was coming from. It could have been echoing through the forest, or it could have been coming from inside Jagger's head— there was no way to tell. It was loud. It was everywhere. The song was familiar. A Beatles song. He wasn't the biggest

Beatles fan in the world, but you didn't have to be. Everyone knew at least some songs by the Beatles. He'd heard this one several times, and Jagger incorrectly screamed out the first line. *"You are me and we are you and we shall be together."* It was the wrong opening line from "I am the Walrus."

Henry wanted to plug his ears, but they weren't his to plug. He wanted to run from this cursed place in the middle of the woods, where this disturbed man performed black magick and chanted at the moon, but the legs he could feel as if they were his own would not obey his commands.

He heard Jagger cackling with glee, and it scared him to death, for the maniacal laughter seemed to spring forth from his own mouth. Then he was screaming. "Coo coo cachoo motherfucker!"

The wrong lyrics from "I am the Walrus" poured from his mouth, and Henry tasted insanity.

In an instant, it stopped. Henry looked out from Jagger's eyes. The fire had died. Crickets chirped. Smoke drifted lazily from beneath the cauldron where dark-orange embers of spent wood glowed. The contents of the cauldron were all but emptied, and Henry saw what Jagger saw as he looked down the length of his body. Crimson stained his clothes from head to toe, trailing away haphazardly from his feet in spidery red rivers through leaves covering the forest floor.

"Welcome to my nightmare, Henry," whispered Jagger.

CHAPTER 17
DARKNESS CALLS

anda sat in silence and darkness across the counter from Jagger Corey. The grandfather clock ticking away back in her safe room, and the soft chatter of snow blown against the front windows were the only sounds.

She wasn't sure what to expect, and she sure as shit wasn't going to speak the first words. The man sitting across from her wasn't exactly stable, and starting down any conversational road with him was bound to end up in a cul-de-sac from hell. This wasn't her first rodeo when it came to the circular logic of insanity.

Paging Mondra Tibbets! she thought. Later, she would realize how close to the mark that statement was.

"Well?" asked Jagger. "Aren't you going to ask me why I'm here?"

"I was hoping you might fill me in on that one," said Wanda.

"Fair enough. But first, let me ask you a question, Wanda. Do you mind if I call you Wanda?"

"Do I have a choice?"

Jagger's mouth smiled, his eyes took a rain check. "Now *that*, Wanda, is the million-dollar question, isn't it? It's one that I've asked myself countless times since I was a wee lad. Do I have a choice? Well, as it turns out, I do. But that wasn't always the case. No no no. As Walter Mosley wrote, 'If it wasn't for bad luck, I'd have no luck at all.' Truer words were never spoken."

Jagger stared at Wanda, daring her to contradict him. She held his gaze and held her tongue.

"I was born to parents who, to put it kindly, couldn't find their asses with a map and a flashlight. That is to say, they are *galactically* fucking stupid. Society, however, has certain rules. One of those rules is that the aforementioned parents get to raise a child." Jagger bowed deeply. "Yours truly, until the ripe old age of eighteen. Said child has no say in the matter. Are you with me so far, Wanda?"

"Yes."

"Good. Good. Now, when one is burdened with circumstances such as these, one tends to find outlets. You see, one of the things I realized I was good at was magick. And I'm not talking about pulling rabbits out of hats. Well, at least not living ones."

Jagger barked a laugh. Wanda jumped in her seat.

"Too much caffeine? Anyway, I've never been good with people—"

"You don't say?" asked Wanda. She immediately regretted it, but his smarmy, know-it-all attitude was getting under her skin.

He glared at her. "As I was saying, I'm not exactly a people person. I keep to myself. One day, I went for a walk in the woods. I was about," he closed one eye and tilted his head toward the ceiling, "oh, I'd say thirteen. Yes, thirteen. That's a great age, don't you think?"

Wanda kept her mouth shut this time.

"Cat got your tongue? I can arrange that, you know?" He winked. "So, where was I? Ah, thirteen. Such a complicated time for a young man. Hormones. Curiosity. Rage. All those *good* things. You'd be surprised what you attract when you've got all those things just bubbling up inside you. And when you're walking alone... in the woods of Maine... at night... you don't even have to be looking for it. *It* finds *you*."

Wanda was afraid to ask, but curiosity got the better of her. "What does?"

"The darkness. It lives, Wanda. It knows. It cares. And it provides. When you feed it, it feeds *you*. Do you know what happened to me on that walk?"

Wanda was trembling. She didn't trust her voice, and simply shook her head.

"I met someone. One minute I was alone, the next—she was there. I never heard a sound. Never heard so much as a leaf crunch or a branch break. And do you know what she showed me?"

Wanda couldn't move, she simply swallowed.

Jagger smiled. "Me."

MERCY SAT in the beanbag chair in the middle of her living room, chewing a thumbnail and waiting. Jo was shaken. After Mercy, Fermina, and Luci had all confirmed what they'd seen, she wasn't sure what her next move should be. She wasn't even sure what the eye looking out from the obsidian orb *meant*. Well, other than she was positive there was no way it came from Henry.

"Do you think Moreland might be responsible for it? He was obviously acting a bit strange tonight," said Mercy.

Jo shrugged. "I was wearing it before my walk in the park. He wasn't in the store today. But that doesn't mean he wasn't there. You know how vampires are."

Mercy nodded, "Yep. They seem to appear out of nowhere. Still, I don't get that vibe from Armand. Not anymore, anyway. But there *is* something you need to know."

Jo's eyes narrowed at the caution in Mercy's voice. "What?"

"I probably should have mentioned it earlier, but I wasn't completely sure what I was *seeing* actually meant something. I wish we'd had more time with Jazz tonight, because she was the one I wanted to ask about it. When Moreland left here, earlier tonight, and you'd run upstairs, I watched him as he left. There was an aura surrounding him."

"Do vampires have auras?" asked Jo.

"My question exactly!" said Mercy. "And that's what I wanted to find out from Jazz. But there was also something about the aura that seemed just a bit too coincidental, considering what we saw later on with that healing scar on your shoulder. There was green in it, Jo. *Your* green."

Jo was quiet as she churned the new information around in her head. She didn't know enough about vampires to start making assumptions. And she didn't blame Mercy for being cautious about jumping to conclusions before having the facts. What she *did* know, and there was no doubt about it now; Moreland had been blocking her. Jazz *had* said he was probably doing it to protect her from acting out on a desire to please him and repay the debt. That was most likely true; Jazz wasn't some magical bullshit artist, and she knew her shit when it came to the vampires of Salem. But what if there was more to it?

With Armand Moreland, there's always more to it, Jo thought.

"Let's go," said Jo.

This took the other witches by surprise, and it showed on their faces. Mercy 's surprise seemed like genuine curiosity. Fermina and Luci looked troubled.

"What?" asked Jo. "You didn't think I was gonna sit around here all night, did you?"

"Where are we going? And how are we getting there? It's kind of a blizzard out there tonight," said Mercy.

"Where else? Jazz's shop. I know she didn't want me there. But I'd bet my life Moreland was already there when we dropped her off," said Jo. "I'll see if Penny can come back and get us. If not, it's just snow, right?"

They all looked doubtful, and a bit scared. No one wanted to get on the wrong side of Jazz. And then there was the small matter of the blizzard.

Jo sensed their unease. "Guys, relax. Jazz will be mad at first, but I'll smooth it over. Once I tell her what you guys saw in the pendant, her being pissed will probably be the least of our problems."

She pulled her cell phone from her back pocket and tapped the screen. It rang seven times, then went straight to voicemail. Frowning, Jo left a message asking Penny to call them back as soon as possible. "That's weird. She just left here not even ten minutes ago."

Mercy said, "Well, she mentioned she was gonna try and

contact Byron. Maybe she didn't mean by phone. You know how she gets on nights like these."

Jo nodded. Mercy, and everyone in the League of the Moon, knew how Penny liked to check on her husband. It had nothing to do with modern technology. "Okay. I'll give it a bit. But then I'm outta here. You guys can stay here if you want, but one way or the other, I'm talking to Jazz."

PENNY PULLED INTO HER GARAGE, using the remote to close the door behind her. She exited the 4Runner and stepped into the muted silence. The blowing snow sounded like giants flinging fists full of sand at the garage door.

Leaving the giants to their fun, she climbed three steps, opened the interior door, and stepped into the kitchen. It was dark. The only light, thanks to the power outage, came from the battery indicator on the emergency floods. The lights themselves weren't working.

"Just when you need 'em most," she told the kitchen.

She'd shut off her cell phone as soon as she'd left Mercy's apartment on Witch Hill Road. *They'll understand*, she'd thought. Besides, it was only for a short time.

The only thing on her mind since dropping them off was the whereabouts of her husband. It wasn't *like* him not to check in on a night like this.

Unless something was happening and he couldn't.

Out of an abundance of caution, and knowing his cell phone going off might get him killed under the wrong circumstances, she avoided calling him. Byron was the one to call. Always.

That last thought made her nervous.

Penny placed her bag and cell phone on the kitchen table, removed her snow gear, then went upstairs to the bedroom. She didn't need lights to locate the items she needed.

Cones of Dragon's Blood incense, a lighter, and candles were in the top drawer of the nightstand. She lit a tall, white candle and placed it in a holder atop the same nightstand, then placed a cone in the burner and sparked it up.

The spicy-powder aroma of Dragon's Blood filled the room and her nose. It calmed her immediately. She laid back on the bed, laced her fingers together, and rested them right below her sternum. Three deep breaths in and out and she was ready. The astral plane awaited. The search for Byron began.

CHAPTER 18
SCREAMING IN THE NIGHT

Once out of the cellar, the first order of business was finding something to light his way. It was pitch black in the store. Earlier, before the power outage, he'd caught sight of the register over Jagger's shoulder, where he was currently opening and closing drawers and cursing him out. The chains hanging from both arms clattered loudly as he searched.

"What kind of asshole doesn't have a—" he stopped as his hands closed around what he'd been looking for, then said, "—flashlight. Okay, at least there's that. He's still a fucking idiot."

Byron turned the flashlight on. It was a cheapo job you could buy at the front of any grocery store. He'd seen them more than once as he checked out at Market Basket.

"What kind of asshole buys a piece of shit like this?" It worked. And it wasn't half bad, but Byron wasn't in the mood to let the pasty bastard off the hook. "Doesn't even have the common sense or decency to by a Maglite! Shithead!"

Finished ranting, Byron aimed the flashlight to his right. "Jason tap-dancing Vorhees!"

Eyes gleamed back at him. Bared teeth shined. The giant wolf to his right remained silent, poised to rip his throat out, but couldn't—because it was dead. Mounted on a stand and posed for attack. "That just earned you points on the shit list, asshole. I'm gonna bust you so hard."

Once his heart settled, Byron didn't dare move from his spot behind the counter until he'd swept the room with the flashlight. Satisfied there were no more taxidermic threats, at least none in the immediate area, he stepped out from behind the counter and began his inspection of Jagger's shop.

From what he could tell from the narrow, barely adequate cone of light, the middle of the main room was wide open. The room itself was circular. The center was comprised of broad planks of pine, stained dark brown, typical of 1800s construction. The planks were ringed off by red marble inlays that stretched roughly two feet toward the walls.

"Spanish marble? Good taste for a shithead psycho."

Byron ran the flashlight along curved walls. They were chocolate brown and mostly bare. Not a surprise, since Jagger had only been in town a short while. Holes dotted the walls where pictures had hung, outlined by squares of slightly darker areas where dust hadn't found a home.

Following the line of missing pictures, he trained the flashlight across the floor once more. Crates of various sizes were stacked against the wall at the far end of the room, forming a semi-circle along its edge. Where the stacks ended, a staircase began. It was neatly inset into the wall, and a thin, cast-iron bannister gracefully curled upward along its length to the second floor. It fused neatly into a railing running full circle around the second level. Byron shone the light on the floor directly ahead, then made his way over to the staircase. Chains rattled against the railing as he climbed.

When he got to the top he paused, remembering his encounter with the Big Bad Wolf downstairs. His imagination ran wild, and he pictured a giant grizzly bear stuffed and mounted and just waiting with bated breath for a chance to make him soil his long-johns. Better to be safe. He ran the light around the circular length of the second floor.

There wasn't that much to it. Bookcases filled with dust-covered volumes from a different time ringed the room, interrupted at fixed intervals by multi-paned windows with cushioned reading nooks at their bases. The word that came to mind, once you discounted the dusty books, cobwebs, and spiderwebs lining the windows, was *cozy*.

"Penny would *love* this shit."

Byron let the light drift slowly from nook to bookcase, following the curve of the walls. He'd started at the farthest point from himself, moving the beam slowly toward his present spot and taking in every detail. When he'd covered the area to his right, he turned to his left. The light came to rest on a door he hadn't noticed when first reaching the top of the staircase.

"I'll be damned."

He reached for the handle then thought better of it, opting to shine the light on it first. Unlike almost everything on this level of the building, the handle was dust free. The detective side of him gave this some consideration, but not much. The guy had to sleep *somewhere*, and this was probably the place where Jagger laid his tortured brain at night.

"Only one way to find out."

Byron squeezed the latch at the top of the handle, but it wouldn't budge.

"Of course. Why would it be easy?"

He reached above the frame of the door, hoping against hope there was a key. There wasn't, and he was rewarded with fingertips blackened by thick dust and the corpse of a ladybug buried in the pile on his right index finger.

Byron shook the dust from his hands, then wiped them across the front of his formerly white thermal undershirt. Combined with the blood from where the chain plate had impaled him, it looked like Freddy Krueger had taken a swipe.

Intuition told him he needed to get into that room. He whirled, looking for something to use as a battering ram, and came up short.

Raising his right arm, he shook his fist at the ceiling. "What the fuck did I do to deserve this?"

The gods were mute.

Byron let his head drop in defeat, and his arm slapped his hip, rattling the chain against his leg and the floor.

"The chain!" Suddenly, he felt optimistic. "Someone up there likes me."

Wasting no time, Byron reeled it up from the floor, stuck the plate through the handle, and looped the links around both the handle and the plate. A two foot length of chain separated Byron and the door's handle.

Left foot against the frame on one side, right foot on the opposite, he pulled for all he was worth. Bracing himself for a long battle, he was taken by surprise when it gave easily. The handle splintered loose from the door with a thunderous crack, and Byron was sent flying backwards and off balance. His legs pumped furiously as he tried to right himself, only to have them catch in the chains. When that happened, his body pitched backwards and into one of the bookcases. Dusty volumes tumbled from the highest shelves, pelting his head and shoulders, pounding him downward until he lay sprawled on the floor, covered in volumes of Salem's history.

He laid in the pile of filthy books for a while, eyes closed and breathing in the dusty air, letting pain leach slowly from his body.

Between the battle with the door on the second floor, and the struggle with the chains in Jagger's makeshift dungeon, he was almost spent. The temptation to just lay where he was and drift into blessed sleep was overwhelming. It was a battle he almost lost, until he opened his eyes.

When he saw the casket through the doorway, any thought of sleep vanished in a soup of adrenaline. Byron kicked the books aside and heaved himself from the floor. The boost of adrenaline was good, but it only revived him so much. Still wracked by pain, he lurched down the hall. Chains hanging from both arms scraped across the floor.

"I must look like the ghost of Jacob fucking Marley," Byron quipped.

When he reached the casket, he felt like he'd walked a mile. The adrenalin rush faded, giving way to a brand new one. Fear drove the bus, and Byron wished he didn't have to get off at *this* stop. Unfortunately, for him, it was the end of the line.

It took every ounce of courage he had to reach for the lid. He ran both hands along its cool, metallic side, wondering who might be in it. Then he thought about the stuffed wolf downstairs, and the question went from *who* to *what*.

Byron took a deep breath and raised the lid.

Then, he screamed.

HENRY WASN'T sure how much time had passed, or where he was. The room was dark, save for the narrow shaft of moonlight on the floor to his right. His head throbbed. When he sat up and gave his eyes time to readjust, he began to remember. Bits and pieces of what he'd seen and heard came back to him: the cauldron; the fire; the chanting; the music he wasn't sure he'd been hearing in the woods or in his head.

Jagger's screwed up lyrics from the song echoed in his mind.

"You are me and we are you and we shall be together."

It was one of the few Beatles songs he would listen to all the way through when it came on the radio. He enjoyed the oddness of the song, but it held no special meaning for him, like some songs did. Music has a way of freezing time and memory, stamping your life forever with the emotions surrounding events in life. Times you can never truly return to, but for those few minutes, wrapped in that sonic cocoon, you're *there* again—as real as the steering wheel in your hand, the wind blowing through your hair, and the tear running down your cheek.

When Henry heard the lyrics forced from his own mouth by the man controlling the visions, he'd felt anger. But it was more than that. Anger was too simple a word. As he sat in the middle of this strange man's messy, cluttered room, he closed his eyes once more and tried to feel what Jagger had felt.

The memory washed over him, but he resisted being swept away by the raw emotion.

Remain detached.

Words Archie'd used describing how he dealt with emotionally distraught subjects of past life regression; it was sage advice, and he employed it now.

Henry pictured himself outside of Jagger, but allowed just enough to remain inside to taste the flavor of the emotion behind the rage. Those emotions, those *flavors*, came to him in the form of colors. It amazed him seeing it this way, and he realized he was harnessing his unique talent for astral travel in a whole new way.

Red leaped out at him first. Anger. No surprise there. Next came orange, but that was only a transitional color as it morphed into what it truly was—yellow. Jagger, for all his bluster, was a coward at heart. Red would always be how things started with him. Anger was the shield of the fearful, but yellow would always and forever lurk beneath the surface until the underlying fears fueling them were dealt with. Cowards and heroes stood on either side of a thin line that could only be crossed with action. Jagger had yet to cross.

Henry, remaining detached, let the memory unfold. Jagger screamed out the nonsense line from the song. *"Goo goo gjoob!"* The red returned. Henry expected yellow soon after, but was surprised when blue appeared. Blue was the telltale sign of sadness, and despite Jagger's outward display of anger, the blue remained.

Then, Henry saw something that shocked him.

It was like watching one of those split screens you might see on a TV news show—one where the pundits argued across the imaginary white line about why their side was right and the other guy's side was stupid. On the left, Jagger was slapped, kicked, punched, and berated by the woman with the greasy blonde hair. She seemed vaguely familiar. As before, he saw it through Jagger's eyes.

The scene on the right was what shocked him. He saw it from a third-person point of view. A tall, pretty lady with long, auburn hair handed a child an ice cream cone. It was a sunny day. The air roiled with the wonderful smells of the sea, sunscreen, and cooking hot dogs. The boy was happy, and in the vision, though the words were never spoken, the feeling of a mother's love for her son was as real as those smells. It was the exact same vision from Henry's regression session of over a year ago in Archie's office. *Somehow* it was playing out in the mind of another person.

Remain detached.

It wasn't easy. Henry fought for calm.

Jagger's colors morphed from the anger of red, to the sadness of blue, followed by the yellow of cowardice. Once more, Jagger screamed out the nonsense line from "I am the Walrus."

'Coo coo cachoo, coo coo coo cachoo. Motherfucker!'

Jagger's auric colors swirled violently together, and the result was a whirlwind of brown. A literal shit-storm of emotion. When it slowed and settled, his true color emerged. His entire body radiated green. Muted, dark, and dull, it paled in comparison to Jo's brilliant emerald. It was the green of Envy.

"Welcome to my nightmare, Henry. And now it's yours."

That last line was *new*. Something was changing. Henry felt it. He did *not* like it. No sir, not one bit.

The vision receded.

Henry was more confused than ever. Not only did this

strange and angry man have a picture of Jo taped to his mirror, but he somehow possessed memories of Henry's life he had no business having. He felt violated.

Deciding to return the favor, he sprang up and rushed the dresser, ripping open drawers and dumping their contents onto the floor. He pawed through piles of debris, searching for anything to unlock the mystery of this Jagger guy.

Most of what he found were items he'd heard about but never actually seen. Things Wanda brought to his attention in the year he'd learned the ins and out of his new-found faith.

"Not all witches are good, Henry," Wanda had said. *"It's just like any other walk of life, or flavor of faith, sweetie. There's good and bad. Light and dark."*

Judging by the things spilled across Jagger's floor, Henry was pretty sure the creep fell into the 'dark' category. There were books Wanda had brought to his attention. In particular, The Necronomicon. It was rumored that the book was real, but Wanda thought otherwise.

"I've heard of it," said Wanda. *"But it's just something that was invented by H.P. Lovecraft. It's brilliant, when you think about it. He created the rumor of the book's existence, though most believe it was never actually written. So, in effect, the thought of it is real. People to this day believe it's real, and some have even gone so far as selling 'Authentic Copies' on the internet. But I've never seen a copy, nor is there proof it actually exists."*

Henry was looking at it now. Was it real? Or, more to the point, was it something capable of influencing real world events? Either way, he was looking at a copy of something that wasn't supposed to exist.

There was a Post-it note sticking out from the middle of

the book. Strangely, it was spelled Poast-It. What was it with the misspellings? Henry turned it sideways to read the writing on its edge. *Scapulimancy.*

Henry remembered the headline from the newspaper with the misspelling of Portland at the top.

Rituals suspected in disappearance of local pets. Bones found in woods.

Scapulimancy's root word, he knew from his medical training, was scapula—the shoulder blade. Henry dreaded opening the book, but open it he did.

Spidery scrawled notes in Jagger's hand ran down the margins of the page. One passage in particular caught Henry's eye...

"I got it on the thirteenth try. How appropriate! The bone snapped perfectly! And the spell worked! She will be pleased. I knew the moment I met her in the woods, things would be different. Once I set things right here, I can take care of 'over there.'

Scapulimancy, Henry realized, was divination—reading the future—via the bones of animals.

"My God," whispered Henry.

That's when he heard the creek on the stairs.

CHAPTER 19
PICTURE THIS

Archie sat in silence, focused on the flame of a candle burning away on his desk. The tapes had awakened something in him. Not only memories from a past he'd just as soon forget, but something else entirely. Something in need of intense scrutiny. Well, now that he thought on it... several somethings.

With the tape player off, Archie poured over the transcripts from the sessions.

Jagger – "So is that how things work over here?"

Over where, exactly? He'd been so offended by Jagger's suggestion he was involved in a scam with Byron, he never bothered to find out what 'over here' meant.

Archie berated himself. "You fool."

The next item could have answered itself, had he not been so concerned with a teenager accusing him of corruption. It was his own statement.

Archie – "You say you woke up on the Salem Common, and you've no recollection of how you got there."

Anyone knowledgeable on magick in Salem knew portals

existed on the Common. Lots of portals. Even later, when Jagger confessed to practicing dark magick, Archie still failed to realize he'd arrived in Salem via a portal.

On the Common.

It was *so* in his face! He wanted to kick himself.

"How could I have missed that?"

He shook his head in disgust, wondering what other giant clues he'd completely missed in 2004. He traced his finger down the transcript's page.

Fuck-up number three wasn't hard to find. It followed close on the heels of the one he'd just read.

When he'd asked Jagger about the magick he practiced in the forest, he'd focused on the wrong thing. The word *sacrifice* had shocked him. Visions of what this little monster was doing to defenseless creatures enraged him so much, he'd ended the session early.

Normally, he would have walked Jagger into the hall and out of the building, but he didn't trust himself not to smack the kid upside the head. He'd told Jagger to see himself out.

So, he'd missed the most important word in the next two sentences.

Jagger – "The only kind that matters to her, professor. The kind that requires sacrifice!"

Her.

How the hell did I miss that? Archie wondered.

No sooner had the thought entered his mind when an ominous connection blindsided him.

Though the obsidian orb in the claw surfaced in the third session, his failure to pick up on the word *her* from session two caused him to drop the ball in three.

It was a very big ball. A Red Witch sized ball. Somehow, his old girlfriend was mixed up in all of this.

The beat went on. So much missed. So many opportunities to nip current events in the bud. Jagger Corey *had* returned for a reason, of that much Archie was sure.

Jagger – "You keep saying you're gonna help return me to my parents. But I've got a news flash for you, professor. You'll never find them. At least, not in this world."

He traced down the transcript to Jagger's next statement, the one where he feared Jagger might have killed his parents. Parents Archie *never* attempted to contact. Not once.

Jagger – "I won't do it, of course. The repercussions would be disastrous, on a number of—levels."

Levels.

Archie wanted to hurl the transcript across the office. Of all the passages from the tapes, this one was the most obvious, cards-on-the-table clue, as to what was going on back then. The little prick was practically taunting him, and he never even sniffed the truth.

How Jagger must have *laughed* at the old fool behind the desk.

The Train of Mistakes kept rolling merrily down the tracks, bearing down on the fool tied to them. Archie wouldn't even try to untie himself, wishing the train was real instead of metaphorical.

"Choo! Choo! Idiot."

Resigned to his fate, he plunged forward.

What came next spanned sessions two and three. Taken separately and out of context, he could see how he'd missed the complete picture. It wasn't something he was going to use to let himself off the hook, but it made him feel at least a little bit better.

But not much.

From session 2:

Jagger – "You're just like him."

Archie – "Just like who?"

Jagger – "My father. You even resemble him."

From session 3:

Jagger – "I'm taking my leave of you, da— Archie. Where I'm going, you can try to arrest me. But let's just say... you'd be out of your jurisdiction. And that's putting it mildly."

That first sentence... *"I'm taking my leave of you, da— Archie."*

Jagger had almost called him Dad.

"My father. You even resemble him."

Archie thought, *not something uncommon.* People resembled other people. No shocker there. But coupled with the previous statement, it set his intuition on high alert, leading him to examine something else more carefully: the *comments* about his parents, and where they might be.

"You'll never find them. At least, not in this world."

He added *that* to the last words he'd heard Jagger speak.

"Where I'm going, you can try to arrest me. But let's just say... you'd be out of your jurisdiction. And that's putting it mildly."

Where exactly *was* Jagger going? And *why* would it be out of his jurisdiction?

"And that's putting it mildly." Suggestive of something larger. Something beyond reach.

Someplace only reachable through a portal?

Portals could be used to travel from far away places. Jagger claimed to be from Maine. But what if he meant something else entirely?

Archie closed his eyes, slowed his breathing, and ran the fragments together

So, is that how things work over here...

You'll never find them, at least not in this world...

levels...

my father... da—Archie... you even resemble him...

out of your jurisdiction... that's putting it mildly.

Where had Jagger *been* all these years since? Where was *over there?* And the biggest question of all; why had he returned?

A theory formed in his mind, one he struck down almost the instant it materialized. But he'd just finished kicking his own ass with the past. So, despite his misgivings, and with a healthy dose of skepticism, he made a phone call.

She picked up on the first ring. "Hello?"

"Hi Jeanne, it's Archie."

"Hi Arch. What's up?"

"This is going to seem like a strange request. And to be honest, I'm embarrassed by it. But since discovering I'm Henry's natural father, I've never asked you for picture's from his childhood. Would it be too much trouble to text me some of them? Particularly from the ages of, say, thirteen to eighteen?"

"Sure. Just those ages? No baby pictures?"

Archie realized how odd the request must have sounded and wished he hadn't been so specific. Too late.

"I'd love to see those too, of course," said Archie. "Maybe I could come up there and check them out another time. We'll make a day of it. But right now I need those specific ones."

Jeanne Trank was nobody's fool. Her next question was no surprise. "Okay, Arch. What's going on? Why do you need specific pictures of Henry?"

The theory he'd come up with was crazy and he knew it. He also knew he couldn't tell the truth to Jeanne. Not yet. It was a Catch-22 situation; he needed the pictures to rule out something crazy, but he couldn't tell her why he needed them without *sounding* crazy. So, he lied.

"Joanne and I are planning a surprise for him. And you know Jo—she enjoys embarrassing the hell out of him whenever she gets the chance. Not in a bad way, but—"

"Arch?"

"Yes?"

"I don't know why you're lying to me, but you *are* lying. I—"

Just then, Archie heard Dominick Trank calling for Jeanne.

"Hang on Arch. Dominick needs to use the bathroom. I gotta help him."

This struck Archie as odd and he told her so.

"Henry didn't tell you?" asked Jeanne.

"Tell me what?"

"Dominick got hurt the other day. Some weirdo just showed up off the street and made an offer to fix our gutters. You know Dom; anything to save money. Turns out the guy was a hack. Didn't even have the good sense to keep his ladder off the front steps. Dom tripped over it and fractured his hip. The guy took off. No apology, no nothing. We never heard back from him. Henry, sweetheart that he is, came up earlier tonight to help out. He was gonna stay for a while until I could manage Dom on my own."

"Is Henry there right now?" asked Archie.

"No. Something happened to Jo. Henry had to go back home. It didn't sound good, whatever it was."

Goosebumps broke out on Archie's forearms. Intuition screamed from a dark corner of his mind. "Jeanne? This contractor, could you describe him to me?"

"In a minute. I gotta help Dom."

Archie waited out the five minutes with his eyes closed, listening with bated breath for the toilet to flush. When he heard it, his pulse quickened.

Jeanne came back on the line. "Okay. He was a scrawny guy. Tall. About Henry's height. Six-two, six-three. Scraggly beard. Why do you want to know what he looks like?"

"Just curious," he lied. "Maybe we can catch him. Make him pay for Dom's medical bills, perhaps."

"Judging by the look of him and the condition of his car," said Jeanne, "we'd have better luck getting blood from a stone. Now, are you going to tell me why you *really* want those pictures? Is it because of what happened to Jo tonight?"

Archie's pulse jumped another notch. "What happened to Joanne?"

"I'm surprised Henry didn't call you. Byron called him earlier tonight. From what I could tell, someone or *someones* attacked Jo. She was pretty shaken up. I told Henry to head back home and take care of her. He's on his way there now. Although with this storm he—"

"Jeanne. I need those pictures. And yes, I was lying earlier." Archie threw caution to the wind. Suddenly, time felt very precious.

"Okay, now you're scaring me," said Jeanne.

"I don't have time to explain. But everything you've told me tonight is possibly related. I don't know how yet, but those pictures could go a long way to answering that question."

Jeanne didn't press the issue. "Okay. Hang up. I'll grab the photo albums and snap a few. Give me five."

Archie didn't bother with a goodbye. He tapped the red icon and waited.

Less than five minutes later, his phone dinged. With shaking hands, Archie tapped the text notification the second it popped up on his home screen. Blank thumbnail images, four in all, arrived on his phone. Little, round white icons in the corner of each file slowly filled as the images downloaded. It seemed to take forever.

Archie slapped the top of his desk repeatedly. "Come on! Come on! Come on!"

The first image download completed.

Ding!

"Oh my God," whispered Archie.

BLACK AND SILVER

CHAPTER 20
DÉJÀ YOU

"**H**ave you ever experienced déjà vu, Wanda?" asked Jagger.

"Yes," said Wanda. One word answers were all she was willing to give him. It seemed the safest course.

Jagger nodded. His head was tilted down, and he was pacing the front of the shop, his hands clasped behind his back as he spoke.

"Silly question. I'm sure you have. Everyone has," said Jagger.

He stopped pacing and turned toward Wanda.

"But what I'm talking about is... different. It's *similar* to that feeling—déjà vu, that is—but at the same time, not. The best way to describe it is a feeling that you're not living the life you were meant to live, but you get a glimpse, from time to time, of the way things could have or *should* have been. That eerie recognition crawling through you when you enter a place you've never been before, but it's familiar all the same. Almost like a memory. For just that brief, shining moment, things seem right. Are you with me so far, Wanda?"

"Yes."

"At the same time, it's a feeling of not fitting in *anywhere* —like a duplicate puzzle piece placed in the box at the factory. You know where you *should* fit, but the other piece has your spot. It's not long after that the spare piece gets put on the shelf and forgotten. Only, the spare can see the finished puzzle hung proudly on the wall, just across the room."

Jagger slapped the counter. Wanda jumped in her seat. He leaned toward her, his voice low and angry.

"And that one motherfucking piece, sitting where *you* should be, sticks out like a sore thumb, surrounded by all the pieces that *you* should have been surrounded by. Everything fits nicely around him. He's supported. Loved! And the spare? Cast aside on the shelf with the other forgotten items. Left in the dust to rot with the rest of the misfits. And some-times, those misfits—the ones that came before you—they're just as pissed off as you. Even more so, because they've been there longer. They take it out on the new guy."

He straightened. Jagger clasped his hands behind his back once again and resumed pacing. "So, what's a puzzle piece to do?"

Every time he turned away, Wanda put her foot on the floor and inched her chair away from the counter and closer to the hallway leading to her safe room. She'd been doing just so for a while. Jagger seemed not to notice. Or, for some reason Wanda hadn't worked out, he didn't care.

"Do you know what a doppelgänger is, Wanda?"

"Yes."

"Humor me. Define it."

Is this guy for real? Wanda wondered. "It's a German word. It means double-goer. Today, it's used to describe a ghostly twin or someone who physically resembles a person but has no genetic relation. Urban myth claims that if you see your doppelgänger, it means you're going to die soon."

"Exactly! Though I disagree with the last part of that statement. I've *seen* mine. And yet, here I am. Funny thing is —you've seen him too. As a matter of fact, you see him all the time." Jagger showed Wanda his first genuine smile of the night.

In that smile was something eerily familiar, yet she couldn't put a finger on it. Like she'd caught a fish but it wriggled from her hands after the hook was pulled out.

His smile dropped, the feeling fled, and Wanda was getting pissed off at being toyed with. She decided it was time to turn his own shit against him.

"What did you mean earlier. About the "me" business?" asked Wanda.

Jagger rolled his eyes. "You haven't figured it out yet?"

"Humor me. Define it."

Jagger golf clapped. "Touche, Miss Heinze."

What an annoying fuck, she thought.

"Let's rewind the tape then. Shall we?"

Wanda waited.

"You'll remember I mentioned the person in the woods. The woman?"

"Yes."

"Did I leave out the part where she told me to give you a message?"

Wanda's mouth ran dry.

"I can see by the look on your face, you may have figured

out this little portion of the program. The message was, *'You can count on it, sweetie.'*"

Wanda shuddered as she felt the dead hands of the Red Witch reach out from beyond the veil.

"What does she have to do with all this?" asked Wanda.

"Let's just say, the lady was supremely prepared. I am the result of that preparation."

So much for turning his shit back at him.

Jo was putting on her peacoat and getting ready to head out. Mercy didn't bother to question Jo's decision. What would be the point? When Jo made up her mind to do something, it pretty much happened.

Mercy went to the front hall, strapped on her winter boots, shrugged into her ski jacket, and pulled an orange and black knit hat over her head. "Just add broom" was embroidered in gold across its front. It was a birthday gift from Wanda, and she was smiling with the memory when she entered the living room.

"All ready, Jo. I—"

Mercy stopped dead in her tracks. What she saw before her made no sense, and she wondered if Dragon's Blood incense could make you hallucinate. Fermina, Jo, and Luci stood in the middle of the room at the center of the ring of beanbag chairs. Luci dangled the onyx eye necklace in front of Joanne; it swayed gently left and right. Jo's green eyes were glazed over, and her head followed the path of the necklace slowly back and forth. Fermina stood behind Jo, with her arms raised as if ready to catch her when she fell.

"What the hell are you guys doing?" asked Mercy.

Fermina trained her hazel eyes on Mercy. They glowed softly, and all at once Mercy felt the energy drain from her body. Her eyelids weighed a thousand pounds, and she had to lean against the wall to keep herself upright.

Fermina swept her right hand toward Mercy and said, "Sleep."

She fought with everything she had and tried to remain upright, but it was useless. Mercy's legs gave way, and she fell forward and face-first into one of the beanbag chairs, landing with a soft *fwump*. Still clinging to consciousness by a thread, Mercy caught the last bit of conversation between Fermina and Luci.

"She's going. Get ready to catch her," said Luci.

A second later. "Got her," said Fermina. "Call Eljin. See how he's doing with Professor Whackjob."

Then, all went black.

ARCHIE COULDN'T BELIEVE his eyes. The pictures Jeanne had sent him all but confirmed what he feared they might. His first instinct was to call Wanda. He'd let her know what he'd found and then send her the pictures. At least she would have a heads up on her new neighbor. He put the phone on speaker. As it rang, Archie closed its window and opened the photo gallery. Another pass through the image files was needed, just to make sure his eyes weren't playing tricks on him. It had been *that* kind of night.

The phone rang several times, and his focus was pulled from the images of Henry as a boy and a young man. The overly-patient, robotic voice mail lady told him to leave a message.

"Wanda, it's Archie. Call me back as soon as you get—"

Archie's message was cut off as three loud raps rattled the frosted glass of his office door. It made him jump in his seat. He stabbed the red hang-up button on his iPhone and said, "Thanks for the heart attack! Who is it?"

"It's me, Arch. Open up."

"Byron?"

"Yeah. Your sister sent me to get you."

Byron never addressed Penny, to Archie or anyone else, as "your sister." Immediately, Archie was on high alert.

"What's the matter, Byron? Did something happen?"

"She wouldn't say. Just sent me here," said not-exactly Byron.

"Why didn't she just call me?" asked Archie.

No answer.

"If it's you, Byron—"

"Why wouldn't it be me?"

"It sounds like you, but then again, it doesn't."

Archie raised the phone, his finger over the number for Penny, when the frosted glass door to his office exploded inward. Pieces of the frame went flying left and right, and the glass shattered and twinkled buttery-yellow in the candlelight. A man stood where the door used to be, his gun drawn.

"Bring the phone here, please," said not-exactly Byron.

Archie did as he was told, rising slowly and studying the man in the doorway. He was Byron's height, he kind of looked like Byron, but one would only make that mistake from far away. And then there was, of course, the small matter of the kicked in door.

"I knew I was right," said Archie. "Byron never knocks first."

Not-exactly Byron actually cracked a smile. "I prefer a more direct approach. I'm Mister Black. Please come with me."

"Would you mind telling me where we're going?" asked Archie, as he handed over his phone.

"I would, yes. You'll find out soon enough." Eljin took the phone, turned it so Archie could see its face, and said, "You won't be needing these." He proceeded to delete the images sent by Jeanne Trank. Archie was surprised when the creep handed it back.

"If you try to use it, I'll shoot you and then your friends."

Well, at least Annie's going to get her new door after all, he thought, as he stepped over its remains.

Eljin Black ushered Archie into the hallway, then walked him down the hall at gunpoint and outside to Byron's Ford Explorer. It was parked a few feet from the entrance.

"In the back, Professor."

"No cuffs?" asked Archie. He was being a wise ass, fully expecting the Byron imposter to cuff him and then shove him in the back. The man's answer took him by surprise.

"I don't see the need for those, sir. But I can oblige if you'd like."

Stunned, Archie took a second to answer. "No, no. Forget I asked."

Eljin Black opened the door for him, keeping the gun trained on Archie until the door was closed. The partition and doors in the back answered the question of why no cuffs were needed. The plexiglass partition looked at least two inches thick, and the back doors had no pop-up locks or door handles. It wasn't Archie's first time riding in a police cruiser, but it *was* the first time he'd ever sat in the back seat.

They drove on in silence. Archie paid close attention to

the landmarks floating by as the Explorer wound its way through the empty, snow-covered streets of Salem. Once they turned onto Proctor Avenue, then Mansell Parkway, he knew the next left would lead to Witch Hill Road.

Mercy's place.

As the Explorer drew closer, Archie moved into the middle of the back seat to get a better view. The partition separating front from back was hazy and opaque from years of abuse by the back seat's more uncooperative inhabitants, and Archie couldn't tell right away who awaited them until the Explorer came to a full stop. Two women stood on the sidewalk, appearing to hold something large and dark between them.

Not-exactly Byron rolled the passenger-side front window down. "In the back. Then I'll meet you at the place."

As the women carried their cargo past the window of the back seat, Archie slid over to catch a glimpse. Snow covered most of his view, and he couldn't see what it was. He turned to watch through another partition separating the back seat from the cargo hold.

This partition was somewhat clearer, and when the hatch opened he recognized the twins right away. Whatever they were loading in the back wasn't light, and they struggled just to get it level with the floor. When they finally got it high enough and over the lip of the hold, they stood together and pushed it from the back. The package rolled over once, then slowly came to a stop. Archie sucked in a surprised breath. It wasn't an *it*. It was a person.

Luci slammed the tailgate closed, and the twins moved to the sidewalk. Archie returned his gaze to the person in the hold. As the Explorer pulled away from the curb and back on to Witch Hill Road, the fine layer of hair covering the poor soul's face slid, bit-by-bit, with each turn of the wheel. When all was revealed, Archie's eyes went wide with shock. He was staring into the face of his daughter-in-law.

At first he was distraught, figuring they'd somehow killed her. It was hard to tell in the darkness, and through the partition, if she was still breathing. He held his own breath until he was positive he'd caught the rise and fall of her respiration through the peacoat.

Numb, Archie inched is body around until he was facing the front partition once more. He slid forward and onto the front edge of the back seat. His thoughts were still with Joanne, and how things would probably go when she woke up. Then, as not-exactly Byron had done less than half an hour earlier, Archie rapped three times on the partition.

"What is it, professor?" asked Eljin Black.

"I just thought I'd let you know. You fucked up."

CHAPTER 21

MIRROR, MIRROR

B yron rose slowly to his feet. When he'd opened the casket, he wasn't sure what to expect. He had a good *idea* what might be in it, given it was a casket and all, but in this new world of magical fuckery he was now part of, you could never be sure. What he saw once he opened it had scared the living hell out of him, yet he felt a certain satisfaction knowing he hadn't trusted it to begin with.

The thing at the bottom had been moving. Its hair was an unruly, salt-and-pepper mess. Blood spattered the front of its filthy white shirt. The face was splotched with flecks of dirt and blood. And when Byron had screamed at it—it screamed back. Funny thing was, the thing at the bottom of the casket made no sound when it screamed. By the time Byron's back had hit the floor, he knew what it was. It was time to get up and face it.

Sore, tired, and drained by fright, he heaved himself up. The chains around his wrists rattled softly as he shuffled toward the casket once more. He leaned slowly over its rim, inched his head forward, then peered down into the hideous face at its bottom.

Byron drew in a deep breath, held it, then blew a raspberry at his own reflection.

"That's for scaring the living shit out of me, you filthy asshole."

It was a mirror.

"What kind of asshole puts a *mirror* in a casket?" Byron asked the room.

The room had no comment.

Fatigue stole over him once more. Bracing on the edge of the casket, he sank to the floor and sat cross-legged. Byron rested his forearms on his knees and let his chin fall to his chest. He drew in a deep breath—as deep as he dared in the dusty room—and let it out in a rush. Calm washed over him, and he let his Spidey senses crawl over the mystery of the mirror in the casket.

Why put a mirror in a casket?

Camouflage came to mind. One of the last things anyone would suspect to be in a casket was a mirror. And that was exactly why it made a twisted sort of sense. You'd either think body, obviously, or nothing. There really was no in-between. It was either the worst thing you could think of, or a simple prop to add to the shop's eerie atmosphere.

"Just like the Big Bad Wolf," mumbled Byron.

The only reason it seemed suspicious was because the move took place in the dead of night.

Suspicious? Yes. Nefarious? Not necessarily.

That reasoning partially satisfied Byron, except for the small matter of the wiry prick chaining him in the basement.

So, Jagger felt threatened—enough to kidnap a cop. Why was that?

Was there something about the mirror itself? Jagger, Byron guessed, knew Wanda had watched him. If the casket was harmless, then why all the attempts at secrecy?

"He wasn't taking any chances. No matter what anyone thought or saw," whispered Byron.

Her words about the casket came back to him— *"He was doing his damnedest to hide it."*

Jagger hadn't wanted that casket seen *at all*. It was never a prop. It was always supposed to be a secret; assumed body or not. But it only needed to remain a secret, Byron reasoned, for what was *actually* inside it.

The mirror was valuable to Jagger. This... made Byron smile. If it was valuable to Jagger, important enough to keep from prying eyes, that meant he *needed* it. The reason didn't matter in the least to Byron, but he suspected it had to do with magic—or, more correctly, black magick.

Ole Jagger wasn't pulling rabbits out of his hat. Magick, spelled with a K at the end, was more closely associated with wicca. The other spelling was more for the likes of Houdini. Byron didn't care either way, he was gonna smash the fucking thing into little, tiny pieces.

"What kind of asshole leaves his casket mirror unguarded?"

Suddenly, Byron wasn't all that tired anymore. Suddenly, he was downright cheerful—but he was also sore as hell. Even as visions of smashing the psycho's mirror danced in his head, and even as he smiled through the groans as he lifted himself from the floor, it took all he had to get himself upright.

He gathered the chains from the floor, pulling the one tethered to his left hand all the way up until the plate rested in his right. Then he wrapped the chain around the plate until it formed a nice solid ball. A wrecking ball.

Byron started humming "Wrecking Ball" by Miley Cyrus through a closed-mouth smile.

"What kind of asshole smashes a perfectly good mirror? *This* happy asshole!"

He raised the newly fashioned implement of destruction to ear level, then let it dangle just over his left shoulder and halfway down his back. Maximum damage was what he was going for, and he figured a little extra arc as he swung it from behind his back then over his shoulder was *just* what the doctor ordered.

Byron readied himself. He leaned back, took a deep breath, then froze. Someone whispered, "My God," and it stopped him cold. But it wasn't just the whisper. The voice sounded... familiar. He rolled the chain from over his shoulder, dropping his wrecking ball with a crash. Byron replayed the whisper in his mind, and his eyes went wide.

"Henry?"

~

SOMEONE, or something was coming. Henry desperately wanted to find out all he could about Jagger. He'd spent most of the last few minutes sifting through the stuff he'd dumped all over the floor, finding most of it useless. Most, but not all.

There was the information he'd found in the Necronomicon, which had both creeped him out and scared the hell out of him. There was the picture of Jo taped to the mirror, which had both creeped him out and pissed him off to no end. And now, there was this note.

He'd almost missed it as he tossed aside piles of useless crap from the dresser drawers. It was one of dozens of crumpled slips of paper. The only reason it stood out from the crowd was it clung to something that, to Henry's eyes, seemed more than just worthless junk. It was an obsidian gemstone clutched in a silver claw. The corner of the note was wedged between the stone and the claw. The writing on it had fortuitously been facing out, and his eyes caught three words that sent a chill down his spine. *The Red Witch*.

Henry pocketed the onyx pendant, then unfurled the note.

The Red Witch is dead. Her demons are captured. It's time. ~ Gemini.

He didn't have the foggiest idea what this guy had to do with Mondra Tibbets, but he knew he had to get back to Salem and warn the others.

"And who the fuck is Gemini?" he whispered.

Henry nearly jumped out of his skin when he heard the crash. It sounded like metal on metal, and he looked wildly around the room for its source. It was still dark, but his eyes had long since adjusted. Enough moonlight shone through the kicked in window to see by. When he'd needed to see something clearly, like the note, he simply carried it over to the window.

Nothing in the room had caused the crash.

The creeps from the porch heard it just fine. Multiple sets of feet pounded up the stairs, hissing his name as they came. "Hhhhhhheeeeeeeennnnnnnnrrrrrrrryyyyyyyyyy!"

At the same time, another voice called his name. A very

human sounding and familiar voice. It came from the area of the dresser.

"Henry?"

It sounded like Byron.

The dresser was next to the door, and Henry had one of the best ideas of his life. He bolted across the room, then stepped to the right side of the dresser. In one fluid and terror-inspired moment, he slid the dresser across the width of the door, then stood in front and pushed it flush, save the space created by the knob. There were two inches of space behind the dresser and on the right side of a door that, he saw by the hinge at the top, opened inward. Had it been the other way around...

"Thank God for small miracles," said Henry.

"What?" asked the voice from the dresser.

"Byron, is that you?"

"Yeah! Henry? Where the hell are you?"

"I was about to ask you the same thing," said Henry.

"I'm in some lunatic's shop in Salem. Asshole's name is Jagger Corey. He got the drop on me and chained me up in his basement. It's a long—"

Every hair on Henry's body was standing at attention. "Did you say Salem? And then say Jagger? Did I hear that right?"

"Yeah. I can't see you in here," said Byron. "Where the hell are you?"

The door behind Jagger's dresser slammed against its back, and the mirror that once held a taped up image of Joanne rocked in its frame.

"Oh fuck," said Henry.

"I heard that, Henry. Where are you? I'll help you!"

Henry put one hand on the mirror to steady it, and one

hand on the edge of the dresser, along with a foot to shove it back. Something from the hallway outside screamed in agony as the door slammed most of the way closed.

"I'm in Maine, Byron. I'm in this Jagger guy's shop!"

Byron stood up straight, tilting his head like a confused dog. "Come again?"

"You heard me right," yelled Henry.

"How the fuck is that even possible?" asked Byron.

Despite the situation, Henry laughed. "Are you seriously asking me that *now*? After everything you've *seen*?"

Slam! The dresser grated against the floor and moved a good six inches. Henry fought with everything he had to gain two of those inches back.

Byron said, "Good point! Since we're talking about crazy shit at the moment, you wouldn't happen to be standing in front of a mirror right now, would you Henry?"

Henry was stunned by the question, causing him to loosen his grip on the dresser, giving back the two inches of floorspace he'd reclaimed.

"Fuck! Yeah, I am. And the natives are restless as hell just on the other side of it. I'm in trouble here, Chief!"

Henry looked down at the top of the dresser. The obsidian gemstone glowed, and the mirror responded in kind. In Salem, the mirror lying flat in the casket before Byron did the same.

"What the hell?" asked Byron.

"What is it?" asked Henry, his voice now strained with terror, exertion, and desperation.

"The mirror is glowing."

"Mine too!" yelled Henry.

Byron went with his gut. "Henry, I know this is gonna sound nuts, but put your hand in the mirror!"

"What!?"

"Just do it!"

Henry didn't relish the idea of letting go of any part of the dresser, but his options were dwindling. He planted both feet firmly on the floor and leaned against the edge of the dresser. Then, he braced the mirror with his left hand. Slowly, and with a healthy dose of doubt, he inched his right hand forward until it rested on the mirror's surface—except it never came to rest. The tip of his middle finger breached the surface, and the mirror rippled outward as if a drop of water had hit the surface of a glass-smooth lake.

Sensing their prey's escape, the children of the void went nuclear. They battered the door relentlessly, and though Henry used every ounce of strength he possessed to push back, the dresser lurched two feet into the room, following the arc of the opening door. It teetered on its front legs, then rocked on all fours. The mirror wobbled, and the frame holding it atop the dresser splintered. Another whack from behind and it would surely topple and smash. *That* would be a problem.

Henry was thrown back by a fresh assault on the dresser, and his hand flew from the mirror. The fingers of his left hand tingled as if asleep, but along with the pins and needles feeling, it also felt freezing cold. As if the mirror was fashioned from the frigid ectoplasm of souls long passed. What came next filled him with dread.

As he readied himself to leap into the mirror, the door flew open. The charcoal-grey silhouettes of the void dwellers slunk into the room. Their eyes glowed a murky yellow, and they hissed Henry's name. He dove for the mirror. As he flew toward the rippling, silver oval, his eye caught the obsidian gemstone resting precariously on the dresser's edge. He snagged it just in time, and gripped it tightly in his right hand.

Henry's sudden burst from the casket mirror surprised Byron, startling him backward. He almost fell over, but somehow managed to keep himself upright. Luckily, Henry hooked his right arm over the rim of the casket, but the mirror, unlike its counterpart back at Jagger's Magical Treasures, was laying face-up. Gravity, on the Salem side, was now a factor.

"They've got my legs, Byron!"

Henry felt the frigid embrace of the void dwellers as they groped his legs from a room miles away. He seized the handle on the casket's side just before he was yanked back hard, his head sinking momentarily below the surface on the Salem side of the mirror. A wicked sense of vertigo seized him as his mind straddled two worlds, and he felt his grip on the coffin handle waning.

Byron recovered quickly, plunging his hands through the mirror's surface and under Henry's armpits, then heaving him up, and almost through. Henry's body straddled two worlds. Byron grabbed the beltline of his jeans, ready to haul him the rest of the way through, when charcoal-black hands emerged from the roiling surface of the mirror, followed by a face. The entity grabbed fists full of Henry's jeans, and was trying to climb him like some bizarre obstacle course from hell.

Byron reacted with adrenaline-fueled rage.

"Not happening, fuckface!"

He reared back and punched the thing right between its glowing yellow eyes. Its grip fell away in an instant, and both Henry and Byron flew backwards and came down hard on the dark pine floors. They laid where they landed, sucking wind.

Miles away, in a place where they spelled Portland the wrong way; a place where snow failed to fall just over a low fieldstone wall; a place where stars burned brightly but were slightly out of position, a mirror toppled from a dresser, and a man's fate changed forever.

CHAPTER 22
CHESS

Penny was starting to get nervous. For the first time in recent—and not so recent—memory, she couldn't get a fix on her husband. Astral travel was by no means a science, but she was skilled enough to know how to locate him at a moment's notice. The connection between them was rock solid. Always had been. Even when they communicated in the normal, everyday way, there was an intuitive bond between them since they'd dated in high school. It only grew stronger in the last thirty years, and with Byron's recent foray into the realm of the spiritual, the bond solidified.

So why isn't he coming through?

She asked herself this question as she donned her winter gear. She hopped in the 4Runner, hit the garage remote, and backed out into the storm once more.

Penny pulled her cell phone from the inside pocket of her coat, turned it back on, then slapped it on the magnetic stand on her dashboard. There were notifications from Joanne and Mercy. They'd have to wait.

"Alexa, call Raul Martinez."

The phone rang twice before Raul answered. "Deputy Martinez."

"Hi Raul, it's Penny Miller. Have you heard from Byron?"

"Hi Penny. No. Not in a while. What's up?"

"I'm trying to locate him. And before you ask, I haven't called him on his cell."

"Why not?" asked Raul.

"He usually calls me when he's on. I don't want his cell phone going off while he's in the middle of something. Especially if that something is dangerous. Know what I mean?"

She wasn't about to tell him about the *other* way she kept tabs on her husband; she didn't think Raul, despite having encountered Chesrule in the Salem library, would believe it. And, she suspected, he might think she'd been spending too much time alone and in the company of spirits of the liquid persuasion.

"I hear you Mrs. M. But I haven't heard from him since he was checking on that new shop over on Essex. That's the last thing he called in."

"What new shop on Essex?" asked Penny.

"I don't know the name of it, but it's near Wanda's place. Like three doors down and on the other side, if I remember right. I can try and raise him on the two-way if you'd like."

"Please, Raul."

"No problem. Gimme a sec."

Penny listened as Raul made the call.

"Chief, it's Raul. Over."

She heard the return call coming through. Static filled syllables crackled through her Bluetooth connection, and she wondered if Raul was able to understand it.

"Copy that, Chief."

Raul came back on the line. "He said he's near the Lynn border helping clear an accident. Car slipped off the road. He'll call as soon as he can."

"You understood that?" asked Penny.

"Most of it. With the interference from the storm it's hard to make out, but spend a thousand hours on the business end of these things and you'd be surprised what you can hear."

Penny had her doubts, and not hearing Byron's actual voice didn't ease her worries. There was no logical explanation for the fear she was feeling.

Since when had logic ruled the roost when it came to Salem?

After asking herself that question, she thanked Raul and hung up.

She never saw the Explorer coming until the last second. A glint of something shiny flashed to her left. When she turned toward it, the last thing she saw before the steel-on-steel crunch was the grill of Byron's police issue Ford. Penny stomped the accelerator, narrowly avoiding being t-boned. The Explorer slammed into the side of Penny's truck, catching the back end. The wheel spun in her hand, the truck fishtailed, tipped on its side, then slid on the snow-slick street until it slammed into a row of parked cars.

Dazed, Penny hung sideways in her seat, suspended by the seatbelt Byron always insisted she wear. Even in her current state, she sent him a silent thank you.

Through the haze of adrenaline and confusion, she heard a vehicle door slam, then the crunch of snow under heavy footsteps. They drew closer.

The door to the 4Runner opened skyward, and the silhouette of a large man appeared above and to her left. He reached in and put an arm around her waist, then unsnapped her seatbelt. For a moment it felt like he would drop her face first into the passenger side window, but whoever he was, the guy was strong as an ox. He braced himself against the frame of the truck, then hauled her out and tossed her over his shoulder like a sack full of feathers.

"What are you doing?" asked Penny. "Who are—"

Penny's voice caught in her throat. As she rode the shoulder of her "rescuer," she faced his chest, her legs dangling down his back. Reading upside down wasn't something she'd done many times in her life, but the name on the badge could have been sideways and backwards and she still would have recognized it. She'd married into it a long time ago.

The man bent low and shrugged Penny from his shoulder. When she tried to stand, she stumbled and had to brace herself against the back door of the Explorer. When she righted herself, Penny was staring into the angry face of her brother.

"Archie? What the hell are you doing in the back of Byron's truck?"

Archie pointed over her shoulder, and Penny slowly turned to face the man wearing the badge of her husband.

At first, she was speechless. It was Byron, at least physically. The face. The build. This man was a bit heavier, and the buttons of the khaki uniform shirt, visible above the zipper of his leather coat, strained where they joined the shirt together.

Up close, the resemblance held. But the eyes... they were the same shade of hazel as Byron's, they had the same sympathetic droop at the corners, too. That's where it ended.

Byron's eyes were always so full of life. *Byron's* eyes brimmed with mischief, humor, and love. There'd never been a time since the day she'd met him—even when they'd been mad at each other—she hadn't seen all the wonderful things in those eyes that made her love him madly. In that moment, looking into this imposter's eyes, she wanted to shrivel up and die. For she was seeing something she hoped she'd never see while she still drew breath. Penny Miller saw what her husband looked like dead, and wondered if he was.

When she tried to speak, nothing came out. The Byron-thing didn't say a word as he reached around her to open the back door of the Explorer. He pulled it open, stood to the side, and placed his hand on the butt of Byron's gun. Penny slid in next to her brother. The door closed behind her. The nightmare was real.

WHEN MERCY CAME TO, the living room was empty. Her head buzzed unpleasantly, and her mouth tasted like she'd been chewing copper wire. When she wiped drool from the side of her chin, her hand came away bloody.

She pushed herself up from the beanbag chair. The room whirled in front of her. She reached for the nearest wall and leaned against it, closing her eyes until the gyroscope of her mind settled. Once it did, the memory of what happened came flooding back.

"Jo," she whispered.

Her first instinct was to try and call Joanne on her cell but realized if Fermina and Luci had taken her, they were probably smart enough to take away her cellphone. When she called Wanda, it went straight to voicemail. The same happened right down the line with Archie, Penny, and Byron.

Where the hell is everybody?
She tapped the contact for Jazz...

∼

"IT'S MERCY." Jazz held up the phone so Armand Moreland could see. "Should I answer it?"

Moreland, for the first time Jazz could recall, seemed unsure what to do next. There was no better ally to have than the powerful, young witch. The need to have her by their side, however, had to be weighed against what could happen if things went sideways. As they'd witnessed during the events out in Satan's Kingdom the previous month, Mercy's power in the wrong hands was potentially devastating.

Armand Moreland had other things to consider. Things no one else knew about yet. Not even Joanne, and she had been there when it happened. It was why he'd had to shield her. It was also something which, if revealed at the wrong time, could set in motion a chain of events that, once started, could not be stopped. People could die... or, if his hunch was right, worse.

"Answer it. Tell her you'll call back in five minutes. That should be enough time for me to tell you something you need to know. Something *I* need you to know."

Jazz gave him an *'are you serious'* look. Then she saw the expression on his face, and saw he was *way* past serious. The man looked scared... and sad.

"Mercy, let me call you b—"

Jazz's eyes went wide. "They did what?!" She listened some more, then said, "Honey, slow down. I'm gonna put you on speaker so Armand can hear this. Start from the top."

Mercy said, "Penny dropped us back at my apartment. We were getting ready to go back out and I was just coming back in to the living room after getting dressed for the cold. Luci had something in her hand and she was hypnotizing Jo, Fermina was behind her. When I confronted them, Fermina used a sleep spell on me, and I went out almost immediately. But I did catch something before I hit la-la land. Fermina told Luci to call someone named Eljin. And then she told Luci to see how Eljin was doing with, and I quote, "Professor Whackjob.""

"Archie," said Jazz.

"Mercy?" asked Armand.

"Yes?"

"Stay where you are. We're on the way."

Jazz closed the call.

As they left the warmth of Jazz's shop, Armand Moreland felt somewhat relieved. The decision to involve Mercy, and all that entailed, had been taken from his hands. He closed the door behind them, then stepped into the storm wondering if a higher power just moved a piece on the chessboard of the universe—or if they were being played.

CHAPTER 23
TWO FOR ONE

"What do you mean when you say you're 'the result of that preparation?' Preparation for what?" asked Wanda.

Jagger put a finger to his lips and looked thoughtfully toward the ceiling. As if the answer were some great and complicated mystery and he was considering how to explain it to a lesser being.

Wanda desperately wanted to punch him in the face. Or, at the very least, use a spell on him that would cause his balls to shrivel up and roll out the bottom of his pants—just so she could stomp on them. She'd make sure pain receptors in his brain remained attached, of course. A list of ingredients she thought might work had just begun to form in her mind when Jagger deemed her ready to receive wisdom from on high.

"When I first met the Red Witch, I was thirteen, going on fourteen. As I told you, it happened during one of my walks in the woods. One moment I was alone, the next—there she was. I'm not afraid to admit, I almost soiled myself. Thankfully, everything stayed where it was supposed to stay, elsewise I would have been mortified. To soil oneself in front of a woman as beautiful as Mondra Tibbets is not in the least desirable. *She*, however, I found quite desirable. A fact of which she was well aware."

"On the *last*, we can both agree," said Wanda.

"Do I detect jealousy, Wanda?" asked Jagger.

"Hardly. Try disgust."

Jagger tipped his head from side to side. "Be that as it may, she—to quote that famous movie—'had me at hello.'"

Internally, Wanda rolled her eyes.

"She said she'd been watching me for some time. I asked her first, why? She laughed, and then reminded me I'd been calling to the darkness. Her appearance was the answer to that call. At this point, I'd been working on spells straight out of the Necronomicon. I—"

Wanda stifled a laugh, then said, "The Necronomicon? You do realize that book is a fake, right? It was a rumor created by H.P. Lovecraft. There is no *actual* Necronomicon. There are physical spoofs, but no original text was ever created. It's just—"

Jagger held up a hand. "Where *you* come from, Miss Heinze, *that* is a truth. But not in my world."

What the hell is this guy talking about? Wanda thought.

"I can see the confusion on your face. I'll make it plain to you very soon, I promise. For now, back to the Red Witch. She held out her hand. I took it. Instantly, I felt the power she possessed. Every nerve in my body went slack, and though no words were spoken, I felt compelled to follow her."

Probably staring at her ass the whole time, Wanda thought.

"For some time, we walked. As we did, I saw things. They

were memories, and they felt as if they *should* be mine, but I knew they *couldn't* be. The people and the places I saw in those '*almost*' memories seemed familiar to me. Imagine my astonishment when I realized they were the very people in my life at that time. Only, they were *nothing* like them."

Wanda was confused, and it showed on her face.

"When I mentioned déjà vu earlier, this is what I meant. Everything was familiar, you see. But at the same time, nothing was."

With that statement, something clicked for Wanda. The picture wasn't clear, but the shape was definitely there. She thought about the connection to the Red Witch, and paired it with a guess on how old Jagger was now. If he'd met her at the age of thirteen, that would have been roughly seventeen years ago. The year would have been 2001. This was 2019, which would make him thirty or thirty one years old right now. The same age as Henry.

Another thing that didn't sit right with her was all this 'my world' crap. What exactly did he mean by that? If she could get him to elaborate on that point, (and so far, he seemed to have diarrhea of the ego), then another piece of her fledgling theory would click into place. She decided to ask him.

"Where do you come from, Jagger? You keep saying things like 'my world.' What does that even mean? Or am I missing something?"

The question seemed to throw him. She'd arrived at a conclusion he was not prepared to discuss. At least, not yet. Jagger had every intention of revealing his motives in advance of what was about to happen tonight, but everything had to be in place first. Wanda was only the first piece, but her current line of inquiry was dangerous. To throw her off the scent he decided, on the fly, to shift gears.

"What do you know about mirrors, Miss Heinze?"

"I'm going to assume you mean something beyond using them for shaving?"

"I do," said Jagger. "Did you know there is a scientific study claiming if you stare into a mirror under low illumination for longer than ten minutes, you'll begin to see all kinds of strange things?"

When Wanda didn't react, he continued.

"It's true. People have reported seeing anything from distortions of their own faces, to the faces of relatives, (living or dead), to animal faces, and sometimes even monsters. And that's just a *scientific* experiment. But what of the supernatural? There's the Bloody Mary thing, where you light a candle in a dark room and say her name three times into the mirror and she's supposed to appear. I've tried it, of course, but nothing happened. I mean to try that one again sometime."

"Good luck with that," said Wanda.

Jagger ignored the jab. "There are other legends: Seven years bad luck if you break a mirror; Don't keep a mirror in your bedroom because the spirits will steal your soul as you sleep. All interesting. And there may even be some truth to them. Far be it from me to say otherwise. There is, however, an urban myth that I'm almost *certain* is actually real."

Wanda rolled her eyes, but only on the inside. She said, "And how would you know that?"

Jagger broke into a huge grin. To Wanda, he looked like the Big Bad Wolf from the Three Little Pigs fairy tale. Only this wolf was already inside the brick house and ready to start a'chomping.

"Let's just say, the casket you watched us move into my shop the other night... it's a two-way mirror, of sorts."

~

MERCY WAITED for Jazz and Armand at the end of her walk. She would have preferred to stay inside and wait, but there was no clear view of both ends of Witch Hill Road and the power had yet to return. The only light on the entire road was one almost useless back up lantern, and that was at the far end of the road to her right. Knowing where Jazz's shop was situated in town, she expected them to come from the left.

When two figures rounded the left corner, it felt as if a weight had been torn from her shoulders. Mercy wasted no time and headed for them, figuring the sooner they got moving, the better. She broke into a trot. The relief she felt at the sight of the two, however, was short-lived, and she slid to a stop. There was no mistaking, even in the almost pitch-black, the figures cut by both Jazz and Armand; one tall and lithe, the other short and stout. Neither fit the bill.

Fermina and Luci had returned for her.

The twins were far enough away that Mercy figured the girls hadn't seen her yet, and probably believed she was still unconscious in her apartment. She ducked quickly behind a pickup truck parked to her right and crouched behind the tailgate, then waited for them to pass.

Mercy heard them draw closer, the crunch of snow under their feet growing louder with each step. They were talking, but every other word was obscured by footsteps, and Mercy strained to make heads or tails of the conversation. They were almost to the pickup when suddenly, they stopped.

"What is it?" asked Fermina

"Why are we doing this?" asked Luci.

"What do you mean?"

"The guy may be our father," said Luci "but you gotta admit—he's a little bit nuts."

"Granted. But you're forgetting something. The whole reason we even exist is because of what he's done... and who are mother is."

"I know. But it doesn't mean I have to feel good about it. Mercy and Jo were good to us," said Luci.

Mercy could hear the guilt in the girl's voice, and the doubt in both voices, but they'd also done something unforgivable to Joanne. As forgiving a soul as she was, Mercy desperately wanted to confront both girls and put a stop to what was happening before it went any further. But what was said next kept her rooted to the spot.

Fermina sighed. "Remember what he said though. Joanne, Mercy, and everyone else, when this is all over, won't know the difference. Even Wanda won't know. It'll be like nothing ever happened. Well, except for Jo's husband and that fat little vampire. They're the only ones who stand to lose anything."

"And you're okay with that?" asked Luci.

"*Okay* has nothing to do with it," said Fermina. "You're forgetting something, and it's kind of a big something, my sister. If we don't help him, we're dead. Remember?"

"Dead? I don't think that's *exactly* true. More like... erased," said Luci. "Like we never existed at all."

"What the fuck is the difference?" asked Fermina. "You're alive now. *We're* alive now. I don't know what it's like to have never existed. But I know what it's like *existing*.

I'll take what's behind door number two, thank you very much."

"Yeah. You're right. I just wish it didn't have to be done they way it's being done is all. And I feel bad for Henry. The vampire—not so much. Do you think Mercy will stay asleep until it's over?" asked Luci.

Mercy held her breath. If they went into the apartment and didn't see her there, whoever was behind all this would be on high alert. Any chance of changing the course of events might go out the window.

"Oh yeah. Most of the power in the sleep spell came from her, anyway. She should be out for hours. If you're worried, we can check on her."

Several moments passed as she waited for Luci's response. If they decided to go in, Mercy was going to have to do something drastic.

"You're sure Mercy won't remember a thing, Fer?"

"She's strong, but I don't think she's *that* strong," said Fermina. "It'll be fine. Now let's go. We have to be there when it starts."

For once in her life, Mercy was grateful to be underestimated.

The crunch of footsteps resumed, dwindling to silence as Luci and Fermina continued on. Where they were going still remained a mystery. One which she'd bounce off Jazz and Moreland when they got to her.

CHAPTER 24
THE MANDELA EFFECT

"What's that thing you got in your hand?" asked Byron. He was still lying on the floor, propped up on his left elbow. His breath had finally returned after the struggle to birth Henry through the mirror and into the room.

Henry was lying on his back, facing the ceiling. Every muscle in his body ached after the struggle through the mirror, but the ache wasn't just from physical strain. Whoever those fucksticks were back at Jagger's place, they had drained a ton of energy from his body.

When he felt strong enough, he turned his head to look at the strange item. In all the excitement, he'd almost forgotten he was holding it.

"It was glowing in time with the mirror. I'm not sure what it is, or what it does, but something told me to take it."

"Probably a good idea. I always like to bring souvenirs back from other states," said Byron. Then he cracked a broad smile. "Especially when I come back home through a mirror. Makes the trip that much more special. Ya know?"

Henry smiled at the ceiling. He was still too drained to turn and face Byron. "Yeah. It does. The people there were so nice, too! I almost couldn't leave the place."

They laughed for a long time after that. They needed to. Nothing drains the puss from the infection of fear faster than laughter.

"What the hell is going on with all this shit, Henry?"

For the first time since crossing over, Henry turned to face Byron. "Holy shit! What the hell happened to you?"

Byron filled him in from the moment he stepped across Jagger's threshold until he'd heard Henry from the other side, finishing with, "I still can't believe the scrawny bastard got the drop on me."

"I wouldn't beat yourself up too much over it. From what you've told me, the guy's got some serious mojo."

"Yeah, he does," Byron conceded. "But I didn't listen to myself. So what was the deal over there?"

Henry started with how he'd gone to Maine to take care of his father, then followed with the call from Moreland, the Jeep crash, following someone or something through the storm, the wall separating the storm from the calm, the photo of Jo taped to Jagger's mirror. It was at this point Byron stopped him.

"He had a picture of Jo?" asked Byron, his voice laced with menace.

Henry, even in the dark, could see Byron's face turning beet-red. He knew the chief had assumed the role of father to Jo, and he loved the guy for it. There was no person he'd rather see in that role than Byron Miller. And no person in the world he thought was in deeper shit than Jagger Corey. Byron, Henry knew, was pissed at himself for being suckered into this place. Those feelings were now amplified ten-fold by this new revelation.

"There's more, Chief. I need to bounce some things off you, see if you can make sense of it."

Byron sat up. Suddenly, he didn't feel tired. "Hit me."

"The place was protected by the children of the void. That thing you punched off of me earlier was one of them. The whole first floor porch was being guarded by them."

"I knew what he was. After that night in Satan's Kingdom, they're kinda burned into my memory. What else?"

"This," Henry held up the obsidian gemstone, "had a note attached to it. It must have got lost in the shuffle, but it said 'The Red Witch is dead. Her demons are captured. It's time.' It was signed by someone named Gemini."

Byron nodded. "Keep going."

"When I first touched the picture of Jo on the mirror, it caused me to have a vision. I saw some of the shit this guy's been up to. Animal sacrifice is part of it; he uses the bones for divination, the sick fuck. And I saw memories. Some were his... and some were mine."

"Is it possible you know this guy, Henry?"

"Not that I'm aware of. It's one thing to have a picture of my wife. That's fairly recent. But the memory I saw in his mind came from when I was nine, Byron."

"No shit?"

"That's not even the strangest part. The whole thing was nuts. At the same time I saw the memory from when I was nine, I saw one from his point of view. He was roughly the same age, and someone was slapping the shit out of him. The lady doing the slapping looked familiar. A lot like my biological mother, now that I think about it. Only, she was much heavier and her hair was filthy."

Byron had the beginnings of a theory forming in his mind. It seemed ludicrous, and he knew it had only come to him because, well, he'd come to accept his role in this new world of witches, magic, and general insanity. The logical part of him, the facts and evidence part, forced him to keep his powder dry and wait for the rest of Henry's story before he rolled it out.

Henry continued. "When I came out of that vision, I was back with him in the woods, and I was seeing things through his eyes. Archie once told me the key to objectivity in his regression therapy sessions was to remain detached, so I tried to apply that to the memories I was seeing through Jagger."

"How'd you manage that?" asked Byron.

"I adapted astral projection in a new way. It left me mostly outside of him, but I could feel his emotions and see their true colors."

"Emotions have colors?"

Henry nodded. "They do. And you've probably heard a lot of the sayings attached to them, you'd just never know that emotions actually *do* have colors. You know, 'he's yellow' would be what you'd say about a coward. Or, 'I've got the blues,' would mean you're depressed. Stuff like that. I'd bet my left nut it was a witch or someone who could read auras who came up with those sayings."

"Makes sense," Byron agreed.

"Anyway. Jagger was off the walls at this point. The guy was in the middle of the woods and either he was *listening* to "I am the Walrus" by the Beatles, or he was *hearing* it in his head. You remember the lyrics to that song, Chief?"

"I do. The Beatles are my favorite band."

"I'm more of a Stones guy, but I do like that song. Or I did. I don't think I'll ever be able to listen to it again. Especially that opening line. It's like he meant for me to hear it. Like he wanted to rub it in my face. For the life of me, I can't figure out why."

Byron sang the lyrics quietly to himself, then Henry told him Jagger's screwed up version. Byron asked, "Did he say anything else after that?" He had an idea what came next. If he was right, or even close, he was going to tell Henry what he suspected.

"Yeah. He screamed out the '*coo coo cachoo*' line, ending it with 'Motherfucker.' And then he said, like he knew I would hear him, 'Welcome to my nightmare, Henry. And now it's yours.'"

Byron was silent for a time. Henry was used to this now. Byron liked to churn things over in his mind before offering up a theory, much the same way a serious chess player will mull over his next move. In the long run, it saved time and got him to the solution, or next move, much faster.

Byron came out of it. "Henry. Have you ever heard of the Mandela Effect?"

"As in Nelson Mandela?" asked Henry.

"Yeah."

"I've heard of the man. Not the effect part."

"A couple of years ago, I went down one of those YouTube rabbit holes. It was during a snowstorm and I was on vacation from work. Penny was down the cape visiting the kids and I was stuck in the house. I came across a video about the Mandela Effect. It's this weird thing where a whole bunch of people have the same memory of Nelson Mandela dying in prison in South Africa in the 1980's. It—"

"Nelson Mandela died in 2013, though. Right?" asked Henry.

"Right. But that's why it's such a big deal. And why it's so strange a huge number of people are convinced it actually happened."

"That's weird."

"Yep. But there are a bunch of theories on it. Some interesting, most just the usual internet conspiracy crap. But there was this one video I saw that was related to the Mandela Effect, and it blew my mind. It had nothing to do with him, but it came up in the feed."

"Ahh. The legendary YouTube algorithm," said Henry.

Byron nodded. "Yep. They'll feed you new stuff all night. So this other video, it had to do with a kids book called 'The Berenstain Bears.' This guy was holding it up for the camera, and you could clearly see the name of the book in the frame. Now, mind you, this was a one shot video. There were no edits that I could see, and the camera never left the cover of the book."

"Yeah, but video's can be doctored in so many ways," said Henry.

"True enough. And the guy might have been a wizard with that shit. But doctored or not, it was a really interesting thing to watch. So, he's in one room and he walks forward and through the doorway to his bedroom. The title on the book changed from 'The Berenstain Bears' to 'The Berenstein Bears.' The spelling of the title *changed*. That camera never moved from that cover, Henry. And I'll be damned if it didn't look real. And you *know* how skeptical I am about *that* shit."

"Okay. So what was the guy trying to prove?" asked Henry.

"That there's more to this world than meets the eye. Or, to put it a different way, he was saying that the version of the world we're living in might have similar versions existing at the same time, and those versions might be as close as the next room over."

"Or the other side of a mirror," Henry whispered.

"Didn't you say something about falling over a stone wall? And that the snow didn't just stop, but the sky was clear just on the other side of it?"

Henry was numb. "Yes."

Byron was on a roll now. "Didn't you find a bat in the parking lot with your initials on it too?"

Henry nodded slowly. He was starting to understand. And then his eyes went wide. "Oh shit!"

"What is it?" asked Byron.

Henry sprang to his feet, shoving the obsidian gemstone into his right pocket. He rooted around in that pocket, then the other three, finally pulling a worn and yellowed piece of paper from his left back pocket. Carefully unfolding it, he held it up for Byron.

Byron squinted. "I can't make it out. It's too dark in here."

Henry pulled his cell phone from inside his winter coat. The battery meter was at two percent, and he silently cursed himself for not turning it off when it didn't work at Jagger's shop. But all he needed was the flashlight app before the battery died. He shone it on the paper, and Byron read it aloud.

"Pourtlande Press Herald. And Portland is spelled differently," whispered Byron.

"I've never seen any major newspaper screw up their own name. Have you?" asked Henry.

"No."

"He got the first line from "I am the Walrus" wrong. Or maybe he didn't." said Henry.

Understanding dawned on Byron's face. "I know. Let's get the fuck out of here and find Jo. Like yesterday."

CHAPTER 25

FACE TIME

The moment the twins rounded the corner at the end of Witch Hill Road, Mercy scooted out from behind the pickup. She ran as fast as the snow would allow in the opposite direction; the one she hoped— prayed—Jazz and Armand were coming from. As if her thoughts had conjured them, they rounded the corner.

Mercy was hauling ass when they suddenly appeared. Out of pure reflex, she dug her heels into the snow and started sliding. Her arms pinwheeled, and her feet were about to come out from under her when Armand Moreland reached out and saved her at the last minute.

Ever since the night at Wanda's Wicca'd Emporium, when he'd laid his soul bare to the witches of the League of the Moon, he'd been extremely careful not to touch Mercy. It seemed no matter who she came into contact with, especially if the person had magical abilities, that person's abilities magnified. He'd experienced it to a degree at Satan's Kingdom, but any power Mercy might have imparted him was minimal at best as she was close to death. The effects faded soon after he'd turned her over to the archangel Raphael.

Whether it was fate, luck, or the universe making another move on the chess board, what Mercy saw in the instant she made contact with Armand Moreland shocked her deeply. When he set her straight after saving her from the fall, he saw the dawn of understanding in those mysterious and depthless hazel eyes. She *knew* what he planned to do, and he could only hope she understood why he had to to it. This chance contact—if it *was* indeed chance—had the potential to change everything. His fate, and the fate of so many others, was now in her hands. He was, pun completely intended, at her mercy.

From the moment of impact, Mercy was slow to grasp what she saw. The memory of the collision, though seconds old, already seemed distant. Absorbed by the mind of the vampire, she instinctually fought to break free. Until she realized she didn't want to break free.

It felt as if time stood still. At first, she didn't understand what she was seeing. The black, wrought-iron gate of the Salem Common came slowly into focus. Snow fell gently all around. Something bright and emerald green flashed in the middle of the park, and the eyes she looked out from were instantly drawn to it.

The mind she was attached to went on high alert, and she heard it screaming 'Danger!' The body she inhabited went into action, closing the distance between itself and that danger in a matter of seconds. As they drew closer, something glinted yellow amidst the fallen snow, and she barely registered the vampire reaching for the knife. It seemed to be on the ground one moment, and in his hand the next.

Momentum swung quickly, and the rapid movement of Moreland's body gave way to slow and methodical thought, borne of long existence.

Mercy was he, now, and he was Mercy. Their thoughts became one. When he lifted the knife and brought it down on the void dweller's neck, she felt every movement. When the malevolent being cried out, she felt its anguish. When it tumbled back to the void, she felt its anger as it passed through Moreland's body. And when Moreland absorbed what the being had stolen from Joanne, and then locked it down deep within his own being, she understood everything.

Mercy now knew the reason the being had taken it, and the reason Moreland had wrenched it back and then locked it away deep within himself.

What she'd seen earlier in the evening, as the vampire walked away from her apartment, wasn't an aura, as she thought it might be. She replayed the moment in her mind: Moreland walking down the walkway leading away from her apartment, then turning the corner; a flash of color; a small trace of that color floating briefly in the air and then vanishing. Mercy focused on it now. It was green. Emerald green. *Jo's* green.

In the last second, before the vision faded and she returned to the present, she divined his intentions. What he *knew* had to happen. A million different scenarios of how she might prevent it flooded through her mind, and none of them provided a way out. No words, she knew, could change his mind. No action existed that could change what must inevitably unfold. The hardest part of all was Mercy knew he was right, and she decided in that instant she would help him make it happen. And she saw that Jazz knew it too.

She looked from one to the other through tears forming in her pretty, young, wise-beyond-her-years eyes.

"Is this the way it has to be?" she asked both of them.

They nodded.

"It's okay, Mercy," said Moreland. "I'm fine with it. Now let's get it done."

Mercy knew, by what she'd seen in his mind, and also what was written on his heart, what she needed to do. She took Armand Moreland's hand in hers. Their eyes locked. He heard the spell in his own mind as if she'd spoken it aloud. Once it was done, and they released each other, his fate was sealed.

Jazz was unaware of what Mercy had just done.

"Where do we go next?" asked Mercy.

"Wanda's," said Jazz.

As THEY MADE their way down the staircase, Henry faltered. Halfway down he stumbled and Byron grabbed hold of his right arm to steady him.

"Are you okay?" asked Byron.

"Yeah. I just felt a little weak there for a minute. Maybe that mirror took more out of me than I thought."

They continued on with Byron following a little closer, just in case.

Halfway across the the floor of the circular room, Henry slowed. Byron was still following close behind, flashlight in hand, and had to quickly sidestep to avoid bumping into him. When he turned back around, Henry was bent over, his hands on his knees. He looked like someone catching his breath at the end of a 5k road race.

"What's wrong, Henry?"

"I don't know. All of a sudden, I have no energy. Like something is sucking the life out of me."

"It's Jagger. It *has* to have something to do with him," said Byron. He knelt next to Henry, pulled his arm up over his own shoulder, and helped him across the room. Then he sat Henry down in the chair behind the counter, right next to the Big Bad Wolf.

Henry's energy, by the time Byron eased him into the chair, had dropped even further.

"I don't feel sho gool," said Henry. His speech was starting to slur, and he was having trouble raising his head. Byron couldn't be sure, due to the room's darkness, but Henry looked like he'd lost ten pounds since they'd come down from the upstairs room. He rushed over to the far end of the counter and grabbed another flashlight from the drawer. Turning it on, he flew back over to Henry and shone the light on his face.

"Holy shit!" said Byron.

"Wha? Wassamatta?" slurred Henry.

Byron wanted to tell him what he saw, but thought better of it. Whatever was happening to Henry was happening fast, and telling him so would only make matters worse. Fear had a way of sucking the life out of you, and Byron didn't think Henry could handle much more suck.

It wouldn't do to tell him his cheeks were sunken in... or that his clothes were hanging on him just a little bit... or that he suddenly had the beginnings of a scraggly beard struggling to grow along his jawline.

No, it would not be one *bit* a good thing to tell Henry he was starting to take on the features of the man who owned this building.

Byron needed to do something. Now.

"Henry, which pocket is the gemstone in?"

"Huh?" Henry could barely lift his head now, and he was already beyond understanding anything Byron was asking him.

Terrified of wasting time, Byron leaned down and braced Henry's upper body with his right arm so he wouldn't fall forward and out of the chair. With his left, he rooted around in Henry's pockets until he found what he was looking for. Once he had the gemstone in hand, he pushed the chair up against the counter, sandwiching Henry between it and the chair.

It was the best he could come up with. He didn't want Henry falling out of the chair and face first on the floor, and he didn't have the time or strength to lift him out of the chair and lay him down.

With Henry secured, Byron started looking for a way out of Jagger's Magical Treasures.

WANDA WASN'T sure she was seeing things right. For the last few hours, she'd been sitting in the dark and listening to this lunatic rant. Only, she suddenly had the sinking feeling he wasn't as much of a nut-job as she'd originally thought. But three hours was three hours. It was a long time to sit and jabber with a *good friend*, let alone a magick-wielding psychopath.

She rubbed her eyes, trying to make them work right. All of a sudden, Jagger looked slightly different to her. It was subtle, and she had a hard time putting her finger on it at first. There wasn't a lot of light to work with, and she had to wait until his pacing brought him past the candle once more. In the last few moments, however, he'd taken to communicating from the far corner at the front of her shop, and she wondered why.

"What did you mean when you said the mirror was two-way?" asked Wanda.

Jagger's head snapped up at that. He appeared lost in thought, and he asked, "What was that?"

"You said the mirror in the casket was, and I quote, 'a two-way mirror of sorts.' What did you mean by that?"

Jagger drew closer, as Wanda had hoped. When the candlelight once again lit his face fully, she had the answer to her question—and the confirmation of the budding theory she'd been working on.

She was looking into the face of Henry Trank.

CHAPTER 26
ALL ROADS LEAD HOME

A rchie watched from the back seat of Byron's cruiser as not-exactly-Byron drove them through the storm. Penny had offered her hand and he held on to it tightly. They took turns looking into the cargo area to check on Joanne, but she hadn't stirred once the entire ride. She looked like she was sleeping peacefully. Neither Penny nor Archie were surprised when Eljin Black turned into the parking lot behind Wanda's Wicca'd Emporium. It always seemed to come down to this place.

It gave them hope. But that hope was short-lived.

Eljin Black backed the Explorer up until it came to rest three feet from the back door to Wanda's shop. It was just enough room for the tailgate to open.

The big man killed the ignition, exited the Ford, and made for the cargo area without so much as a glance in Archie's or Penny's direction. They turned and watched as he opened the cargo area, picked up Joanne, slung her over his shoulder, closed the hatch, and turned around to rap three times on the back door.

WANDA HEARD the distant and muted knocking coming from the back of her store. Someone wanted access to her safe room. She hoped it was Byron, and he'd come back from Jagger's place with a posse of Salem police. When she turned to look at Jagger, hopes of rescue fled. He'd been expecting this.

"That should be my assistant," said Jagger. He pointed to the back of the room, where the swinging doors next to the cash register sat. Behind those swinging doors, the hallway to the safe room at the back of Wanda's shop awaited them. "Please, lead on, Wanda."

Now Wanda understood why he hadn't bothered to say anything as she scooted away from him and closer to the safe room.

She didn't move. It wasn't out of any sense of rebellion, or some kind of calculated move to stall—she was simply too stunned. In a matter of a few hours, this scrawny, psychotic, apparent Henry wannabe had subdued the Chief of the Salem Police, trapped her in her own store, and managed to somehow turn himself into another person, (*at least on the outside*, Wanda thought), and all with what seemed a minimum of effort. For the first time in as long as she could remember, she was at a loss for what to do next.

Jagger brought a fist down hard on the counter, and the candle wobbled in its holder. The disturbance of light contorted his face into an angry perversion of Henry's. It was an expression of which her young friend was incapable, because what drove this man could not be found anywhere within Henry.

He leaned down low, sliding his hands across the glass

countertop, and spread his arms wide. Bangle bracelets at his wrists scraped across the glass, making a hissing sound like a quiver of cobras. When he smiled, shadow and candle-light danced across his teeth, somehow making them look like the fangs of the Big Bad Wolf, and making Wanda feel like one trapped little piggy.

"The pentacle room awaits, Miss Heinze."

BYRON TRIED the front door first, not expecting it to open, but it made sense to start with the obvious on the off-hand chance it actually worked. It didn't.

He turned to look at Henry, who was still slumped forward in his chair with his head resting on the counter. It looked like he was sleeping, and Byron prayed that's all it was. The rapid decline in Henry's physical health had scared the shit out of him, and he was desperate now to find a way out and get Henry over to Wanda's.

Something about Henry being back in Salem, having come from what Byron was pretty sure was a place on earth—but not exactly *this* earth—connected to this. The thought of taking him to Salem Hospital crossed Byron's mind, and he quickly pushed it aside. Henry's ailments were of the magical variety. An IV bag and a couple of Tylenol weren't going to do the trick.

When Byron turned back around, he was staring through a thick, arched window which reached all the way to the ceiling. Its edges were surrounded by four-inch-wide, stained glass panels separated from the main window by lead framing. It looked thick and hard to smash.

Byron scanned the room for something he thought

might do the trick. There wasn't much to work with. The crates stacked near the staircase were bulky and way too big. Furniture was a scarcity, which didn't surprise him; the pasty bastard had just moved into the place and apparently seating wasn't high on his list of priorities. Other than the chair Henry occupied, that was it.

The clock was ticking. Byron spun around, frantically searching for something heavy and with a pointed edge that might, at the very least, crack the glass. The rattle of chains hanging from his arms was getting on his nerves.

The chains!

Byron chastised himself for not thinking of it right away. "Miller, you dumb son of a bitch."

Wasting no more time, Byron played out the length of chain from his left hand; the one with the plate still attached at its end. He grabbed it up with his right hand and then moved as close as he dared to the window. If it shattered, he wanted as much room between himself and flying glass as possible. If the wind was blowing against the window, it probably wouldn't be enough room. It was a risk he had to live with.

Byron stood sideways, left shoulder facing the window, and began twirling the chain with the plate at its end in his right hand. Once the chain reached speed, he let it fly with a scream. The corner of the plate smacked into the glass, and Byron turned his head in the opposite direction to protect his eyes from flying shards that never came. Instead of the crescendo of falling glass he'd hoped for, there was a muted cracking sound akin to the snapping of a celery stalk. When he turned to take in his handiwork, he saw the edge of the plate impaling the middle of the huge window. Glass remained, cracked but unified. It looked like the shattered windshield of a car.

Frustrated, Byron yanked the chain free, and the plate clanked loudly on the floor. He repeated the process, once again swinging the chain and launching it at the window, but managed only to knock out a two or three inch section of glass. It didn't take a rocket scientist to realize how long it would take to finish the job. He needed something big and heavy enough to throw through it, and knock out most of it all at once.

Across the room, Henry started snoring. Loudly. It drew Byron's attention, and he thanked the power greater than himself Henry snored like a buzzsaw, for directly above Henry were the gleaming eyes of the Big Bad Wolf. Byron ran across the room, as fast as the dragging chains would allow. He hopped over the counter, grabbed the stuffed wolf by the legs, and then heaved it over Henry and the counter, where it landed, right-side-up, on its base. Already tiring from the effort, he walked the length of the counter instead of vaulting it. When he reached the wolf, he grabbed it by the ear and dragged it toward the shattered window. The night had taken its toll, and he had to rest, if only for a few moments, until he felt strong enough to do what came next.

When ready, he bent and grabbed the wolf once again by the legs, spun in a circle like a high school shot-putter, and released the wolf when he reached maximum torque. The wolf hit the window, and stuck there. Its massive head and the front part of the base were the only parts to make it through. It looked like a freeze frame from a movie.

"You gotta be shittin' me," said Byron.

Dejected, he moved toward the center of the room. He was preparing to make a flying leap at the wolf's backside when the window gave way. It sounded like the wrapper being ripped from a giant-sized candy bar.

Snow flew in through the window, and Byron flew toward Henry. The adrenaline pendulum swung in his direction once more, and he vaulted the counter, pulled back the chair, and tried rousing him. All he got for his troubles were sleepy grunts.

He'd have to carry him, there was no other way.

"After this shit is over, I'm going to sleep for a week," he told Henry.

"Shleep fur avweek," Henry mumbled.

Byron bent down, slid an arm under Henry's left arm, then one under his legs. The first thing he noticed was how Henry's clothes hung loosely from his body, the second was how little trouble he had hoisting him over his shoulders. It made the task ahead of him much easier—that was the good part. It also meant whatever was happening to his nephew was happening fast—not one bit good—and the sooner he got him to Wanda's, the better.

"I hope that's true," Byron said to himself.

As he made his way toward the ruined window, he had a funny feeling it would be much more complicated than that.

Isn't it always? he wondered.

CHAPTER 27
GEMINI

"Who's that in Byron's truck?" asked Mercy.

"It looks like Penny and Archie," said Jazz.

"It is," said Moreland. "

They'd made good time getting across town in the storm, all things considered. As they'd drawn closer to Wanda's shop, Moreland suggested a stealthy approach, and then a period of surveillance before making a move.

The strategy proved its worth. Less than a minute after arriving, they lucked out. The cargo door of the Explorer was open, and they glimpsed the big guy's back as he carried Jo through the door. Once he'd gone inside, they took position at the back of the parking lot behind the shrubs and settled in. They'd been focusing so much on Jagger's co-conspirator, they'd almost missed the passengers in the back seat of the Explorer.

"I'm gonna let them out of there," said Jazz.

She started to slip from behind the shrubs when Moreland put a hand on her arm. Jazz didn't like that, and went to give it to him with both barrels when he pointed toward Explorer. Eljin was on his way back out. Jazz froze in place, then slowly slid back to her original spot.

They watched in silence as the man who looked like a slightly larger version of Byron opened the rear driver's side door and ushered Penny and Archie out at gunpoint. After a few minutes inside, he returned to the Explorer, executed a three point turn in the parking lot, and backed it into the spot directly in front of the stand of shrubs in which they hid.

"What the hell do we do now?" Jazz whispered just loud enough to be heard over the running exhaust a mere three feet in front of her.

"We wait until he exits the vehicle, then we deal with him," said Moreland.

Mercy asked, "Why not just take him out now?"

"Nothing would please me more, Mercy. But two of us are still unaccounted for. Byron, judging by the Explorer in someone else's possession, is persona non grata at the moment, and Henry, when last I talked with him, was tending to his ailing father in Maine. As for Wanda, she may or may not be inside. My gut tells me she's inside. Do both of you agree?" asked Moreland.

Mercy and Jazz nodded.

"Has she reached out to you?" Moreland asked Jazz.

"No. I keep trying to reach her telepathically, but she's off the grid."

Moreland pulled the obsidian gemstone from his pocket. "He probably has one of these. My guess is it can block that kind of communication."

"How do you know that?" asked Mercy.

"I don't. But it was powerful enough to knock Joanne out cold, and then subdue you. Is it beyond the realm of possibility it could prevent telepathy between Jazz and Wanda?"

Jazz was nodding before he got the last word out. "He's right. And with Jagger having a gemstone in there, and there being one out here—"

The loud crunch of snow under heavy feet stopped her sentence cold.

"It means he knows you three are out here. The gemstones are connected," said Eljin Black.

Jazz, Mercy, and Armand Moreland looked up at the same time. Eljin Black stared down at them with his creepy, not-quite-Byron face, and his very large gun resting two inches from Jazz's face.

Under normal circumstances, Moreland would have attacked him before he could make a move to defend himself. With a gun so close to a non-vampire's face however, a face he'd come to know and love and respect, he wasn't willing to take the chance for fear of the gun discharging in the process. No matter how fast he was, Jazz could die. Something, it seemed, of which Eljin Black was well aware.

The shapeshifter was only following orders.

As Moreland handed the gemstone over, he found himself wishing he'd never involved Jazz. He'd assumed she would have found him tonight eventually; the gypsy was the only one in town good enough and experienced enough with vampires to track them down. So, he'd sped up the process and called her to the store, figuring it was better to have her with him than wasting time with the chase. Big mistake.

"You two out first," said Black. He never looked at Moreland or Mercy, but kept his eyes and gun trained on Jazz. All business.

They did as told. As they stepped out, Eljin slid around Jazz and put the gun to the back of her head. Jazz rose from a crouch, both knees popping loudly.

"Inside, please," said Black.

The headlight beams of the Explorer were trained on the back door to Wanda's Wicca'd Emporium—brightly lighting the way through the snow and toward the unfolding darkness within.

As WANDA ENTERED the safe room ahead of Jagger, the first thing she saw was Joanne unconscious and lying in the middle of the gold-encrusted pentacle. She ran to her, knelt, and tried to rouse her.

"Save your energy, Miss Heinze. She sleeps until I need her awake," said Jagger.

"Why are you doing this?" Wanda asked as she fought back tears.

"To take what should have been mine all along. As you can tell just by looking at me, I'm the one who belongs here now. Not Henry Trank."

As he spoke, Jagger circled the pentacle. When he got to the compass point for north, he removed the obsidian gemstone from his pocket and placed it facing toward the pentacle. He circled around Wanda, then stopped at the southern compass point.

On cue, Penny and Archie walked through the door, followed by someone who Wanda thought was Byron at first, then quickly realized wasn't. The resemblance, from a distance, was close. To her horror, she realized this was the man who'd waved to her from the entrance to Jagger's shop. Wanda cursed herself for airing her suspicions to Byron earlier in the night. If she hadn't brought it up, none of this would be happening.

Jagger read her reaction perfectly. "This was going to happen, whether the cop came to my door or not. Don't be too hard on yourself, Wanda. This is my destiny—and yours too. It's just happening much quicker now."

The big, not-quite-Byron guy pointed at the pentacle with his gun, and Penny and Archie joined Wanda and Jo at its center. Without a word, he pivoted and went back outside. When he returned, Jazz, Armand Moreland, and Mercy were directed to the same spot. Then he put something in Jagger's hand and moved to the far end of the room, standing guard next to the bar.

Jagger placed the second obsidian gemstone directly on the south-facing compass point at the edge of the outer ring, exactly seven feet from the inner circle.

Two were down. Two to go.

The bell over Wanda's front door tinkled, and soon footsteps echoed from the hall leading to the pentacle safe room. When the twins stepped into the room, Wanda, Archie, and Penny each drew in a surprised breath. To Moreland, Mercy, and Jazz, there was no surprise. And as they circled around the pentacle, Jagger moved to join them at the east compass point.

He hugged both of them, and each planted a kiss on his cheek.

Luci reached into into her coat pocket and pulled a third

obsidian gemstone from it. Jagger took it and repeated what he'd done with the earlier two.

"Such wonderful daughters," said Jagger. "Their mother would be proud."

Fermina and Luci stood on either side of Jagger. Each reached out a hand and he took theirs into his. Jagger tilted his head back, closed his eyes, and spoke:

> *Conceived in darkness, the apples of my eye*
> *Reveal the daughters Gemini*

A fine red mist swirled around the heads of the twins; a mist this room had seen before. The three obsidian gemstones at the north, south, and east compass points glowed to life—a watchful eye at their centers. The lustrous, straight black hair of the twins began to morph, first retreating into their scalps, then spawning outward anew. Auburn hair sprouted slowly at first, slinking its way out like rust-colored and hungry serpents in search of prey. The deep blue of their eyes glowed a fierce, bright white, illuminating the skulls beneath like a flashlight in a jack-o'-lantern. White gave way to red, like coals burning in living sockets that, once cooled, revealed the hazel that had always been there—a shade identical to their mother's.

BYRON STOOD in the middle of Essex Street, Henry hanging over his right shoulder like a limp dishrag. With every step closer to Wanda's shop, Henry seemed to diminish further, as if something (or a certain someone, Byron suspected) was taking from Henry everything that made him who he was. There was no way for Byron to know where Jagger was for sure, but the scant evidence indicated he was in Wanda's Wicca'd Emporium. For what reason? God only knew.

"Time to find out what God knows, then," said Byron.

"Whaf gosh nose," slurred Henry.

If he needed any more proof Jagger was in Wanda's shop, he got it right away. The obsidian gemstone grew warm in his right hand. When he pulled it up to see why, it glowed red. An eye stared back at him, one he'd seen up close and personal just a little over a year ago. One which had stared into his mesmerized brain as it jammed a tongue down his throat.

The memory made him gag, and he closed his hand around the medallion, if only to thwart any satisfaction the eye's owner might get from viewing his reaction. He still sometimes saw it in his dreams.

Byron shook his head, trying to shake the memory away like a wet dog drying itself. It helped bring him back to the present. He looked up and down Essex Street, trying to decide on his next move, but there were no answers to be gleaned from the rounded edges of snow-covered buildings. The bloated snowflakes falling in lazy, tumbling silence offered no advice. And the unnatural darkness of Salem's streets kept the answers to itself.

Byron had never felt so alone, and so at a loss as to what came next.

"Time to wing it, Henry," said Byron.

It was then, for the first time in well over an hour, Henry spoke clearly. It was weak and barely loud enough to be heard, but any doubts Byron had about what came next were erased.

"He's in Wanda's, Chief. Let's go," croaked Henry. Then, just above a whisper, he said, "Welcome to *your* nightmare, Jagger. *Coo coo cachoo, motherfucker.*"

Byron headed for the back door to Wanda's Wicca'd Emporium.

CHAPTER 28
CIRCLES

Wanda's safe room had been set up as an after-work refuge for herself, and as a protected area from the encroachment of dark magick. Which, more and more lately, had poked its ugly head above the surface throughout Salem.

As a matter of history in the Witch City, things had always been this way. Darkness has many forms, sometimes packaged in light. In the last few years, however, it seemed to have ratcheted up another level or two. It was nothing the average citizen (or, to borrow a famous description—muggles) would notice, but to those in the know and those with abilities beyond the norm, it was terrifying. All the evidence needed to prove the town was going in the wrong direction was in this room.

Five witches, a gypsy, and a witchcraft-practicing vampire were held captive in the center of a room devoted to keeping dark magick at bay. A psychotic dark witch, his equally psychotic and crafty daughters, and a shapeshifter with a gun posing as the Chief of the Salem Police, had taken over this haven for white magic. With what had seemed a minimum of effort, Jagger Corey had shifted the balance of magical power in the town.

In one day.

If Wanda and the others hadn't been scared out of their minds, they might have been impressed by this feat. As it was, they *were* scared, but not so scared they couldn't try and figure a way out of this mess.

The first glimmer of hope came when Jazz entered the circle. Now that she was on the inside of the not-quite-complete circle of obsidian gemstones, her telepathic link with Wanda was no longer blocked. When she tested this, Wanda had startled slightly. It was subtle, like the reaction one would have when touching something metallic after walking across a carpet. Jagger hadn't noticed; he was too busy casting a spell and revealing the true natures of Fermina and Luci.

It went like this:

Jazz – *Boo!*

Wanda- *Oh! I can hear you now, sweetie.*

Jazz – *I noticed.*

In her mind, Wanda could see Jazz's mischievous smile. They never made eye contact; there was no need. It was also safer that way.

Wanda – *What are we going to do about this nut job?*

Jazz - *I have an idea. But first, tell me what you've found out about him. We need to compare notes.*

Wanda – *Okay.*

Wanda ran it all down for her, from the moment Byron had left for Jagger's place, right up until she'd made it into the safe room. It was only a matter of seconds, for in place of clunky words, Wanda simply presented her memories to her friend. It allowed Jazz to cherry pick the information she needed.

They'd done this a million times in the past, (often separated by miles), and practiced it together frequently, just to keep the telepathic muscles strong. It helped keep their relationship strong, too. They rarely got the chance to spend time together because their shops were at opposite ends of the town and their business hours were identical. Whatever spare time Jazz *did* have was usually spent with her husband, Scott.

When Jazz was up to speed, she returned the favor, letting Wanda know of Moreland's plans. She was shocked, but she never let it show, save for a small furrow at her brow line.

Wanda – *Is he sure it has to be this way?*

Jazz – *That's what he says.*

Wanda – *Do you think Jagger suspects anything?*

Jazz – *No. I don't see how he could. As far as he knows, the attack on the Common was a success. Fermina and Luci bringing Jo here is all the proof he thinks he needs.*

Wanda – *I wouldn't want to be them when he finds out.*

Jazz – *Screw those two-faced bitches. They'll get what they deserve.*

Wanda – *We need to let the others know.*

Jazz – *You're right.*

Wanda – *What do you need me to do?*

The six of them sat in a circle around Joanne. Jazz, Moreland, and Mercy hadn't planned on being captured by not-exactly-Byron, but it turned out to be a blessing in disguise. When they entered the room and saw Wanda sitting between Penny and Archie, Jazz took the spot in the circle directly opposite Wanda. Moreland sat to Jazz's left, Mercy to her right.

Jazz – *As subtly as you can, take a hand from Penny and Arch into yours. I'll do the same with Mercy and Armand and tell them to connect with the other two. Once we do, I can show them what's up. Got it?*

Wanda – *Will that work?*

Jazz – *It will with Mercy in this circle. Remember, she augments whatever powers we have. Even if they see us do it, and stop us, it'll already be too late.*

Wanda first took Penny's hand into hers, then Archie's. Jazz did the same with Mercy and Armand, the latter two intuiting in an instant what Jazz wanted. The circle was complete, and lasted for only a few seconds before Eljin Black told them to break it up, half-heartedly raising his pistol for emphasis. The damage was done, however.

Instantaneously, the circle of six understood it all. A kaleidoscope of images from separate minds swirled together as one, and the mystery of Jagger Corey became *almost* completely clear. The transcripts from Archie's sessions with Jagger, and the pictures Archie received from Jeanne Trank on his phone dovetailed perfectly with Wanda's memories of her conversations with Jagger.

What the six of them came to understand about Jagger was he hated his life, his parents, and himself. But his fatal flaw was blaming everyone else for his problems. Pour on a little encouragement from a dark witch and a healthy dose of black magick... and then show him the life he could have if things were slightly altered, and Voila! The only thing missing was why the hell it was happening in the first place.

As their minds swirled together, it prompted a memory

within Archie, which spread to the group. It was a conversation he'd had with Darren Biltmore, the head of the physics department at the U. They'd become good friends since the League of the Moon had saved his life—and soul—from the Red Witch.

On Friday nights, they'd taken to capping off the week by meeting at Rockafellas restaurant for dinner, drinks, and discussion. They'd come to realize the worlds of quantum mechanics and parapsychology had more in common than either man thought possible.

"So, let me get this right," said Archie. "You're saying there are worlds... universes even, that are exactly like ours? And they're as close as a fingernail away? That sounds more unlikely than anything I've ever taught in any of my classes."

Archie expected Darren Biltmore to take offense, but was instead surprised by his answer, "I know. It sounds like complete bullshit. And that's what I though too, at first. But think about it, Archie; we are the result of every decision we've ever made. The very fact of you and I having this conversation is the result of decisions each of us made. I could have just as easily decided, after all that craziness with the redhead went down, to bury my head in the sand. Stake my claim on the shores of denial river."

"I see what you did there," said Archie, smiling.

Biltmore smiled back. "It's not just a river in Egypt, after all. Anyway, for argument's sake, let's say I did remain in denial. I hid from it all. Somewhere, there is a version of me that actually *made* that choice. He's living out the life that resulted from it. Right now. And next to *that* probability, there's another version of me who made a slightly different choice, and now he's hiding in a room, shut off from the world and sucking his thumb."

"Let's say I accept your premise. All of it," said Archie.

"You're a scientist, so there has to be some concrete scientific basis for this. Right?"

Biltmore sipped his Guinness Stout, placed it on the table, then steepled his fingers as he wondered how best to lay it out for his curious friend.

"Have you ever heard of Schrodinger's Cat?" asked Biltmore.

"Is that the kid from the Charlie Brown comics?"

Biltmore smiled. "No. But Lucy pulling the football away every time just as Charlie Brown goes to kick it isn't that far off. Anyway, Erwin Schrodinger was a physicist, but he wanted to put his theory in words the layman could understand. It goes roughly like this: There is a box on a table. In that box, there is a cat. There are two possibilities for said kitty before opening the box. It is either alive, or dead. The possibilities, before opening the box, exist *simultaneously*. In other words, they cannot be known until we open the box and *observe* the outcome. If we decide not to open the box at all, we'll never know. So, in effect, there is a third possibility. Each has its own effect, and each branches off in a different direction once the box is opened. All outcomes are possible, and all exist at the same time. The one we eventually *observe* ends up being *our* reality."

"Is it possible to observe other realities from within another?" asked Archie.

Biltmore raised his Guinness. "That, my friend, is the million-dollar question! Answer that, and there's a prize out there beginning with a capital 'N' waiting for you."

As Archie sat on the floor in Wanda's safe room, he realized he had the answer to that question, and it was a resounding 'yes.' The Nobel prize would probably have to wait, however.

Jagger Corey had not only glimpsed one reality from the safety of the other, but had traveled back and forth between them multiple times. The scariest question was how many things in *this* timeline had he already altered? And to what end?

Archie was positive now that his aunt dying, as Jagger had predicted in the 2004 sessions, was probably a set-up between himself and the Red Witch. They'd murdered his aunt for no better reason than to get Jagger released early, and to inflict pain. It was payback for Archie's uncovering of the black magick love spell Mondra had put on him.

But that was then. Mondra the Red Witch was dead and gone. Yet, all this seemed tied to her somehow. Was she spiteful enough to set up something and curse them all from beyond the grave? It seemed so.

Archie was pulled from his thoughts as the obsidian gemstones flared to life in their claws. An eye opened in each. Brilliant crimson light illuminated the the center of the room, and tendrils of red mist, identical to the mist Archie had seen coming from Jagger's gemstone from the sessions, crawled their way toward Joanne.

The witches within the circle of gemstones tried desperately to wave the mist away. It had no effect. Their hands passed straight through, and the crimson fingers slunk forward with hideous purpose. It was as if the mist emanated from a place and time other than the present. Because that's exactly what it was. Wherever Jagger came from, this mist was of his world—this black magick *his* creation. A living curse born of dark witches and birthed from a portal connecting worlds.

Jagger stood at the western compass point, Fermina and Luci to either side and holding his hands. Eljin Black stepped from the bar and approached the circle, his gun raised in his right hand and cradled in his left.

The awe and wonder in Jagger's voice was unmistakable, and he whispered, "The fourth stone is nigh!"

~

THE LAST THING Byron wanted to do was walk through the front door to Wanda's shop. The second to last thing Byron wanted to do was go in through the *back* door to Wanda's shop. As he walked through the snow and along the side of the Emporium with Henry still on his shoulders, he was shaking his head and talking to himself.

"I got a bad feeling about this," he whispered.

"Calm dow, Han Salad," slurred Henry, mutilating Han Solo's name in the process.

"Jesus! Even in the middle of a snowstorm, with a psycho dark witch trying to do God knows what, I gotta deal with a Star Wars nerd?"

Henry gave him a weak but passable Chewbacca roar, then giggled his ass off.

Byron cracked a smile. "Save it for Darth Numbnuts inside, okay?"

"K," said Henry.

They reached the end of the building, then turned right into the parking lot. Byron stopped in his tracks. "I'll be dipped in shit," he said.

"Wazzit?" asked Henry.

"It's my truck. And it's running."

"Thas good, righ?" asked Henry.

"Does the pope shit in the woods?" asked Byron.

Before Henry could answer, Byron took off at a fast walk

and made a beeline for the Explorer. He opened the passenger-side door and placed Henry gently in that side's seat, then scrambled around the front and hopped in, pulling the door slowly closed until it clicked shut. Then he grabbed the two-way radio's mic and keyed it.

"Raul, you out there?" asked Byron.

The static-laced voice of Raul Martinez crackled to life. "Here, jefe. What's up?"

"Leapfrog," said Byron.

"Oh, shit. Copy," replied Raul.

Leapfrog was a phrase the two of them used exclusively. It was something they'd come up with after Raul had survived both being kidnapped by the Red Witch, and possessed by the demon Inanis. With the use of that one word, Raul instantly knew some supernatural weird shit was about to go down. Ditto if Raul said it to Byron.

Once the word was mentioned, all chatter across the publicly monitored two-way instantly ceased between them, and they immediately switched to a different, predetermined frequency.

"What's going down tonight, Chief?"

"It's another dog in the library situation, Raul."

"Dios mio! Again?"

Raul sounded terrified, and Byron didn't blame him one bit. That Byron *wasn't* terrified spoke volumes about how much his own life had changed.

"Again, buddy. It ain't my cuppa tea either. But Salem happens."

"I'm moving to Maine, I think. Shit's gotta be safer there, right?"

"Maybe," said Byron. "But that guy who writes all those

horror stories comes from there, I think. If Maine's anything like Salem..."

Raul sighed through the static.

"For now, I just need you to park close to the place and keep an eye on it, just like last time."

"Okay. I hope it don't end up like last time," said Raul.

"Me too, amigo. Me too."

"Copy. On my way, Chief."

"Thanks, Raul."

Henry was all but passed out, his head resting against the window. With every breath, an egg-shaped bloom of condensation grew and shrank against its cold surface.

Byron slipped from the Explorer, eased the door closed once more, and headed for the back door to Wanda's shop. As he drew closer, the obsidian gemstone began to glow in its claw, and a familiar eye watched him.

CHAPTER 29
MAGICK

Archie was still thinking about his conversation with Darren Biltmore when the obsidian gemstones flared to life in their claws. He was pretty sure Jagger Corey was here from an alternate reality. The brief mixing of the minds in the middle of the pentacle had also confirmed for him things he'd suspected about Jagger back in 2004. The life he'd had out of Archie's "jurisdiction" explained a lot about his personality, or personalities. That Jagger and Mondra had connected somehow was now beyond doubt, but he wondered how Mondra had come to discover him in the first place.

It must be Jagger's last name, he realized.

Archie knew the history of Salem like the back of his hand. So did Mondra the Red Witch. She had been crazy, narcissistic, beautiful, and horny beyond belief, but she was also brilliant. If there was a link to be found between Jagger and Giles Corey, (the man who'd been pressed to death by Salem authorities during the witch trials), she would have found it, and exploited it—using that history to fan Jagger's anger.

When he thought about it further, cold dread filled him. Because if Jagger was related to Giles Corey in the *other* Salem, Henry was almost definitely related to the Giles Corey of *this* reality. Which meant Archie was too, since he was Henry's biological father.

Oh what a tangled web we weave, thought Archie.

It was rumored that Giles Corey had cursed the town right before his defiant death. The curse, obviously, went back hundreds of years. It would span generations in both dimensions. This was also something he had no doubt Mondra knew, and was positive she'd made Jagger quite aware of it. He couldn't help but think it played into Jagger's plans.

Oh shit! he thought, as another realization spawned.

A lecture he'd given at the university came back to him. It was titled Genetic Memory, and it dealt with a supposedly debunked theory that certain memories of a person's ancestors were passed down through generations via DNA. The example Archie had given to his students was connected to the 'fight or flight' response.

"...regarding the question of genetic memory. We don't need an instruction manual to know we must run for our lives when a tiger is chasing us; it's natural, intuitive, and automatic. But in modern society, the need to use that response has dwindled significantly. Yet, like our ancient need to survive predators, it still remains. Today's dangers, however, are more connected to money and status, and they manifest in the form of anxiety. Suffice to say that Twitter and Facebook are the modern day equivalent of the saber-toothed tiger. The need for status and approval from others based on the rosy and

227

unrealistic lives presented on social media can trigger that response just as effectively—and sometimes more effectively—than a giant predator. But without the flight component, which drains the initial adrenal surge. Is it any wonder half the world is on anxiety meds? Genetic memory is as real as short-term memory, in my opinion."

What if genetic memory worked in other ways? And what would be the consequences of a dark magick spell used to alter those memories? You wouldn't just be taking over someone's life... you'd be outright manipulating an entire family's history, and *every* memory and feeling attached to them. If a person were able to do something like that, he'd be indistinguishable from the real McCoy.

Either Mondra or Jagger must have visited the grave of Giles Corey, incorporating whatever they'd brought back with them into the spell.

The six in this circle were, with the exception of Jeanne and Dominik Trank, the closest people with the most intimate knowledge of Henry. The Trank's however, were far away in Maine. They also saw Henry every two or three months if they were lucky. Archie guessed the effects of the spell Jagger was readying were meant to have the greatest impact on the seven within the circle. Once complete, it probably would expand outward to those less immediate in Henry's life.

The door behind him slammed open. When Archie turned, he saw the terrifying silhouette of a man in chains. The fourth pendant glowed in his hands.

~

BYRON WAS HALFWAY across the parking lot when he lost control of his body. It was nothing dramatic, just a voice in his head (one attached to really bad memories of a certain redhead) calmly commanding him to walk slowly into Wanda's shop. He'd had every intention of doing just that, but on his own terms.

That's out the fucking window, he thought.

Yes it is, sugar lips, the voice taunted.

Eat shit! he fired back.

The voice remained silent.

Byron fought for control. Every step was a battle, and his footsteps dug long furrows through the snow, highlighted by the blinding brightness of the Explorer's headlights.

He reached the door, fighting for control of his arms. They raised of their own accord—the left holding the obsidian gemstone, the right reaching for the latch to Wanda's back door. The entity in control flung the door open, and forced him forward and into the room.

PENNY, Archie, and Wanda had their backs to Byron. Jazz, Moreland, and Mercy were facing the entrance. When the door flew open and slammed against the wall, they all jumped. When they turned, what they saw looked like something straight from the cover of a Halloween comic book.

The silhouette of a tall being, lit from behind by intense, blue-tinged LED lights, filled the doorway. Its shadow stretched across the gleaming black floor of the darkened room. Eerie red light, identical to the light streaming from the gemstones already set at the compass points, painted the entity from head to toe. Its hair rose in tangled knots. Stains, black in the reddish light, criss-crossed its shirt, its leggings... and its socks.

Jazz broke the silence, "That's either a bargain basement Frankenstein, or a really fucked up chief of police."

Penny went to run to her husband. Eljin Black stepped forward and changed her mind.

"No need, Mrs. Miller. He'll be joining you soon enough," said Jagger.

"Okay, Hen—"Penny caught herself. She'd almost called him Henry instead of Jagger. It scared the living hell out of her that it *felt* right.

Byron continued his slow, forced progress into the room. The chains clanked with each step, and hissed across the floor.

Clank. Step. *Hiss.* Step.

Jagger waited patiently, savoring the moment.

And then it arrived.

When Byron reached the western compass point, he stepped over it, turned, and lowered himself to the floor. Kneeling, he placed the obsidian gemstone in its spot, then turned it so the eye faced inward... toward Joanne and the center of the pentacle.

The red mist pulsed now, turning first bright and then dimming, as if tuning itself to a beating heart. As it settled on Joanne, covering her from head to toe, her body became almost transparent. Every vein and artery shone through, and the engine at the center of her life's blood was plain for all to see. The red mist found its rhythm, beating in time with Jo's heart.

As this happened, Jagger took position at the northern compass point, Fermina went east, Luci west, and Eljin Black completed the outer circle by sealing off the south.

A tendril of red slowly rose from the center of Jo's heart. It stood tall above her, wavering in the air like a cobra drawn by a snake charmer. It swayed in time with the beat of her heart, its featureless head seeking.

It stilled, dropped to the floor, then slithered its way toward the northern compass point, mindlessly obeying the call of its master. When it reached Jagger's left foot, it wound its way around his leg, then climbed and wrapped around his waist. The mist-snake leaned its thickening body out and away from the dark witch's chest, weighing its options, seeming to prepare for entry. The pulse from the mist quickened, and it flashed and dimmed in a random spasmodic sequence. To the horror of the captives in the circle, they realized the beat of Jagger's heart was changing. It was mating itself to Jo's.

Jagger closed his eyes and tilted his head toward the ceiling. Spreading his arms wide, he began the incantation:

> Fates entwined, what's his is now mine
> Souls once apart
> Now joined at the heart
> Old love fades
> New love draws near
> Darkness now shades
> The ones you held dear
> So mote it be!

Wind blew in through the open door. Snow flew inside like angry white bees aflame in a blueish LED sun. Candle flame wavered, casting shadows wildly about the room, painting monsters on the walls. In the pentacle, the League of the Moon, in spite of the whirlwind around them, were still. With the residual connection they'd retained from Mercy, with the exception of Byron, each saw the other's memories begin to change. It wasn't anything monumental; it didn't have to be. The only thing necessary for the spell to be successful now was to wipe the memory of this day from their minds.

This part, Jagger feared, would be most dangerous, for it relied on Henry to do his part.

~

HENRY AWOKE in the passenger seat of the Explorer, not sure where he was or how he'd gotten there. It was snowing hard, harder than it had been all day. The windshield was covered and dimly lit by an eerie blueish light. The only sound was the low, smooth rumble of the truck's engine.

He looked all around the interior, searching for a clue as to why or how he'd ended up in this place, and came up empty. As he opened the door and stepped into the snow, the first thing he noticed was the source of the blue light. Bright beams lit the back door to a building in front of him. The door was closed. When he turned and looked up, he saw the bubble lights on the top of the Explorer.

"How in the world did I end up in a police vehicle?"

After he'd spoken, he tilted his head, wondering why he'd just asked that question in the fashion he had. The words which had come to mind were *Why the fuck am I getting out of a cop car?* It was somehow lost in translation between his mind and his tongue. No sooner had he thought this, it was forgotten.

232

Jagger Corey now stood in the parking lot at the back of the store he knew belonged to the diminutive witch. It seemed absurd to him he should be standing in the middle of this parking lot during a raging blizzard. He pulled his scarf up tighter around his neck, pulled his black silk top hat down a little tighter over his head, and quickly shuffled out of the parking lot and across the street to Jagger's Magical Treasures.

The door was locked, but he was in luck. If you could call it that. Vandals had apparently been at work tonight. The window facing the street had been smashed to bits. His prized stuffed wolf sat in the middle of the sidewalk. 'Jagger' pushed it up against the side of the building, right beneath the shattered window, and with great caution used it as a step stool to enter the store.

"I'll have to bring this to the attention of the authorities. But tomorrow, not tonight," said 'Jagger' to the empty store.

The change was complete. The spell was working. Joanne was the final test.

EVERYONE inside the circle of obsidian gemstones slept. Three of four outside of the gemstones also slept. Jagger Corey, alone, remained conscious. If he was to truly claim the life he *knew* should be his, he would have to cross one final line.

The red mist had faded to nothing. Joanne began to stir. Jagger stood outside the circle and waited, his breath caught in his throat, his mind strangled by anticipation.

It was now or never. Jagger Corey had—he hoped—utterly taken over Henry's life. Though the man across the street knew nothing of who he used to be, Jagger still retained memories of both lives. He'd wanted it this way, of course. Where was the fun in all of this if he couldn't remember how he'd gotten here? What was the point if he couldn't enjoy his conquest?

He'd wanted this life badly since the moment the Red Witch made him realize it was within his reach, but he wanted to keep part of the old one alive if for nothing else than to have it for comparison's sake.

He knew the risks. If too much of his old personality surfaced before enough time passed, the people in Henry's life would know. Mondra had known this, and warned him against doing it this way. Well, threatened would be closer to the truth. Of course, he'd assured her he wouldn't do such a thing, had even gone so far as to promise he would avoid doing exactly what he was doing right now.

"They'll know, Jagger. Especially that little purple-clad midget that owns the shop," said Mondra. *"If you don't go all the way, it could ruin everything. If the green witch Joanne finds out, she'll kill you. That one's got a temper."*

"I have no intention of doing it any other way. I promise," Jagger had said. *The whole time he'd been crossing a pair of mental fingers behind his back.*

"It might not come to that, anyway," she'd said. *"Once I have Mercy's powers for myself, I can open any portal I want. In this world or yours."*

"Then why are you doing this at all?" asked Jagger.

"Because there is a chance, albeit slim, that things might not work out. If they kill me, I want them all to suffer. You are my insurance policy."

After that, there hadn't been much in the way of talking. But Mondra had other ways of getting her point across, and he hadn't minded *that* in the least. He'd been looking forward to it since they'd first crossed paths.

But that slim chance had turned out to be more of a sure thing than the Red Witch had expected. She was dead. He wasn't. Ces't la vie. Things would unfold as *he* wanted.

They'd created Fermina and Luci together in a ceremony in the woods of that other world. In effect they were, for lack of a better term, his children.

Witch's familiars didn't usually come in the form of human beings. They were either normal creatures with magical qualities, or outright magical beings themselves. These two were an exception, and also Mondra's little security system, in case Jagger decided he might want to do exactly what he was doing now.

He could deal with them later. Or, more correctly, Eljin could. Mondra wasn't the only one who prepared well.

Jagger came back from his thoughts, and just in time.

The cop and the Explorer! If anything could derail all of this, it was the cop not checking in. He shuffled quietly over to Eljin and roused him. Together they walked to the back door, and Jagger said, "Call on the radio, tell whoever's listening you made a routine check of this place, and everything is fine. Then come back here and get the cop. Clean him up, dress him, and park out in front of my store. It's the last place he was before this all started. Then wait for my next instructions."

Eljin obeyed, though his obligations to Jagger had been fulfilled.

CHAPTER 30
MRS. G!

Raul Martinez was about two minutes away from going into Wanda's Wicca'd Emporium. His hand was on the two-way's microphone, and he held it against his chest.

"Come on, Chief. I'm gettin' nervous here."

To his relief, the door to the back of the witch's shop opened, and Byron strode toward the Explorer. The mic crackled to life in his hands.

"Oh-one checking in. Just leaving Wanda's Wicca'd Emporium. Everything's okay here."

That struck Raul as odd. Byron had sounded the alarm by using their code word for the new and wonderful type of trouble to be found in Salem these days. A trouble of the type Raul would just as soon like to forget.

Sensing something was off, he decided to play it cool.

"Okay, Chief. I'm a few blocks from there. I got that thing you wanted for the station, but I gotta head out for a car sliding off the road. Why people are out in this crap is beyond me. You want me to drop it with you before I go?"

"Negative. I can grab it later. I'm probably done for the night after I leave here," said not-exactly Byron.

Raul shook his head. There was nothing to drop off at the station. And the way Byron had called in was way too casual, especially since they'd switched channels for the whole Leapfrog thing. Whoever was in that car looked a lot like Byron from a distance—but it sure as shit wasn't him.

"Copy, Chief. I'll catch you later. Have a good night."

Silence. No return message, no good night wish. Not very Byron-like.

The urge to turn on the bubble lights and floor it into the parking lot of Wanda's shop was almost too much to resist, but something told Raul to hang back. So he did.

Byron's Explorer crawled slowly from its spot, executed a three-point turn, and reversed until the tail faced the back door. The Byron impostor got out of the vehicle, opened the tailgate, and then turned to go back into the shop. Raul's view of the back door was blocked by the raised cargo hold door.

After a minute's wait, he saw the cargo door slammed shut, never glimpsing what had been stowed there. Then, the Explorer made its way from the lot and down the street, stopping three shops away and on the other side of Essex Street.

Raul had heard there was a new occupant at that address, but couldn't recall the name of the guy, or the shop's name.

The Explorer pulled up tight to the front door, parking at exactly the right angle so the reflection of its headlights partially blinded Raul. He wanted badly to move the cruiser and get a better view, but with the empty, snow covered streets, he knew any movement might advertise he was watching.

That was the last thing he wanted right now. Raul wished he'd ignored his gut feeling from earlier and just barrel-assed his way into Wanda's parking lot. Too late. Now, he'd have to wait.

Ten minutes later, someone exited the shop, got into the Explorer, and sat for a few minutes. Then, Byron's cruiser was on the move again. Raul once more fought the urge to follow, letting events play out before him.

He was rewarded with total confusion.

Whoever was driving the chief's cruiser had taken it right back to the lot behind Wanda's shop, parking it in exactly the same spot. Raul gave it a few moments, then keyed the mic.

"Chief? You there?" asked Raul.

"Hey, Raul. What's up?"

Raul was through playing it cool. "What happened with Leapfrog, Chief?"

There was a brief pause, then, "False alarm, amigo. Everything's fine in Wanda's. Bet you're relieved, eh?"

Raul held the mic a foot from his face, staring at it like he'd never seen one before. The guy on the other end of the mic now *knew* what Leapfrog meant, where just moments ago he hadn't a clue. At the very least, whoever this was, he was a world-class bullshitter. Time to find out.

"Chief?" asked Raul.

"Yo," said Byron.

"Tell me what Leapfrog means," said Raul.

"What? You know what it means. Why you asking me to tell you something you already know? I know this is a secure channel, but you never know," said Byron. He sounded pissed off.

"Humor me, Chief."

Byron keyed the mic, and Raul caught the tail end of an aggravated sigh before he spoke. "It's our word for magical fuckery in progress. Satisfied?"

Raul tilted his head in confusion, then said, "Okay, Chief. Just checking. You seem a little off tonight. That's all." Then, just to make sure he wasn't losing his mind, he decided to try what he'd tried earlier. "You want me to bring that thing we talked about to the station? Or you want me to drive over and give it to you? I'm on my way to help out a slider, but I'm close enough."

"What thing? What the hell are you talking about?" asked Byron.

"Sorry Chief, forgot it was for the deputy chief. My bad," lied Raul.

"And you think I'm the one who's a little off tonight?" Byron fired back.

Raul's confusion deepened. This *was* Byron, there was no doubt. And he'd readily identified the meaning of Leapfrog. So why hadn't he known it before the trip to the store down the street?

As the chief exited his vehicle once more, then made his way back toward Wanda's shop, Raul tossed his mic to the floor in frustration. The cruiser idled quietly a mere three hundred feet from Wanda's shop, but an explanation of what was happening seemed miles away for Raul.

~

As Byron was being cleaned up and put back into his uniform at Jagger's shop, Joanne had been slowly returning to the land of the living.

Jagger, armed with memories from Henry so clear and bright after the spell, knew his "wife" was a heavy sleeper to begin with. Add a sleep spell on top of that, it was a surprise she wasn't still snoring away.

She sat up, looked around, and caught Jagger's eye. "What the hell's going on here, Henry?"

Good! At least the packaging has passed the test, Jagger thought.

"What do you mean, Jo?" asked 'Henry.'

"Why's everyone passed out like a rave just ended?"

"Tonight was the meditation meeting, remember?" asked 'Henry.'

She looked doubtful. It worried Jagger. Part of the spell had been fashioned so that their most recent, and dangerous, memories were wiped. Any recall of events from earlier in the evening would unravel everything like a thread yanked from a sweater.

"It's probably got to do with the storm. Right after I dropped Delilah at my mother's, I headed right back. The storm wasn't all that bad in New Hampshire and Maine, but it was a bitch getting back once I hit Mass. I just got here like ten minutes ago."

"I thought you were gonna help with Dom," said Jo, rubbing the sleep from her eyes.

"I was. But my cousin Billy was already there. He was unpacked and set up. Mom kept DeeDee and sent me back. She figured we might like some alone time. You gotta admit, it's been a while now."

When she shot him a crooked grin, he did the same in

return. Feeling confident now, 'Henry' said, "How about we get outta here?"

"What about—?" Jo asked, sweeping her arm out in front of her and towards their sleeping friends.

"I don't think they're into that kinda thing, Jo." It was a very Henry-like line, and her mischievous laugh only confirmed it.

"You are so bad!" she said, covering her mouth to stifle a giggling fit.

'Henry' held out his hand. Jo took it. They exited the store from the front, where Eljin Black had earlier placed Henry's red Toyota Camry. Returned from the portal, where it had served its purpose in causing Henry to crash in Maine.

Jagger wanted to cry with joy. Not only was the spell a rousing success, but he was about to spend the night with this beautiful, green-eyed witch.

~

IT WAS A TERRIBLE NIGHT. One of the worst she could remember in all her years living in Salem. Well, at least the worst she'd seen this early in the year. It snowed a fair amount here in the winter, but shite as bad as this mostly happened in January and February. The blasted Blizzard of '78 had been in February, and to this day it was the worst. Hands down.

Iris Greenblatt, Mrs. G to everyone in the building, was worried. Henry Trank hadn't come home yet. She knew Joanne and little Deliliah were still out there, too. She was scared for all of them.

Mrs. Henry didn't seem to like her all that much; you didn't have to be a brain surgeon to figure that out. Of the two, Joanne seemed to be a little bit more... protective of her privacy. Mrs. G was sure there was a story behind that protectiveness, but the last thing in the world she was going to do was pry open that kettle o' fish. That green-eyed terror was likely to rip her head off if she caught wind of her snooping.

Mrs. G was okay with not knowing. Things had a way of coming to the surface when you least expected. Thirty-five years of living in this building had taught her that.

Chronic insomnia plagued her for the last twenty of those years, ever since Herbie Greenblatt had shuffled off the ole mortal coil. Part of the insomnia was losing the man she'd loved and slept next to since they'd been married at the ripe old age of eighteen. His absence, especially at night, was something she'd never overcome.

The other half was empty nest syndrome. She'd had three children with Herbie. All were grown and scattered across the country. They kept in touch. Good kids, all of them. They came with their spouses for Thanksgiving some years, Christmas and Hannukah others, with the occasional birthdays sprinkled in between. But, for the most part, she was on her own.

She knew most of her snooping and seeming nosiness sprang from that loneliness, but she also thought of her fellow tenants as a surrogate family. As with most families, she was closer with some than others. Henry Trank was, by far, the current apple of her eye. And, God bless him, he was kind in return. Mrs. G's way of returning that kindness tonight was to keep watch and make sure he was home safe.

Her vigilance was rewarded. Henry's red Toyota Camry rolled around the corner of the building and into the parking lot behind it.

Mrs. G shuffled down the hallway to the window over-looking the parking lot. She watched Henry and Jo as they exited the Camry, walked the few feet to the door, and made their way inside. As fast as her legs would allow—*they ain't what they used to be,* she thought—she took up her post at the top of the stairs.

"Nice to see you two home safely, Henry and Mrs. Henry," said Mrs. G. "And where is little DeeDee tonight? I saw you leaving with her earlier, Henry. Is everything okay?"

Jagger knew this was the building's busybody from Henry's memories. He was hoping against hope the old bat wouldn't be at her usual post on the entire drive over here. From what he could gather from Henry's past, it was a long-shot. But a guy could hope, right?

Now that he stood before her, he realized she reminded him of someone from the *other* place. Iris Greenblatt, on Jagger's side of the portal, had been the librarian at the reform school he'd been forced to attend. After he'd been caught in the woods practicing the dark arts on the forest's innocent residents, the powers that be came down hard on him. Iris Greenblatt had not only been the librarian at the school, however, she ruled detention time, too.

Unsurprisingly to Jagger, she'd lived alone... with lots of cats. Iris loved those cats. Ergo, Iris despised Jagger Corey with every fiber of her being, and she made sure he knew about it. The fat bitch had made his life a living hell.

Though deep down he knew this was a different person, and to act out might raise suspicion, he couldn't help himself. Through gritted teeth he said, "Is it too much to ask, just for once, Iris, for you not to bug us when we're coming home? Maybe mind your own fucking business for once?"

Mrs. G's mouth dropped open, and she placed the flattened palm of her right hand between her chest and her throat. Her eyes filled up at their bottoms. "I'm sorry, Henry. I didn't know you felt that way."

With a savage grin, and through still gritted teeth, he said, "I do. I've put up with it long enough. Jo has too. Good night, Mrs. G."

The moment the words left his lips he regretted them. Jo was looking at him sideways. As if seeing something within her husband she'd never seen before. Henry was no saint, for sure, but if someone pissed him off, he usually kept his powder dry and talked about it later, either with herself, Wanda, or his mother. He wasn't a fly off the handle kind of guy.

Something must be really bugging him about her tonight, Jo thought. She tugged his hand. "Come on, Henry. Let's go inside."

'Henry' stared at Mrs. G a bit longer. The absolute, out-of-place hatred and malice on his face shook her to the core. When the Tranks finally disappeared into their apartment, she stared at their door a long time before moving. Mrs. G swiped at her eyes, turned on her heel, and marched down the hall. She'd built up a full head of steam when she suddenly stopped.

"He called me Iris," she whispered to herself.

Henry had been a tenant in the building now for almost a year and a half. They'd had hundreds of conversations in the halls of this building. Not once had he ever used her first name.

Not once.

He'd never even asked her what it was.

Mrs. G liked to think she knew him well. One thing she was sure of, and she knew this from the very way he treated her—even when she knew *herself* she was being a pain in the arse—Henry Trank's parents had brought him up right and proper. He always, without fail, called her Mrs. G.

Always.

"If that's Henry Trank I just talked to, then I'm an elephant's anus."

Iris Greenblatt strode the rest of the way down the hall with purpose. She never closed her apartment door when she was out on 'patrol.' Two steps over the threshold, she slammed the door behind her.

There was an old-fashioned Rolodex beside the phone on a table next to her couch. Her kids had urged her to get a cell phone, but she'd politely declined. Mrs. G didn't trust the blasted things for a number of reasons.

"Nothing but trouble those things," she'd said, on more than one occasion.

Her big, red touchtone phone was all she needed.

She flipped through the Rolodex and found the number she was looking for, then dialed Wanda. The two of them had hit it off when Delilah had first been born. Wanda was in the building daily for the first few weeks. The old witch had handed her a card with her cell number on it. Other numbers were scrawled on the back, just in case she couldn't reach Wanda at her cell.

"Call me anytime, sweetie," she'd said. "There's bound to be more odd shit happening around here. If you ever see anything you don't quite understand, or something that seems a little off, you just ring me. We both know Salem can be a strange place." Wanda then winked at her.

Now seemed like one of those times, but there was no answer at the other end. She tried one of the other numbers Wanda had given her, and crossed her fingers as it rang.

"Hello?"

The voice on the other end sounded sleep-bleary.

"Yes, hello. I'm trying to reach Wanda Heinze. My name is Iris Greenblatt. To whom am I speaking?"

"This is Archibald Love."

"Ah. You're one of the names she put on the back of her card. Wanda told me to call her under certain... circumstances." Mrs. G wasn't sure if she could trust this guy, even though she believed Wanda wouldn't have put his name on the card if he was risky.

Archie, though groggy, picked up on her unease. "Hold on, Iris. I'll try and wake her."

Several seconds passed, then Wanda came on the line. "Hi Iris. What's the matter, honey?"

"Well, you said to call if something strange happened in the building, you know, with this being Salem and all?"

"Yes?" asked Wanda.

"I don't know any other way to say this other than sayin' it. I just talked to Henry Trank in the hallway. And if that man is Henry Trank, then I'm Donald blasted Trump."

"I'm putting you on speaker, Iris. I have friends who might want to hear this. Repeat what you just told me."

Mrs. G let out an aggravated sigh, then repeated herself.

"Was he by himself?" asked Wanda.

"No. He was with Mrs. Henry. When *whoever* that was told me to, and I quote, 'Mind my own fucking business for once,' even Joanne looked at him like she didn't know him. And you know she doesn't exactly see me as the Rose of Tralee."

"You know, that's funny. I could have sworn Henry told me he was going to Maine to take care of his father—"

246

Mrs. G leaned forward. Someone was mumbling something to Wanda. "What's that all about?" she asked.

"Two of his friends are coming to check on him. Their names are Armand and Mercy. Would you mind letting them into the building when they get there?" asked Wanda.

"Okay. Please hurry. This shite feels all wrong."

CHAPTER 31
MEMORIES

Armand Moreland and Mercy Glass left from the front of Wanda's store, just as Jo and 'Henry' had done roughly thirty minutes earlier. They waited until they were far enough away from the building before they spoke.

"Armand," Mercy began, "are you sure this is the way it has to be?"

Moreland kept his eyes forward. "Yes. Jagger knows I have it. What happened on the Common tonight was no accident. He knows I've been watching, and he knows a permanent change is only possible if he controls what I was forced to take."

"And that's why you had me do what I did?" asked Mercy.

"Yes. Joanne must be the one to do it. And she will. Remember, she's alive by my blood. The obligation will force her, if I demand it."

Jagger's spell had not had any effect on them. They were the only two who'd glimpsed what was taken from Jo. It was

248

an integral part of Jagger's spell, but the dark witch hadn't accounted for the effect it would have on other's who'd seen what it was. It shielded them from it. They had endured the entire ordeal fully conscious, fully aware... and fully informed. Their memories were intact.

What seemed a chance encounter earlier near Mercy's house, when she'd slid into Moreland, had been anything but. Mercy had every intention of confronting the vampire about his 'aura' the first chance she got. When Jazz and Moreland appeared out of nowhere at the end of her street, it had startled her, but only for a second. Taking advantage of the slippery conditions, Mercy turned her startled slide into a purposeful collision. The moment Armand had wrapped himself around her, preventing her fall, she'd used her considerable power to peer into him.

At first, he struggled to keep her out. Were he mortal, he wouldn't have stood a chance from the start. Mercy would have shredded his defenses and gotten in with little resistance. Armand Moreland was a vampire and a powerful witch, however. It would still have been difficult to stop Mercy—which he saw from the start—but he would have eventually succeeded. In the short few moments of their power struggle, he'd seen the plea in her eyes. They screamed 'Let me help you.' And so, Armand relented. He'd let her in.

Time, in moments such as those, is flexible. Events, conversations, emotions—all of it—seem to unfold much as they do in linear time-space. Entire lives can be lived from start to finish in those moments, yet upon return, the clock has barely moved. The world of spirit did not occupy the same train tracks as the physical world. There, all things happen—exist—at the same time. There is *only* the present.

Moreland had once heard a vampire friend make a very clever comparison of the physical world juxtaposed to the spiritual.

"Armand. If you could imagine a vinyl record, all its songs laid out neatly from the edge to the inside, everything is there. All that wonderful music is just waiting. The physical world is the needle. Life plays out in the grooves, but only in the spots touched by the needle. Nevertheless, regardless of where you put the needle down, it's all there. It always has been."

Armand had loved the analogy. It was the closest he'd come to truly understanding the nature of time on both sides of the veil. It helped him grasp what happened when he and Mercy had connected. But there was more to it. Mercy had died and come back, once upon a time. She'd *seen* the vinyl record from one edge to the other. Though she was in the physical world presently, the knowledge of things to come was a part of her. Not as accessible now as it was *over there,* but still there. It went a long way to understanding how déjà vu worked. Something they were both feeling now. And something that gave them an advantage over Jagger. He always seemed to be one step ahead of everyone.

As if he could read the future.

Mercy and Armand understood the dimension he came from must be on a slightly different time track. Events in Jagger's universe likely happened before they did here, or maybe foreshadowed things to come. Though neither heard the other's thoughts, they both wondered the same thing; *Maybe that's how premonitions work?*

What they were gambling on, now that Jagger had completed his goal of becoming Henry, was that his connection to that other world had been severed. The needle on his record now played in time with *this* world, effectively cutting off access to the other and thus negating his advantage.

They were betting everyone's lives on it.

When they arrived in front of Henry's apartment on Lafayette Street, the flicker of a candle's flame drew their eyes to the second floor. A round face full of concern hung suspended above it, buttery and soft and floating in a sea of darkness. Mrs. G mouthed the words *hurry up*. Mercy and Armand obeyed. They took off at a run for the glass enclosed front foyer where the door had already been propped open with a brick.

Armand reached the door first and ushered Mercy through. The main hallway's emergency lighting was dim, and they ran its length to the stairs at the back end of the building. When they reached the second floor, Mrs. G was at the far end, candle held before her, urging them forward with her free hand, and whispering, "Come on! Come on!"

In seconds, they were by her side.

"What have you heard, Iris?" whispered Moreland.

"Not much since they went through the door, but I know that bastard in there with Jo ain't Henry Trank. No farkin' way!"

"You're right," said Mercy. "Are you sure you're not a witch?"

Mrs. G smiled. "No, but this is Salem, sweetheart. Even the non-magical get something. It's like a contact high from a Tom Petty concert. Everyone smokes the funny stuff at those. You can't help but get a little yourself."

Mercy was surprised. "You like Tom Petty?"

Armand Moreland cleared his throat. "I think there are more pressing matters than Tom Petty at the moment. But I do love '*Runnin' Down a Dream.*'" He shrugged, admitting he couldn't help himself. Then he turned serious. "Iris. You need to go inside your apartment now. What comes next is going to be dangerous."

Mrs. G frowned. "I'm a big girl. I can handle meself."

Moreland nodded. "I've no doubt. Should we need your help, I won't hesitate to call you. But your being in there could put Henry—the *real* Henry—in jeopardy. I'm sure you don't want that."

That got through. "Okay. I'll be right on the other side of that door with my ear pinned to it. You call me if you need me."

"Without hesitation," said Moreland.

Mrs. G stepped across the threshold to her apartment, shooting one last glance at Mercy and Moreland over her shoulder as she closed her door.

"What comes next?" asked Mercy.

Armand Moreland smiled. "We knock on the door."

JAGGER'S SPELL was supposed to make them forget. Life, from that moment forward, was supposed to go on as if nothing had changed. He'd all but guaranteed it to Fermina and Luci. They'd trusted him. Believed in him. The evidence of that betrayal, however, was clear to see now that Elvis had left the building.

Jagger had ignored 'mother's' advice.

The first dent in the armor was the phone call. Neither Fermina or Luci knew who this 'Mrs. G' was, but her call had set in motion the first seeds of recall.

The sweater unraveling had begun.

Jazz, the gypsy, was the first to notice something wrong.

She pointed at the cop and asked, "Byron. Where is your gun?"

The chief looked down and saw his holster was empty. When he looked back up, confusion reigned.

"I don't know," he said. "Be right back."

He ran outside.

Fermina and Luci slowly moved to the far end of the room, where the unused beanbag chairs were stacked, and stood in the shadows. Watching and waiting.

The next domino to fall came from the tiny witch in purple. "What are we all doing here?"

Archie said, "I don't know. But that call from Henry's neighbor seemed strange."

"What are *you* doing?" Wanda asked Penny.

"Trying to find my phone. I seem to have misplaced it."

Wanda shoved her hands into both pockets of her purple cloak. "That's funny. I don't have mine."

Penny said, "Found it." She pulled it from her pocket. "Hey... it's cracked." She squeezed the button on the side. "It's still working. How the hell did my screen get cracked?"

Jazz held up hers.

Fermina exchanged a worried look with Luci, the message crystal clear.

Eljin fucked up.

No one was supposed to be left with a phone. They were to be returned the next day, conveniently located in places their owners would 'find' them. Destroying them wasn't an option; it would've caused too much suspicion.

Penny checked her notifications. "I've got a text from Jeanne Trank. She wants to know if you got the pictures. What pictures, Arch?"

Archie tilted his head. "Why does that ring a bell?"

Penny said, "Let's find out." She put the phone on speaker for everyone to hear.

Henry's mother said, "Hello?"

"Hi Jeanne, it's Penny Miller."

"Penny! Where the heck is that brother of yours?"

"He's right here, in Wanda's with me. I'm just calling about the text you sent about some pictures Archie's supposed to have? He's wondering what it's all about."

"He should know, he's the one who asked for them. He thought it might be connected to what happened to Joanne tonight and some contractor guy up here. That idiot is why Dom's all messed up," said Jeanne.

Penny looked to Archie for an answer. Archie's head was tilted toward the floor, looking for one. She snapped her fingers.

Archie looked up, chewing his left thumbnail and holding up his right index finger, asking for a minute.

"Hold on, Jeanne," said Penny.

After a few seconds, he snapped his own fingers. "Jeanne? I don't know why I can't remember, but maybe if you send the pictures to Penny's phone, it'll clear things up. Could you please do that now?"

"Yep," said Jeanne. "Gimme a sec."

Everyone in the room, including Fermina and Luci, heard the keyboard tapping sounds coming from Jeanne's phone.

The twins shot each other a worried look, thinking the same thing at the same time; *Shit's about to get real.* Luci went to whisper something to Fermina when her sister held up a hand to stop her, mouthing the word *wait.*

Penny's phone dinged. "Got 'em."

Archie crowded in next to Penny. When he saw the pictures, he looked confused. "Who are these pictures of?"

"Your son, Arch. You asked me to send pictures of Henry when he was younger because you've never seen any. Remember?"

He knew she was right, but couldn't remember why he'd asked for them in the first place. Archie told her so.

Jeanne said, "It sounded like you needed them bad. Like it was life or death. You seriously don't remember that?"

"No. But he looks like someone I used to know. What was his name...?"

With an open palm and closed eyes, Archie gently slapped his forehead, trying to will the answer forward. His eyes shot open, and he said, "Jagger Corey!"

The memories from before the spell were cracking open. The details from six minds brought together as one would not be far behind.

Fermina reached for Luci's hand and squeezed until the bones rubbed together.

~

RAUL DECIDED ENOUGH WAS ENOUGH. When Byron emerged from Wanda's shop and ran toward the Explorer, he sped toward the lot. As he got there, Byron was slamming the door and brandishing a shotgun.

Raul pulled up next to Byron and lowered his window. "What's going on now, jefe?"

"You ain't gonna believe this... I lost my gun somewhere."

Raul was nodding. "Oh, I believe it. I've been watching from down the street for the last few hours. You've been acting squirrely, Chief."

Raul gave Byron a rundown of the things he'd seen him

doing, and also of his strange amnesia when it came to Leaprog.

"You're shittin' me," said Byron.

Raul shook his head.

"And I was over there for how long?" Byron asked.

"No more than ten minutes. You sat out front for a bit, like you didn't know where you were. Then you came right back here. It was weird."

Byron was staring in the direction of Jagger's shop as Raul spoke. As his words sunk in, flickers of strange images danced in his head. He saw chains. He saw a wolf. He saw a mirror lying face up in a casket.

Then, he saw his own battered face staring back at him from a mirror.

Strangest of all, he saw the face of Henry Trank emerge from that mirror, and Henry looked terrified.

The spell lost its hold on Byron. Thanks to Raul, the effects were wiped away; his memory was restored.

"Raul?" asked Byron.

"Yeah?"

"I know why I said Leapfrog now." Byron cocked the shotgun.

It sounded like a bomb exploding to Raul. He swallowed hard, pulled the chained crucifix from under his shirt, and kissed it.

Byron smiled. "Let's roll."

CHAPTER 32
STORM CLOUDS

"Y ou didn't have to talk to her like that," said Jo. "She not my most favorite person in the world, granted, but that was mean, Henry."

'Henry' shrugged. "I've been nice to her long enough. I just figured I'd put my foot down. You should be happy about it."

Jo tilted her head, confused. "Did you hit your head or something?"

Jagger was starting to get nervous. Was she seeing through 'Henry' already? "What do you mean?"

"Since when have you taken to deciding what *I* should be happy about? If *I* wanted her not to bug me, *I* would have told her. I don't need *you* speaking for *me*."

He knew he should apologize; it's what Henry would have done. He was about to say something he knew he'd regret when there was a knock at the door. "She never gives up!" said 'Henry.'

As he moved to answer the door, Jo put a hand on his chest. "I'll get it."

Jagger fought an urge to slap her hand away, but rage colored his face, and Jo noticed. As she went to answer the door, she kept an eye on him, asking "What's wrong with you tonight?"

He didn't trust himself to answer, choosing to remain silent and let her deal with Mrs. G.

Jo gave him one final look of warning as she placed her hand on the knob, then turned and opened the door.

"Mercy? Armand? What are you doing here?" asked a surprised Jo.

"May we come in?" asked Armand.

Jo pulled the door wide and ushered them inside.

'Henry' locked eyes with Armand. He'd expected this confrontation. Orchestrated it. The attack of Joanne on the Salem Common had gone exactly as he'd planned it. Right down to the vampire coming to the rescue. When you saw things from one dimension before they happened in another, it wasn't all that hard.

It had worked when he'd predicted the demise of Archibald Love's aunt.

It had worked to cause the crash which had sent Henry to Jagger's shop in the other reality.

And, most important of all; it had worked to force the vampire out into the open to do his bidding.

All that remained was possessing the part of Joanne belonging solely to her husband. It was contained in a memory. A sacred moment between two people who fall in love.

The transition.

The moment when you *know*. Having Henry's memories, he saw the night it happened.

They'd come home from dinner at a place called

Rockafellas. Joanne threw her coat on his couch, and she was dressed in a strapless black dress. The green-eyed beauty had beckoned him with a come-hither crook of the finger, and they'd joined in a passionate kiss. Then, she pushed him down on the bed, so hard he'd bounced. Jagger felt the joy, surprise, and delight Henry'd felt when she'd done that, then felt the desire rise when she'd crawled on top of him.

After that, there was a long and frustrating blank spot. For some reason, the moment everything had changed for them—the moment they fell completely and utterly in love—was simply not there. At first, he couldn't figure out why.

Jagger *had* been in love. More than once. The objects of his desires, however, either had no idea how he felt—for he lacked the courage to tell them—or they found his strange ways off-putting. He'd never experienced the transition. Not with anyone. Mondra was as close as he'd come, but even *he* knew it was a lust thing... he'd never been in love with her.

Though he was, in almost every way, Henry now, Joanne could never be his completely. Because that memory belonged to *both* of them. It wasn't something he could take from her directly by attack, because a physical attack to acquire something that wasn't physical simply wasn't possible.

And it wasn't something easily solved with a black magick love spell. Those were for people who would never love you any other way. And, without exception, they inevitably unraveled—usually with the object of the spell ending up despising the caster.

It had to be ripped from her by a non-physical entity.

The Red Witch had unleashed the children of the void. Those lost souls could do part of the job, but they couldn't be trusted not to just devour Joanne's soul on the spot. After all, they'd been promised the souls of everyone in the League of the Moon by the Red Witch. They'd be claiming their due.

That was where the vampire came in. The void dwellers could get the memory out, but a vampire—a soulless entity —was needed to preserve that memory outside of the soul it belonged to. It could not possibly exist within the body of another person, there was simply no room. Trying to house something like that could lead to madness. It was a sacred thing, belonging to two souls, and shared in one glorious moment.

It had to be released when they were both present. And it had to be absorbed by both souls at the same time.

The vampire had to die. And he had to die now.

ELJIN BLACK WAITED PATIENTLY inside Jagger's shop for the cop to awaken and then drive away. Though his master's spell seemed successful, there was much work to be done. Once the Explorer pulled away, he stepped back outside and into the waning storm.

Things were coming to a head. The weakening storm was the first sign. Eljin knew, from long experience, magical events had profound effects on weather. Events of the magnitude of tonight's spell drew vast resources of earth elements to power them. A black magick spell of the likes Jagger Corey had cast drew those resources from more than one reality. Eljin had seen, firsthand, the effects of the spell in both realities. It was after he'd placed the Camry in the road in this reality's version of Maine. One side was consumed by a raging blizzard. The other was calm and peaceful.

Henry had followed him not long after. For this, Eljin had taken the form of an owl, turning his head now and again and guiding Henry with eyeshine. A dicey proposal, given the sparse amount of light available in the storm, but there'd been just enough to do the job. From the placement of the car, to the walk through the woods, then Eljin's trip back through the portal to this side, less than twenty minutes had elapsed. It had relieved some of the boredom of waiting outside the professor's office.

Eljin wondered about the fate of the man upstairs in Jagger's mirror room. As he raised the wolf display over the window sill, leaned over it, and then gently lowered the piece to the shop floor, he thought he'd probably be alright. Still, once sent back through the mirror and then sealed from this world, Eljin wondered if the man would carry on Jagger's pathetic existence. Would he pick up right where the other had left off?

He wiped the snow from his suit, then shook it from his hair. He laughed, realizing what he'd just done, saying to himself, "Old habits die hard."

Eljin stood next to the wolf, absently placing a hand on its head. Then, he started for the stairs.

THINGS WERE UNRAVELING FAST. Fermina and Luci watched helplessly from the darkened corner of Wanda's safe room. They were biding time, wondering if and when retribution from the witches might come. Or if 'father' would return to save them. Both had their doubts.

When the big cop came in carrying a shotgun, they decided it was time to get out. Neither Fermina nor Luci believed they would die from a shotgun blast; they weren't human. But they did occupy flesh, and all the glorious pain such an event would entail wasn't the part of the human experience they'd signed up for.

Fermina reached for Luci's hand, and they made their way toward Wanda's beaded door. Luci stuck a hand between two strands of beads, slowly parting them to avoid advertising their departure. She waved Fermina through, then just as carefully lowered them back into place.

Fermina tapped Luci's shoulder, just as Luci released the beads. She said, "Whatever you do, don't touch the walls."

Luci nodded and whispered, "Holy shit!" Her eyes were wide with amazement and fear. Fermina's matched. The protective sigils covering the walls and ceiling blazed brightly. Evil was not welcome here. Given who they were, both were surprised they hadn't simply burst into flames. Once they reached the front of the store they bolted for the door to Essex Street and disappeared into the night.

WITH THEIR MEMORIES RESTORED, the League of the Moon were on the move.

Byron, Raul, and Jazz were in Byron's Explorer. Jazz had told everyone what Moreland knew, and what he intended to do about it. The way Byron understood it, he didn't see where the vampire really had a choice. If something that made Jo what she was had been sealed inside Morcland to protect her, and the only way it could be recovered was for the vampire to die, then he had to die. And Byron was okay with that.

He liked Moreland a lot, but he loved Jo. If he had to kill

the vampire with his own hands to save her, then that's what he'd do. Jo was family now. She'd had a lot of guys treat her like shit in her life, and he was determined that ended with him. Her biological father and mother were scumbags of the highest order, though at least her mother seemed to have gotten her shit together. Daddy-O wasn't around to worry about after he self-cremated in a crack house in New York.

Henry was a great guy, and he loved Jo madly. That made Byron happy. He wasn't worried about Henry's ability to protect his wife and daughter, he'd already done quite a good job at it. Henry, however, didn't figure into the equation tonight.

Byron often wondered if he'd been in Henry's shoes when all that shit with the demon had gone down, if he would have acted in the same way. It shamed him a little when he thought about the answer. To go from living a normal every-day life to accepting things almost beyond imagination and belief took guts. But above even that, it took an open mind—something he was developing now, albeit somewhat against his will, but also something he knew, deep down, would have been a roadblock if he'd been in Henry's shoes.

An open mind, Byron had learned, took more courage than facing down a loaded gun. It meant abandoning beliefs so dear it felt like kicking grandma out into the cold. Nobody welcomes radical change like that, but Henry had—all while facing the craziest shit imaginable. Byron admired him for it, and he would die protecting Jo, or Henry, if it came down to that.

As he pulled the cruiser to a stop in front of Henry's apartment building, he stepped out of the car, leaned in and grabbed the shotgun, and then closed the door. Raul and Jazz joined him on the sidewalk.

"You guys ready?" asked Byron.

Jazz and Raul nodded.

They couldn't have been more wrong.

CHAPTER 33
SHIFTING

Wanda, Penny, and Archie remained in Wanda's shop. Penny wanted to go with Byron in the worst way, but resisted bringing it up. If she had to put a finger on why she kept quiet, the only thing explaining it was intuition. Something told her Byron and the others would be better served if she stayed put. That didn't necessarily mean staying in Wanda's shop.

"What are you thinking, Penny?" asked Wanda.

Penny smiled. "You don't miss a thing you old witch, do you?"

Wanda shook her head. "Nope. Can I guess?" The hint of a smile played at the corner of her mouth.

Archie watched them warily. His head bouncing between the two like he was at a tennis match. His ass cheeks puckered slightly for fear of what came next.

"I think it's time we checked out the new store across the street. I hear there's all kinds of interesting shit in there," said Wanda.

Penny feigned surprise. "Ya think?"

265

"I do," said Wanda. "Let me grab a few things. It's rude not to bring something to welcome the new neighbors."

"That's a great idea!"

Archie rolled his eyes skyward, breathed deeply, then closed them. *Here we go again.*

~

'HENRY' stood at the far end of the living room near the entrance to the bedroom. Jo walked past him and into the living room, having lit the last candle in the bedroom. The power remained out, and going by the town's history in storms such as this, it would probably be out for a while. No sense sitting in the dark when you didn't have to.

As she passed him, he stole a glance into the bedroom. At the far end, a balcony with sliding doors caught his eye. Though he had Henry's memories, it didn't hurt to make sure things were where they were supposed to be—you never knew what might happen. With that in mind, he feigned stretching and rubbed the small of his back, reassuring himself the wooden stake, the one with the word *Karma* carved into it, was where it was supposed to be.

Joanne took a seat on the couch, noticing for the first time no one else sat. "Why don't you guys take a load off?" she asked Moreland and Mercy.

They hadn't moved from the short entrance hallway. Armand Moreland answered Jo's question but kept his eyes glued to her husband. "We're fine where we are."

Jo looked from him, to 'Henry,' and then back again. "Is there something wrong?"

"No, Jo," said 'Henry' through a smile. "Everything's perfect."

266

Every hair on Joanne's neck prickled. Electricity charged the room. The smell of roses, fresh earth, and blood filled the air. It was a smell that seemed familiar, yet she couldn't recall when she'd first encountered it. And then, in an instant, she did.

Jo saw herself in the Salem Common.

Running.

Then the gazebo.

She was saying to someone, "Come get some."

They did.

One down.

Three down.

Then, they were on her. Mauling her emotions. Everything she loved in the world was gone. Taken. Sorrow ripped through her. Loss like she'd never known filled every corner of her being. She felt tears streaming from her eyes when she realized they were emptying her soul. Digging deep and devouring all that was good.

Then... it was all given back. One moment, emptiness and sadness reigned. The next, it didn't. All was restored. Hellish darkness gave way to sudden and glorious light. Armand Moreland smiled down at her, then helped her up. In that moment, she would have done anything for him.

Anything.

Just as quickly as the feeling to please filled her, so it was gone. And though she knew she owed everything to the vampire, she also felt suddenly and inexplicably afraid of him.

The last thing she recalled was the relief she'd felt as she flew up the stairs and into Mercy's apartment.

Except... something was still missing. Something dear to her. Unlike the memory she was reliving in this moment, however, it hadn't come back. It was close, though. Whatever *it* was, it was in this room. It called to her now. It meant everything.

Jo's eyes moved toward Armand Moreland on their own, as if pulled by an irresistible force. When they settled on his, he was staring right at her.

No words were spoken. None were needed. Joanne felt something within give way, and a sudden urge to please the vampire overwhelmed her.

A new vision filled her head. A man, a woman, and a child stood together. They were happy. They hadn't seen each other in a very long time.

Jo understood. Her debt would be paid when the vision became reality.

~

'JAGGER' sat in the mirror room, staring at nothing. Eljin Black watched him from the doorway. Thirty minutes, at least, had elapsed since the spell's completion.

Something should have registered with this man by now, thought Eljin, but he hadn't moved from his spot by the fire. Hadn't said a word, or made so much as a peep. It was like looking at a corpse capable of breathing.

Eljin knew he shouldn't do what he was about to. Getting emotionally involved this late in the game could only cause him problems. He didn't know anything about this man. He shouldn't care one way or the other. But he did. There was something inherently wrong about all of this.

Jagger Corey was, technically, his master. Eljin had been the Red Witch's familiar up until the moment she'd died.

Except, she hadn't *died* a witch. The green witch named Joanne killed her when she was a full vampire.

The moment Mondra accepted Xavier Saulis's proposition to turn her into a vampire, Eljin was released from obligation. Her hold on him vanished, the spell binding him dissolved.

Jagger Corey assumed Eljin was his to command because the Red Witch bound him to her in the event of her natural death. But the Devil is always in the details, and Eljin knew better.

His current master had given him strict instructions: Do what Corey wanted, no matter what, until the spell was completed. That had already happened. Beyond that, he was to use his judgment. Eljin's only concern was that the wishes of his new master be fulfilled.

By any means necessary.

Jagger Corey had, to this point, gotten what he'd wanted. In Eljin Black's estimation, it was not what he deserved.

Eljin slowly made his way over to Henry until he stood before him. There was no reaction. The shapeshifter raised his right hand, fingers splayed, and waved them in front of Henry's face.

Nothing.

He snapped his fingers three times right next to his ear.

Nothing.

Eljin cast his gaze around the mirror room until he found what he was looking for. Once found, he circled behind Henry, then lifted him gently from the chair.

Still unresponsive to the point his legs wouldn't support his own weight, Eljin dragged Henry toward a closet at the far end of the room. He propped him against the wall, then retrieved the chair from beside the fire and placed it in the closet. He folded Henry into the chair, but left the door opened.

The closet faced the entranceway at the far end of the room. Jagger, upon return, couldn't miss him.

Eljin didn't know what came next, but he had his suspicions. Cowards like Jagger Corey were predictable. They clung to the familiar when faced with adversity. They ran backward toward what they knew, instead of forward to challenge and conquer the unknown.

"We shall see," whispered Eljin.

With a glance over his shoulder toward Henry, he left the mirror room, descended the staircase, and made his way to the middle of the circular main room. Few of the things transported from the old store to this one had been unpacked. Among the ones that had was the wolf—now standing sentry by the smashed window—and the owl, already hung proudly above the reception desk.

"I claim the wind," said Eljin.

At this command, his body began to shift. He became lighter, almost translucent. A soft violet light glowed from within. Eljin reached toward the snow owl perched above the desk, and as his body stretched, the light within glowed brighter. His essence drifted upward, pouring into the owl like sand in a gravity-defying hour glass, until the owl consumed him. After a few moments, violet light shown in its eyes, and its head rotated almost three hundred sixty degrees. Then, he became still... and waited.

CHAPTER 34

STAKES RAISED

Jo wasn't sure what the vision meant, and she didn't have time to give it much thought. Armand Moreland was ready to attack. The first thing she wondered was why? What had Henry done to draw the murderous ire of the vampire?

And why, in the midst of an imminent attack on her husband, did she want to please the vampire so?

All of these questions flashed through her mind in an instant. It was an instant too long.

Moreland moved with lightning speed. The candle burning atop the coffee table flickered wildly, and shadows sprang to life in every corner of the room—the only evidence the vampire had moved at all. One minute he was next to Mercy, the next he was standing in front of Henry.

The vampire shot his hands into Henry's coat, reaching for the small of his back. When he brought them out, he held a wickedly sharp, rounded wooden stake between himself and 'Henry.'

"Planning an execution tonight, *Henry*?" asked Moreland.

'Henry' smiled, and it was all Jagger. "I'd call it a mercy killing. Pardon the pun." His eyes flicked toward Mercy, wondering why she was here, and also why she hadn't moved from her spot by the door.

Jo was up and out of her seat now, the shock of the moment fading fast. She placed herself between both men, hoping against hope to prevent the death of one or the other. Her eyes glowed emerald green as she faced the vampire, and she slowly placed both hands over his.

When their eyes met, Jo knew what came next. The vision made sense to her now. As a mother, she understood completely. As a wife, she envied his. As a witch, she knew what she had to do.

They communicated without a word. She didn't want to kill him. She'd reluctantly come to love this man. He was brave. And kind. He had honor.

He'd also saved her life—more than once—and she owed him.

Armand Moreland's eyes reached into her very soul at that moment, touching her in ways words couldn't. Tears pooled in Jo's eyes, feeling his loss deeply, as if it were her own. She saw his wife, Katarina, and his daughter Victoria. Their faces melted before her eyes, consumed by fire and hatred and the mindless bigotry of the witch trials, then in Germany and soon to be imported to the New World. Then, the faces transposed. Katarina's became Henry's, Victoria's now Delilah's. It took her down deeper into despair. What would she do if this had been her fate? How could she live?

Jo saw him as he truly was. Any resistance she'd clung to

regarding her debt to him melted away. Her hands moved of their own accord.

His grip on the stake loosened. Hers tightened.

Moreland's hands fell away. Jo's rose high, then flipped so the stake pointed downward.

Mercy closed her eyes, and whispered, "So mote it be." Then lowered her head.

Jagger stepped back, a satisfied smile on his face. Knowing the green witch would soon be his. Henry's life, everything he'd ever wanted, *everything that should have been his from the start! Everything the universe rightly owed him!*— was about to become truly and justly his.

Forevermore!

As the stake came down on him, Armand Moreland smiled, and peace stole over him.

In her mind, Jo heard him say, *"Thank you. I release you. Save your husband."*

Everything slowed.

Jo saw Mercy run from her spot, sliding low and then catching Armand's body before it hit the floor. The vampire's head came to rest in her lap, and Jo saw the reflection of candle light in Mercy's tears as she stroked Armand's head and sobbed.

A green mist slipped from his body. It floated toward Jo, and she watched as it drifted close, then entered the left side of her chest. It felt warm and wonderful. And with it, the memory of the night her life changed forever played once again on the silver screen of her mind as it had a bajillion times before.

The night she fell in love with Henry Trank, the soul she'd loved through eons.

Armand Moreland died protecting *this* for her.

And only her.

Jo turned to face her husband. He was smiling. Henry looked exactly as he always had. Tall, handsome, and smiling that smile that always sent a thrill through her body.

"The Thrill is Gone," by B.B. King began playing in her mind as she stared into her husband's face. Jo said, "Who the fuck are you?"

As the smile faded from Jagger's face, Mercy breathed a sigh of relief; her spell had worked. Jagger was denied. Jo was whole again. Armand had not died in vain.

~

WHEN GREEN FIRE erupted from the second floor window, Byron had already been looking in its direction. He smiled. "Jo's not happy about something!"

When crimson fire followed close behind, he knew there was some serious shit going down. "Let's go!"

Jazz was the last to move, but she quickly overtook Byron and Raul. "You guys need to follow my lead. And put those motherfucking guns away! They ain't gonna do shit up there."

Byron was already huffing and bringing up the rear as they reached the stairway at the end of the hall. "Too many goddamned cigars." *And*, he thought, *being locked up in a dungeon and having to break out of it didn't help.* He quickly cast all that aside. Now was not the time for whining.

As they reached the top of the stairs, Jazz yelled, "Henry, wait!"

'Henry' stopped in his tracks at the far end of the hall-way. Behind him, the door to the Trank's apartment smashed open. The doorknob hit the wall with so much force it impaled the drywall, and the door stuck fast.

Jazz watched in horror as green magic, fired in righteous anger, flew just over 'Henry's' head, scorching the wall above it.

'Henry' looked around frantically for an escape route, and found one. The infinitely curious Mrs. G had cracked her door ever-so-slightly open to watch the festivities.

'Henry' saw a dark brown eye peering out at him and dashed in its direction. Mrs. G saw him coming and slammed it shut, but she couldn't get the chain in the slider fast enough. 'Henry' leapt in the air and kicked the door with everything he had, sending Mrs. G stumbling backwards into her apartment where she tumbled, ass first, over the coffee table and onto the couch she'd dubbed 'The lumpy 'ole piece o' shite.'

As 'Henry' ran past her and toward her bedroom, she yelled, "Jarsus Murphy! Come back here you fake Henry sonofabitch!"

"Eat shit you old bag," 'Henry' yelled over his shoulder.

Mrs. G was struggling to get up from the couch when she froze. Mrs. Henry was at the entrance to her apartment.

Iris Greenblatt's mouth dropped open, and for the first time in her entire adult life, she was at a loss for words. Joanne Trank looked past her, eyes glowing bright green, following the progress of Henry's imposter as he made his escape through the sliding double doors of her balcony. Identical doors to the ones in the Trank's apartment.

Joanne pulled her eyes away and looked down at Mrs. G. "Are you alright?"

Mrs. G nodded, but still couldn't speak. *Those eyes!*

"Let's chat sometime," said Jo, pulling the door closed behind her.

~

'HENRY' whipped open the doors to the second floor balcony of the nosy bitch's bedroom, grabbed the railing, and vaulted it. He landed hard, wrenching his ankle in the process, and thanking the gods snow had cushioned some of the impact. It could have been worse.

He scrambled up from the snow, sliding a bit as he gained his footing, and then lurched his way around the corner of the building and toward Lafayette Street. As he ran, he imagined what he must look like. An image of Quasimodo from "The Hunchback of Notre Dame" flashed in his mind, and he cackled.

As he drew closer to the street, a miracle appeared before him. It wasn't in the form of an angel or demon, however. It was a miracle on four wheels. The cop's Explorer sat at the curb. *And it was running!*

His ankle throbbed now, but he doubled his pace in spite of the pain. As he reached the sidewalk, he saw the snow to his left turning a bright shade of emerald. He looked up and saw the witch through the glass in the front foyer. Their eyes met, but she never slowed. She was double-timing it down the stairs. Two cops and the gypsy were close behind her.

'Henry' unleashed a maniacal laugh that was part fear, part exhilaration. He would make it to the truck before they made it through the front door.

He skidded in the snow across the front of the Explorer, sliding almost halfway into the middle of the road. When he came to a stop, the driver's side door was a good six feet away. In the same moment his momentum slowed, the glass door to the foyer flew open. The green witch was coming fast.

She was on the sidewalk now.

His hand landed on the driver's side handle.

Jo leapt and slid across the hood of the truck.

'Henry' jumped in and slammed the door closed.

Her feet hit the snow, street-side.

He yanked the shift into drive.

Jo's hand reached the driver's side door.

'Henry' hit the gas.

She ripped the door open as the Explorer fishtailed.

He fought to pull it closed but couldn't reach the handle.

Her hand closed around his throat and squeezed.

'Henry' pounded at her forearm, but her grip held firm.

She put a foot on the running board, preparing to rip him from the vehicle.

He kicked out wildly with his left leg.

Her grip loosened.

He kicked again.

Her hand fell away, but her nails dug bloody tracks across his neck.

Jo tumbled head over heals into the fluffy snow. She was back on her feet in a blink and running faster than she'd ever run. At first, she gained ground. The tail lights of the Explorer drew closer as not-quite-Henry wrestled for control of the fishtailing truck. She was inches from the rear bumper when the oversized cop car finally dug in.

Snow flew high from the rear wheels, framing the witch in his rear view mirror. He shook his head in disbelief as he floored it. *She was still coming.*

'Henry' gave it as much gas as he dared. The last thing he

wanted was to wreck the cop car before he retreated to the safety of his shop. He knew if she got a hold of him before he reached Essex Street, he was a goner.

From the Trank's apartment to the front door of his shop was slightly over a mile. The crazy bitch was fast but she wasn't *that* fast. He'd make it there well before her, where he'd have his faithful servant take care of the rest. Eljin Black was exactly who you wanted on your side in a time like this.

As he drove toward his salvation, he felt the weight of the four obsidian pendants in his suit coat pocket. There was nothing stopping him from trying again. He might have to disappear for a little while until things cooled off, but that was okay.

The thought calmed him. He could close the shop until further notice. He owned it outright. It would be there for him again when he needed it. All he had to do was make it back to Essex Street alive.

As for the man who's life he'd captured? Shit happens. It wasn't his problem anymore. He was going to eventually die anyway. Probably within the next few weeks. Henry Trank was Jagger Corey now. Just another eccentric shop owner who'd died before his time.

No one would miss him.

No one would care.

No one would know the difference.

CHAPTER 35
WHAT BIG TEETH YOU HAVE

Archie eased the door to Jagger's Magical Treasures open just wide enough to poke his head through. It took a few seconds for his eyes to adjust to near blackness.

"Arch?" asked Wanda.

"What?" Archie whispered back.

"I brought a flashlight for a reason."

"I know," he said, lying. "I just want to make sure the coast is clear." As nervous as he was, he'd forgotten that minor detail.

Wanda didn't want to hurt his pride. She thought it sweet he was playing the role of protector. So when he held his left hand open behind his back, she put the flashlight in it.

Penny wiggled her eyebrows. Wanda grinned.

Archie aimed it at the floor first, leaning the rest of his body backward. If someone was armed, losing a flashlight was better than a bullet between the eyes. When nothing

279

happened after several seconds, he pushed the door slowly open and stepped inside.

"Nice job, double-oh-seven," said Penny.

Wanda cupped a laugh with her hand.

Archie swept the room with the flashlight, starting at his far right and then making a complete circle. When he reached the far left, near the shattered front window, he started to scream. Penny slapped a hand over his mouth.

"Sheesh, Arch. It's just a stuffed wolf," said Penny. With her hand still clamped over his mouth, she asked, "Are you okay now, fearless leader?"

He nodded.

Penny took the flashlight from him, then pointed it toward the staircase inset into the curved wall. "I think we should head that way."

Wanda and Archie followed her lead.

If they'd waited a second longer, they might have heard the crunch of snow under the tires of the Explorer as it pulled up out front.

As 'HENRY' closed in on the store, he saw the sweep of a flashlight inside the front of his shop. He doused the lights to the Explorer and crawled it the last few feet, right up to the front entrance. It was almost an instant replay of the night they'd moved the casket in. As he killed the engine, he patted the pocket of his suit coat containing the obsidian gemstones for reassurance. They'd already proved their worth tonight, but they were primed for an encore performance.

When the green witch attacked him back at the apartment, he'd barely escaped her lethal magic. The bolt had whizzed by his head, shattering the window behind him. As he dove through the open bedroom doorway, avoiding certain death, his first instinct was to run. The double doors at the Trank's balcony beckoned him toward escape, but he'd ignored their call.

Much to own surprise, he'd *wanted* to fight. His entire life had been spent running from danger, but something in him called out. Some arcane and heretofore untapped resource deep within craved battle. It never dawned on him he was acting as Henry Trank would have in such a scenario. Narcissism, despite the relocation of his essence, clung to his soul like a depraved lover.

Drawing on what he'd observed coming from the green witch, he mimicked her. Crimson fire exploded from his outthrust hands, and *she'd* been the one diving for the safety of the kitchen. It was then he'd realized Mercy was still with them, and instead of testing the limits of his newfound courage, he fired a warning shot at the stove, then scrambled from the apartment, slamming the door behind him.

But the lesson was learned.

The intruder, or intruders, had left the front door wide open. Perfect. A soundless attack was a deadly attack.

He slipped silently through the entrance of the store. As he turned to lock the door, he scanned the length of Essex Street. An emerald glow jounced to and fro at the very far end of the block. His "wife" had never stopped running.

"What a crazy bitch," he whispered.

'Henry' was about to lock her out to buy time, then noticed movement to his left. Snow tumbled gently through the shattered window, rendering a locked door somewhat pointless. With the green witch coming fast, he desperately scanned the store. The soft glow of a flashlight played across the ceiling on the second floor. Judging from its location, he knew they were on their way to the mirror room. He threw caution to the wind and bolted for the staircase with murder on his mind.

THEY HEARD HIM COMING NOW. Archie and Wanda shuffled to the reading nook furthest from the mirror room. It was tucked away at the far end of the curved wall, to the right of the staircase. 'Henry,' they hoped, wouldn't look their way because the mirror room was to the *left* of the stairs. Penny, however, had no choice. She was the youngest and fittest of the three, and their only hope of trapping Jagger Corey in the room with the mirror. After that, they weren't sure what might happen.

She climbed into the nook, then squeezed herself against the window. The bookcase to the right of the nook was barely wide enough to conceal her. She loosened the rope sash sealing the top of a black velvet bag. The brick dust and black salt contained within, along with the element of surprise, were all that separated her from death at the hands of a powerful, and quite delusional, dark witch from another reality.

JO SAW THE EXPLORER FIRST, then the fucker as he closed the door. She'd been sprinting through the snow for the better part of a mile now. A stitch of pain ripped through her left side, and she was at the absolute limits of her endurance. She tried to ignore the pain. Whoever this dickhead was, he was the key to finding her husband again.

What if he's dead already?

"No!" she screamed. "No fucking way!" Her mind was playing the role of traitor now, as it had for so many dark days in her life's history. Henry and Delilah were the best things to ever happen to her. There was no way she'd let them down.

You don't deserve them. You were a nothing before them, and you're going to be a nothing when they're gone.

"Fuck all the way off!" she screamed.

Her mind and body were in full rebellion. Her past, as it had so many times before, waged war with her present. Jo would not let it win.

Anger fueled her. Desperation drove her. The stitch in her side, the pain in her legs, the burning in her lungs, they could all fuck off, too.

She ran faster. Byron's Explorer was less than fifty yards away. Then, as if the gods had issued a ruling from 'on-high,' she saw the shattered window. Her luck was changing.

"About fucking time," she said.

Jo changed course, setting her sights on it.

Twenty yards.

Ten.

Mindful of the slippery snow, she never slowed to brace for the jump. Launching from a dead run, she flew over the stone border of the window, crashing into the wolf on the other side. It broke her fall and she grabbed hold as it slid across the smooth floor of the main room. It came to a stop just shy of the staircase leading to the second floor. Jo pushed herself up, then ran for the stairs.

~

'HENRY' was halfway down the hall of reading nooks when he saw it. It was barely noticeable, and he would have missed it without the soft glow of firelight from the mirror room. It was the toe of a boot. Someone was perched on the last nook before the room.

He drew the obsidian gemstones from his pocket, cupping them in his left hand. They glowed a malevolent crimson. He stepped forward, then turned to face Penny. Her mouth formed a surprised O, and the man who looked like Henry smiled. When he did, her insides quivered like Jell-O. It was the first time in her life she'd ever seen a smile transform someone she loved into a complete stranger. And in that moment, she knew she was about to die.

'Henry' raised his hand, ready to send this bitch flying and paint the snow with her blood. He raised his hand—

A bolt of white shot from the darkness. A deafening screech thundered from wall to wall. Where gemstones glowed in the palm of his hand one moment, darkness enveloped it the next.

Penny was quick to take advantage. As the stunned man with Henry Trank's face turned to track the owl streaking across the mirror room with his pendants, Penny swung her booted foot at him. She connected with his jaw. His teeth cracked together, his arms flew in the air, and he stumbled backward into the room with the mirror. Penny hopped from the nook, tipped the bag on its side, and sealed the room at its threshold with Wanda's light-infused concoction.

The owl circled the room, hovering in front of an opening on the far side. Penny watched as the majestic night hunter, a silhouette framed in pulsing crimson, thrust its talons forward. The pendants landed inside the opening at the far end of the room, landing not on the floor, as she expected, but in the lap of a man.

Wanda and Archie appeared at her side, and Wanda gasped. "My God. He's completely Jagger now!"

The owl swooped away, heading back toward the entranceway to the mirror room. It swung wide of 'Henry' as he pushed himself up from the floor, narrowly avoiding his outstretched hands. Then it flew over the three witches on the other side of the black salt, rose above the bannister ringing the second floor, and dove for the shadows.

On the heels of the owl's triumphant exit, footsteps pounded across the floor below. They were coming fast. An emerald glow bloomed from the landing at the top of the stairs, and Jo burst around the corner.

Wanda and Archie scrambled left. Penny backpedaled right. Jo was coming full speed now, heading straight for the mirror room. The moment her foot crossed the brick dust and black salt barrier, she was instantly repelled. She flew backward into the hall, sliding several feet across the polished hardwood floor, and came to a dazed stop.

As Penny and Archie rushed to help her up, Wanda inched a hand toward the barrier. The air between her hand and the invisible wall which repelled Joanne crackled with electricity. When she touched it, it rippled. As if the scenery beyond it were a mural painted at the bottom of a half-filled bathtub. The disturbance settled after a few moments, and the room beyond once more appeared normal.

Jo, Penny, and Archie joined Wanda at the barrier.

Between heaving breaths, Jo asked, "What the hell just happened? Why can't I get in there?"

A voice floated from the shadows below. "They are balanced. The dark and the light on the other side of the barrier are equal. When the balance shifts, you will gain entry."

"Why should we trust you, shapeshifter?" asked Wanda.

"Armand Moreland was my master, not Jagger Corey. He foresaw what has transpired tonight."

"What do you mean 'was your master?'" demanded Archie.

"The green witch knows," said Eljin Black.

They turned in unison, looking to Jo for an answer.

Jo hung her head. "I killed him."

Silence reigned. When Jo looked up, tears streaked her cheeks. She recounted the Salem Common attack from the beginning until she'd blacked out. "When I woke up, Armand was standing over me. Immediately, I felt I owed him a debt."

Wanda nodded. "That's common with vampires, sweetie."

"Yeah. Jazz filled me in." She swept her friends with her eyes. "At our apartment, about a half hour ago, Armand and Mercy showed up at our door."

Wanda placed her hands on either side of Jo's face and gently swiped her tears away with her thumbs.

"It happened fast. Whoever that shit bag is in there, I believed he was Henry. Armand confronted him. At first, I thought he was going to kill him. But that wasn't it at all. I put my hands over Armand's to stop him, and I could *see* his thoughts. When he killed the last two attacking me on the

Common, he returned what they'd taken. But he also held something back."

"What did he hold back?" asked Archie.

"I don't know the word for it, but it's the thing between Henry and I that's bound us through time. He held it for me, in the hole where his soul once was. Something only a vampire could do. There's only one way to remove it, and he *knew* that. I could feel he was relieved. Like a burden had finally lifted. He *wished* to die. So... he called in the debt. I had no choice."

"Genetic memory," said Archie.

"What?" asked Jo.

"I'll explain it to you later. What he held for you was similar to it, but on the level of *souls*, not genetics." Archie seemed to be explaining it to himself more than anyone else.

It was just how he rolled.

Jo heaved a weary shrug. "Whatever. The last thing I saw was his wife and daughter. He was happy he'd saved us, but he envied what Henry and I have. Not in a bad way. It was loss... and longing." Jo took a deep breath, then said, "The minute the stake went in, I felt what he'd held for me return. And I knew right away that scumbag in there wasn't Henry."

Laughter erupted from behind them. 'Henry' had crept toward the barrier, listening to their every word. "It's not over. I'm him now, and the children of the void answer to me. You'll never be safe. I *will* take what's mine."

From behind him, something creaked. During the commotion, he'd not noticed there was someone else in the room. The frail silhouette of a man emerged from a closet. Familiar crimson light glowed from the spot where his hands were clasped behind his back. As he approached, he released his grip, swinging his arms from around his back and then clutching the obsidian gemstones to his chest. The shadow of his chin painted the middle of his face black—all except for his eyes. They burned crimson with malicious glee.

'Jagger' smiled. His teeth looked sharp and red. "I believe you have something of mine."

CHAPTER 36
REFLECTIONS

'Henry' was terrified. Part of it was the realization the 'Jagger' he saw before him was *entirely* the man he used to be. He knew how that man thought, but being mostly Henry Trank now, the memory was like looking at your reflection in a fogged-out mirror; the outline is there, but the details are obscured. There was too much Henry Trank and too little Jagger within his current self for the recollection to be clear. He'd wanted to become Henry without having to commit all the way; the very thing the Red Witch had warned him against. It would be his downfall.

The *other* part, he'd discussed earlier with the pint-sized witch at the front of her store. He'd given lip service to all the doppelgänger business, not truly believing the myth behind the legend. Now, in front of a transformed version of his former self, urban myth was becoming reality. Henry was completely who he *used* to be now, and this 'Jagger' craved the exact same thing.

"I want what's mine," said 'Jagger.'

"What could I possibly have of yours?" asked 'Henry.' He fought to push the tremor out of his voice and failed.

"Everything. You're living the life that was meant for me. I want what's mine," said 'Jagger.'

Those words struck a chord. It was like hearing a familiar song but muffled and at a distance. You recognize the beat, but only the beat. The guitar and vocals were yet to come clear, but they were there.

The man before him suddenly looked different. At first, he couldn't put a finger on it. Two short minutes had elapsed since he'd laid eyes on him, but he'd *changed*. As fearful as he felt in the moment, he took a cautious step forward, tilting his head to study the man.

The beard!

The scraggly beard framing his chin had receded. 'Henry' absentmindedly raised a hand to his own chin. Fear lanced through him as he felt the first signs of stubble.

'Jagger' cackled. "It sucks to be me, doesn't it?"

'Henry' nodded without realizing he was doing so, then said, "I remember."

'Jagger' pulled up short. "Remember what?"

It was there one moment, then gone the next. The memory rolled ashore like a small wave, but all he'd glimpsed was its retreat.

Music.

Something attached to music. There had been fire. Screaming. Colors.

It almost faded completely when 'Jagger' whispered, "Coo coo cachoo, motherfucker."

That opened the floodgates. As the memories poured back in, 'Henry' screamed in pain. His body became thinner. The beard which was stubble a moment ago sprouted along the frame of his face in all its former ingloriousness. The memories of Henry Trank became harder to hold on to. The chasm of despair and self pity he'd always found himself hovering over threatened to pull him down once more.

A few short feet away, 'Jagger' was also changing. The clouds of gloom that had swallowed him whole began to part.

Anger. Fear. Hatred. Constant companions for what seemed a lifetime, but were mere hours old, melted like ice from a personality frozen in a glacier of adolescent rage. And at the core of these emotions was a green and malignant tumor of envy. One he was about to return to its owner.

'Jagger' raised the obsidian pendants, thrusting them toward 'Henry.' There was no need for a spell, and no use for one. 'Jagger' was still mostly *old* Jagger, enough so that commanding the gemstones provided by Eljin was second nature. They glowed fiery crimson as they bent to his will. The red mist, identical to that of the spell at Wanda's, snaked out and wrapped itself around 'Henry.'

The room grew dark. Where the casket holding the mirror should have been, a fire burned at the center of a stone pit. Suspended above it, a cauldron hung from two stakes supporting a warped metal rod. It was the setting in the woods he'd witnessed from his blackout in Jagger's bedroom.

"Jesus," said Jo. "What the hell is going on?"

Wanda, Archie, and Penny's jaws dropped open as they watched in awe.

"Aye! Dios Mio!" said Raul from behind them.

The four of them jumped, turning just in time to see Raul pull his crucifix from under his shirt and kiss it.

Byron stood behind Raul, shotgun at the ready. He

nodded toward the scene in the other room. "Don't see something like that every day."

It was the understatement of the century.

"It's two worlds coming together," whispered Jazz. "Universes don't like to share. It fucks things up."

"Don't you think we should go in there and help him?" asked Byron. He started to move forward, Jo put a hand on his chest. "Already tried that, Chiefy. Got bounced halfway into the hall for my troubles."

Byron frowned but stayed put. They all turned to watch, anxiously waiting for the moment they could breach the barrier.

'Henry' fell to the floor, writhing in pain. 'Jagger' moved closer, the smile on his face was demonic. Music played from somewhere. "I am the Walrus" by the Beatles filled the room.

As 'Jagger' watched 'Henry' spasm in pain, colors bloomed from his body. Just as they had in Henry's vision.

Jazz stepped forward to be next to Wanda. "Are you seeing what I'm seeing?"

"Yes," whispered Wanda. "His aura. That is one twisted soul."

'Jagger's' aura went from the red of anger, to the sadness of blue, and then morphed to they yellow of a coward. He lurched toward 'Henry,' his body jerking and spasming. Then, he collapsed onto his knees and leaned low, getting right in 'Henry's' face. Anger, rage, and hatred screwed his face into a hellish mask. He took a deep breath, then screamed, *"Coo coo cachoo. Motherfucker!"*

The colors of 'Jagger's' aura swirled violently around both men, mixing together to a whirlwind of brown.

"That," said Wanda, "is a literal shitstorm of emotion."

When the shitstorm slowed, the resultant mix stilled. It hung in the air above 'Jagger' and 'Henry.' The toxic cloud of envy drifted slowly from one man to the other, as if alive and choosing a suitable host. In that moment, neither man could have told you his name. They were between worlds. Henry's vision from Jagger's room had come true. He'd not been looking *through* Jagger in the vision; he'd been divining the future.

The building began to shudder. The fire, the trees, the very ground inside the barrier shimmered in and out of existence like a mirage. The ceiling in the hallway cracked, and plaster dust floated gently but steadily onto the heads of the six outside the barrier.

"Oh shit," said Byron.

The rumbling seemed to last forever before fading. They peeled their eyes from the ceiling once it felt safe, then trained them on Henry and Jagger once more.

Something was different. The man on the left was now bigger, reclaiming his former build.

Henry was Henry once more. Jagger was Jagger. But the poisonous cloud was moving in the wrong direction.

"Give Jagger the stones, Henry!" screamed Joanne. "Now!"

Henry heard his wife screaming something, but it sounded far away and dreamlike. He turned his head and saw her pointing at the floor in front of him. When he looked down, he saw four identical objects glowing before him.

Where have I seen these before?

He looked from the gemstones, back to Jo, and then up. Something green and nasty floated before him, drifting closer. The horrible essence of the man who'd almost stolen everything from him drew near. He felt it begin to taint his soul. It snapped him out of his funk. Jo was telling him the gemstones and the green cloud were *attached*. They sought their rightful owner.

Henry kicked them away, and Jagger scooped them up greedily. He looked like Smeagol gathering up his 'precious.'

The moment he touched them, the barrier separating the room from the hallway flamed a brilliant gold, then collapsed in a shower of glittering dust.

Jagger knew this would be his only opportunity to act. Though he'd planned on returning to claim this life he coveted in the future, the rage at his failure, in this moment, was all-consuming. Henry Trank had to die.

With two obsidian gemstones in his left hand, and two right, he lifted them for a killing spell. They got as high as his hips before he was sent flying. Jo barreled across the room, smashing into him like a Patriots linebacker. Jagger was sent sprawling, sliding face first into the side of the casket. The obsidian gemstones were scattered about. Two clattered in the same direction as Jagger, thonking against the polished black metal of the casket. One landed a few feet to the right of it, and one popped high in the air, coming down hard on the thick surface of the mirror with a loud smack. It rolled to a stop at the mirror's frame.

Wanda saw the surface of the mirror shimmer, just before it turned from a solid to something between liquid and gas.

"Look!" she yelled.

All eyes were drawn to the casket mirror. Jagger scrambled to his feet, realizing this diversion would be his only chance to recover the gemstones and save himself. He'd already recovered the two closest to the casket, he dove for the one lying a short distance to his right, scooped it up, and was on his feet in a flash. All he needed was the last one. In the frantic scramble, his anger boiled over.

I'm gonna kill every last one of these assholes, he thought.

He turned to bolt for the one resting atop the mirror and pulled up short. The green witch stood in front of the casket, her right arm extended, the fourth gemstone dangling from her hand. Her eyes were aflame with dazzling emerald light. When she smiled, he felt a curious pucker in his nether regions.

"Come get some," said Jo.

Before he could speak, she turned, held the glowing crimson gemstone above the mirror, and released it. Silvery gas puffed from the mirror's malleable surface, accompanied by a crackling hiss. Then, Jo whirled and was on him. Jagger put his hands up, gemstones out, in a last second attempt to take her out. Crimson energy shot from his hands and she swatted it aside as if it was a pesky mosquito. When she reached him, Jo put one hand on his shoulder, grabbing a fistful of suit coat, then one between his legs, grabbing a fistful of balls. She clenched hard, and Jagger screamed in a fashion not unlike the legions of female Beatles fans from the 1960s.

Jo hoisted him high above her head, strode to the mirror, and threw him in. Top hat, suit coat, obsidian gemstones, and poisonous personality—everything he'd come to this universe with—went in. He sank below the surface briefly, then rose once more, placing his hands on either side of the frame for support.

"This isn't over. I'll be back to kill every last one of you."

Byron stood next to Jo, shotgun in hand. He asked, "What kind of an asshole threatens a room full of witches and a cop with a shotgun?"

Jagger's mouth formed a surprised O, and Byron knocked the white out of it with the butt of his shotgun. "That's for chainin' me up."

Jagger Corey went limp and slipped beneath the surface of the mirror. His last thoughts, before his consciousness winked out, were about doppelgängers and the warning from the Red Witch. Then, he was gone from this world.

After a few seconds, the mirror's surface hardened. In its reflection, four powerful modern-day witches, a gypsy, a Salem University professor of parapsychology, and two Salem Police Officers looked back at them from the mirror.

The chief smiled at the face in the mirror belonging to the green witch. "You made him scream like a little bitch."

The green witch smiled at the chief's double, then shrugged. "He *was* a little bitch."

The gypsy said to all of them, "That little bitch caused a whole lotta trouble."

The pint-sized witch said, "Chief, maybe you ought to fix it so trouble can't return."

Everyone stepped back. As Byron raised the shotgun, butt down, he said, "I've been waiting to do this all night." He took a deep breath, poised to smash the mirror, then stopped. Byron caught Henry's eye. He lowered the shotgun, held it by the barrel, and offered it to Henry. "You should be the one to end it."

Henry smiled, and took the gun. "Don't mind if I do."

They all moved from their places around the mirror to stand by Henry's side.

Jo put an arm around his waist and kissed his cheek. "Do it, Band-aid boy."

Henry raised the shotgun. "Coo coo cachoo. Motherfucker." Then he fired.

CHAPTER 37
FASHIONABLY LATE

The sun never looked so good. Saturday morning brought an end to the freakish, early-November blizzard of the night before. A beautiful golden-orange sunrise crawled across the blanket of white laid across the witch city. Henry Trank sat on the edge of his bed with one hand on Jo's bare, triple-goddess-tatooed leg, the other wiping the Sandman's gift from his eyes, and watched it in all its glory from his second floor window.

When the mirror went dark, they'd returned to Wanda's shop. Byron and Penny took Wanda, Henry, and Jo to their respective homes in the Explorer. Raul dropped Archie at his place, then Jazz at her shop. They'd agreed a meeting at Wanda's shop was in order for later in the day.

Mercy, at the time, was still unaccounted for. Jo called her the moment they got home, and an apparently sleep-bleary Mercy agreed to meet with them later. When Jo asked her about Moreland, she was evasive.

"I don't want to talk about it now. I'll fill you in tomorrow. Okay?" asked Mercy. There was a hint of a plea in there,

Jo observed, and decided not to press the issue. She was probably traumatized by witnessing the death of Armand Moreland. Jo chose discretion over information, and that was how the early morning ended.

Henry sat in silence as the sun climbed higher into the sky, thinking about all that had transpired over the last twenty-four hours. It was a lot to digest. It was also a meal too big to be consumed by one mind. So, he let it go, opting instead to rouse Jo from sleep—always a dicey proposition —and prepare for the day. *He* might not have to work, but the Cracked Cauldron and its coffee-craving zombies would be pounding at the door if Jo was late.

~

WANDA LIKED TO SLEEP LATE, especially on Saturday. Today would be no exception. Wanda's Wicca'd Emporium was a favorite destination for locals and tourist's alike. It was also well known for keeping quirky, irregular hours; a reflection of its owner's personality. Instead of pissing everyone off however, most agreed it added to the charm of the place.

She rolled over in her bed to check the time. 11:11 a.m. "Always nice when the angels wake you up," she said to the empty room.

Wanda sat up, slipped her feet into a pair of leopard-print slippers, and got ready for her day. She arrived at the shop at one o'clock in the afternoon.

~

PENNY AND BYRON also slept late that Saturday. Not rousing

from bed until almost the exact same time Wanda put the key into the front door of the Emporium.

Byron was sore all over, and Penny had her own set of aches and pains from the crash of the 4Runner. Neither felt rushed to be anywhere. By the time they were ready to head to Wanda's Wicca'd Emporium, it was five o'clock. The meeting was set for seven.

"Let's head to the Cauldron," said Byron. "We can grab a coffee and pick up Henry and Jo."

Penny agreed. "Good thinking, old man."

"After last night, that's exactly how I feel," said Byron.

MERCY HADN'T SLEPT A WINK. The call from Jo was a welcomed one, though she'd had to keep it short. After what she'd been through with Armand Moreland, there was no way she could fall asleep, but she'd wanted to make sure everyone was okay.

Jo didn't need to say much. The call, and her tone of voice, told Mercy all she needed to know. If things had gone sideways, there wouldn't have *been* a call. Jo, Jazz, and God knew who else would have shown up at her door, ready to kick ass and take names.

Thankfully, that hadn't happened. Jo's call, however, wasn't the only thing she'd been waiting for, but she also didn't want to stay on the line chatting, so she'd feigned sleepiness.

After Jo's call, she waited for one more. When it finally came, she let her guard down. It was safe to close her eyes. Four hours sleep would have to be enough, leaving her a half hour to make the trip to Wanda's.

Mercy planned to be fashionably late, but knew her friends would forgive her when they found out why.

IT WAS SEVEN. Raul pulled up and put the car in park. Mercy was waiting at the curb.

She pulled the passenger door open, plopped in the seat, then leaned over and kissed her father's cheek. "Hi, Daddy."

Raul smiled. "Hey princess. How you doin'?"

"I'm fine. I'm a little nervous. Not sure how they'll react."

"They'll be fine. They all love you to death, you know?"

Mercy's face glowed with delight. "I do. I love them too."

Raul saw the envelope in her hand. It was black. Her name was scrawled across its front in gold script. "That part of what's going on tonight?"

Mercy took a deep breath and let it out. "Yes and no. It's separate from the thing you know about, but it'll have to be brought up. I don't know *what* to think about it."

"That's what Wanda's for, right?" asked Raul.

"If anyone can figure it out, she can," said Mercy. She put a hand on his arm. "I know this stuff seems crazy, Dad. And I get it if you don't want to hang around for the meeting."

Raul took a deep breath of his own. "Sweetheart. I just found out not too long ago you're my daughter. What's it been—three months now, give or take?"

Mercy nodded.

"The way I see it, this is the way it's gonna be from now on. No matter how crazy it might seem to me, it's your world. I want to be part of it. So," he pulled the crucifix from his shirt and kissed it. "I'll ask the big guy for protection, and do my best to do the same for you. Let's go to the meeting."

She leaned in and kissed his cheek once more. "Okay."

JAZZ WAS SECOND-TO-LAST ARRIVING. It was seven fifteen on Saturday evening. The streets of Salem were dark. The roads, for the most part, were clear. Despite the blizzard of the day before, an event the locals dubbed "The Shitstorm of Nineteen," it had been a balmy seventy-four degrees. She'd spent the entire day at her shop, doing business as usual on a day when things were about as far from usual as you could get. What was about to happen at Wanda's Wicca'd Emporium would make the warmth of the day seem like an afterthought. She couldn't wait to see the expression on their faces.

Mercy had called on her cell from Raul's car. "Is everything all set?" she asked Jazz.

"You bet. Are *you* all set?" asked Jazz.

"As much as I possibly can be," replied Mercy. "They're gonna shit their pants."

Jazz had laughed long and hard at that. Then hung up.

She said her hellos to everyone, then pulled up a beanbag chair and plopped it down in a spot facing the back door to Wanda's shop. She wanted the best possible view.

MERCY AND RAUL had one stop to make on the way over to Wanda's. They pulled up to the statue of 'Samantha' from *Bewitched,* and waited. Bluish sparkles of light flared around the iconic statue. Mercy could see them quite clearly. Raul only sensed the electricity in the air. When it subsided, their cargo materialized in the backseat. Raul shook his head, put the car in drive, and piloted them a few short blocks away and into the parking lot at the back of Wanda's shop.

He parked the car in the spot farthest from the door, the same spot Eljin Black had used the night before. They exited, meeting at the front of the car. Raul held out his right hand. Mercy took it in her left. The black envelope remained clutched in her free hand. Without a word, they headed for the door.

When they got inside, Henry jumped up and brought two more beanbag chairs toward the center pentacle. Raul's participation in the meeting was an unexpected surprise, and everyone gladly shifted their beanbags to make room.

"Raul!" squealed Wanda. "I'm so happy you're here, sweetie."

Raul made his way over and hugged her. "Thanks for having me," said Raul.

Henry had the foresight to place Raul's chair next to Byron's. He figured the poor guy could use all the support he could get.

Byron was grinning from ear to ear. Raul took his seat next to the chief. "What are you so happy about, jefe?"

"Just happy to welcome you to *my* world, amigo." He clapped Raul on the back.

"It's only *his* world cuz we let him hang out with us," said Jo.

Byron laughed. "Face it, *greenie*. You need me."

Jo ignored him, choosing to address Raul instead. "You wouldn't believe how many times I've had to save his sorry ass."

Raul grinned. "Me too! The guy is hopeless."

Penny piled on. "I think I've got all of you beat. Seriously, the man is a magnet for trouble."

Wanda capped off the assault. "Okay, now that we've established Byron is a lost cause and in need of constant saving, let's get down to business. Mercy? What's the story with the letter?" asked Wanda, nodding in the direction of the black envelope.

Mercy nodded, but tears rimmed her eyes. Wanda had been too busy cutting up Byron with the others to notice the state of the young witch. "Honey? What's the matter? Are you okay?"

She rose from her beanbag and made her way across the pentacle to comfort Mercy. She hugged her, then wiped the tears from her cheeks. When Wanda next looked into her eyes, she saw Mercy smile and realized they were tears of joy.

Everyone in the circle—with the exception of Jazz, for she knew what was to come—was focused on Mercy and Wanda.

"I'm fine," said Mercy. Then, in a voice thick and choked with emotion, she pointed toward the back door. "Look."

They did.

Armand Moreland, as always dressed to the nines, the tears in his own eyes mirroring Mercy's, smiled at his friends.

CHAPTER 38
MY APOLOGIES

S ilence. Disbelief. Wonder. Joy. They all felt it.

Jo was the first to move. She approached the vampire slowly, as if sudden movement would cause this miraculous mirage to evaporate. When she reached him, words failed her. Tears fell from her eyes, and she wrapped her arms around Armand tightly, confirming reality.

Armand returned the favor. "You brave and wonderful woman," he said as he closed his eyes and let the tears flow.

Jo pulled back, staring into the eyes of a man who'd walked the earth since the fourteenth century, and asked, simply, "How?"

Armand looked over her shoulder. Everyone in the room was making their way over. The time for answers was not yet upon them.

The League of the Moon, witches and non-witches alike, encircled Jo and Armand. They embraced as one, staying that way for a long time.

Armand broke the silence. "Come. Let me tell you what happened."

They followed him to the center of the room. Henry, content in his role as "official beanbag snatcher," went to the corner and returned, dropping one for the vampire.

Armand Moreland had the floor.

"Let me start by, once again, apologizing. It seems I'm forever doing so."

"We're just glad you're still with us, Armand," said Wanda.

Moreland smiled. "I hope that's still the case once I've told you everything. First, I want you to realize exactly where all of this began."

The atmosphere in the room was charged with anticipation, and they leaned forward in their beanbag chairs as one.

"Soon after Joanne ended the life of the Red Witch, something happened to me. Not in that moment. And not before we met here to discuss it. The very next night, however, I received a visitor. As you know, I live at the far end of Salem, on the edge of the cemetery. I'm a creature of the night, for the most part. This may seem strange, but a walk in the cemetery is as pleasurable for me as a walk in Salem Willows might be for you on a sunny autumn day."

Smiles all around. They got it.

"On this particular evening, I noticed eyeshine trailing me. Coyotes are everywhere in Salem, and they tend to follow me on my walks. Usually three or four at the same time. I enjoy their company. That night, only one set of eyes followed me, much larger than the eyes I'd grown accustomed to. I'm not positive, but I suspect a predator of that size kept the usual suspects at bay. I halted my walk, curious to see if it approached. From the shadows emerged a wolf of extreme size. This magnificent creature walked right up to me, sat, and spoke."

"The wolf talked to you?" asked Byron, a healthy dose of skepticism underlying his tone.

"Indeed, constable. I know my presentation comes off as "matter-of-fact," but this is not uncommon."

"Go on, Armand," said Penny, glaring at Byron. He ducked his chin, chastised.

The vampire chuckled. "It's okay, Chief. I understand your skepticism. Anyway, the wolf said, 'The Red Witch is dead. The other believes me his chattle to command at will. Upon her death, her vibration matched that of yours. Therefore, I am yours to command. Not his.'"

"Because my mother died as a vampire. Correct?" asked Mercy.

Moreland pointed at her. "Yes. At this point, I was confused. I'd not realized the Red Witch *had* a familiar. And I'd no clue as to the identity of 'the other' the wolf referred to. Eljin Black, the shapeshifter in wolf's clothing, revealed it to me. Jagger Corey became top priority for me from that moment forward. Eljin Black, to the best of his ability, kept me informed."

"What do you mean by 'to the best of his ability?'" asked Henry.

"In order to keep tabs on this new threat, I had to allow the shapeshifter ample leeway. That meant, for the majority of the time, he'd be at the beck and call of Jagger. Which, given I knew so little about the man, seemed the most appropriate course of action. As we're all here tonight, alive and well, that strategy seems to have paid off. Unfortunately, some of you had to suffer as a result. Though I don't know what was done to you on an individual basis, I can only imagine it wasn't pleasant. Hence, the reason I began the evening apologizing."

"Three hours chained to a wall in a dungeon count as suffering?" asked Byron.

Moreland went pale. Well, paler. "He did that to you?"

Byron nodded. He was still pissed about the whole thing, but his anger had been tempered in the light of events as a whole. Jo was alive, she was back with Henry, and everyone had survived the night. With that in mind, he smiled. "It sucked, I'll admit. Scared myself half to death when I looked in that mirror, too. I looked like the lovechild of Freddy fucking Krueger and Frankenstein."

"He did!" said Jazz. She pointed at the back door, laughing. "He came through that door looking like *exactly* that. Arms out and everything!"

With Byron's anger deflated, everyone relaxed for the moment.

Each in turn recounted their own run-in with Eljin. Archie told him about the door to his office being destroyed, adding, "If I'd been quicker to realize what was going on, maybe I could have stopped it. Jagger was in my care back in 2004. If I'd recognized what was going on back then, given the connection to Mondra, a lot of this could have been avoided."

"Archie, you really gotta quit beating the shit outta yourself, it's getting old," said Jo. "*Nobody* saw that asshole coming. Armand had a heads up and even *he* couldn't stop it."

"You're right. You're right," said Archie, raising his hands in surrender.

Wanda was next. "I spent most of the night with him. He scared the hell out of me, there's no denying that. But in the end, I couldn't help but feel pity for him. Not a lot, mind you. There are plenty of people in this world, and apparently *other* worlds, that've had rotten childhoods. It's the ones who stop pointing fingers and get their shit together who survive. He wanted to bypass all of that at the expense of Henry. In the end, he got what he deserved."

Moreland's guilt abated with each account. They all assured him he was forgiven. Then, Joanne spoke. "What about me? Did you know he was coming for me?"

The vampire bowed his head. "I did." Then he looked her in the eye. "I was there to protect you. I've been keeping an eye on *all* of you, to the best of my ability. And with the help of others from the Council of the Realms. When I found out one key piece of information however, I switched my surveillance exclusively to you, Joanne."

Jo looked surprised. "What was it?"

"Through Eljin Black," Moreland started, "I came to understand there was a curse on you. The Red Witch placed it upon you the moment you killed her. It was nothing stated, of course. Most curses are formed within the heart. Speaking them aloud is a mere formality." He cleared his throat, then continued. "The walls of that room, and everything within, absorbed said curse the moment she released it from her dark heart. That included the obsidian gemstone I found in the dresser. At the time, I'd been following a hunch. Eljin's warning about the Red Witch's curse seemed to parallel the events of last evening. I felt compelled to investigate her hideaway in the church. I brought the item to Jazz, and she confirmed my darkest fears. The curse was a dark magic love spell. Its vehicle was Jagger. Its recipient was you. And it could only work if the children of the void captured one single memory of yours."

The room was completely silent. It was a lot to take in.

After a time, Jo asked, "What was it?"

"The night you fell in love with Henry. A memory and a moment you've shared with him throughout time and incarnations. It's a component of your souls. I knew, and I suspect Jagger knew as well that, once removed from the body, it cannot simply be put back. He knew I'd kill them and recover it. Jagger was well aware killing me in your presence was the only way to retrieve it."

Moreland paused, letting the information sink in. Satisfied, he continued. "A memory such as that—precious, historical, timeless—can only be secured by a vampire, because we don't possess a soul. I knew once I took the responsibility, I was destined to die. There's no other way."

"But you're here," said Henry, "and Jo knew right away he wasn't me."

Moreland smiled. "Correct, Henry."

Jo asked, "Am I missing something?"

Mercy took over. "Jagger Corey, for all his planning, didn't count on one thing. Someone else in that room was in love, at one time, with Henry. And you're looking at her."

Jo said, "Come again?"

Mercy laughed. "I love Henry, Jo. Like a brother. That's as far as it goes. The night you killed the Red Witch—I loved him like I'd known him forever. That's how powerful her spell was. When I met Jazz and Armand on the street last night, I put two things together: the green aura surrounding him, and your miraculously quick-healing wound . That seemed way more than just coincidence."

Moreland smiled. Mercy continued.

"When I," Mercy made quote fingers, 'ran into him.' I saw everything that had happened. Including how he was supposed to die. I put the memory of my feelings for Henry from the Red Witch's spell into Armand. So, the spell was attracted to me, not someone *pretending* to be Henry. That's why I had to be there, and that's why you saw through Jagger right away."

"And you made sure to hug him when you arrived tonight, so it transferred back to Henry," said Wanda, smiling. "I saw the aura flare."

Mercy laughed, turning a bit red. "He didn't feel a thing. And Armand is right, it's only for vampires. It was making me a little nutty."

Again, silence reigned. There was only one question that remained. And it was a big one.

"Armand?" asked Wanda. "How are you still with us?"

Mercy and the vampire exchanged a look that went beyond meaningful. It was akin to the bond survivors of a unique trauma shared. Only those who'd been through said trauma could understand. Explaining it to outsiders was always a challenge, but the League of the Moon had been there at Satan's Kingdom when it happened to Mercy, so Armand knew he had a leg up. Besides, he was in a room full of believers. Even Raul was coming around.

"When Joanne went after Jagger, I was in limbo. Unlike Mercy's near-death experience however, there was no light, and no one to greet me. There was nothing—yet, I existed in total, oblivious darkness. When I awoke, Raphael was there."

"*The* Raphael?" asked Raul. "As in the angel of healing?"

"The very one, Raul," said Moreland.

Raul looked on the verge of passing out. Mercy patted his forearm. "We'll talk later."

"I asked him how it was possible I could still be

anywhere *other* than oblivion, for that is the lot of those who forego their souls." Moreland looked at the floor. "I'm ashamed to admit it, but my motivation in protecting all of you has never been one hundred percent pure. I've always assumed my chances of dying while defending the witches of this coven are excellent. As we've all witnessed, my analysis was spot-on. The other motivation is to finally know, regardless of the consequences, if my wife and daughter still exist. I don't want to live forever without knowing. I consider that prospect worse than existence itself."

Wanda moved to be next to him. She sat by his side, reached out her hand, and he took it gratefully. "Tell us," said Wanda.

Moreland smiled. "You are wise beyond your lifetimes, white witch. They live. Katarina and Victoria's essences are intact. They are between lives, and have chosen to wait for me."

"That's wonderful, Armand," said Mercy. She'd witnessed the meeting with the angel, and she knew there was one more shoe to drop.

"It is," he beamed. "But there are conditions, and *they* are the reason I was brought back. Souls are not redeemed easily. Raphael laid out the terms under which this might happen. And I happily agreed to them."

"And they are?" asked Jo, rolling her hand.

"I am to continue protecting and assisting the League of the Moon and its witches in whatever comes next. For as long as needed. Then, and only when my duties are deemed fulfilled, will they consider it."

Byron said, "Aww, shit. We gotta put up with you and *only God* knows how long?"

The room burst with laughter. Armand Moreland's eyes filled. He was home again. It wasn't the home he longed for, but he could live with that... until the day he died.

When the room was quiet once more, Mercy held up the black envelope. "There's one more thing to discuss."

CHAPTER 39
WHAT'S IN A NAME?

" I 've read this already. I'm not sure what to think of it."

Mercy pulled the letter from the opened envelope and started reading.

To Mercy, Joanne, Jazz et al,

Let "us" start by saying what happened was nothing personal. "We" needed you to get to him. Jagger Corey was a pawn, nothing more. He believed he summoned "us," with the help of the Red Witch. "We" did not disabuse him of this notion. Neither were parents to "us." Their actions, however, drew "our" attention. When you call on the darkness, the darkness listens. When you think you control it, it controls you. And when you use it to take what you want, you are taken.

Jagger found this out the hard way. He overstepped his bounds.

"We" are still in Salem. You might even catch a glimpse of "us" from time to time.

You might have noticed you never saw "us" apart. That is to

313

say, "we" are always together. Try and think of it this way. Gemini is the sign for twins. And you saw "us" that way. But it is possible for one to be Gemini, yet not be a twin. Now take it a step further.

The world is about to change. It has already begun.

Henry Trank will be the first of you to understand. Jagger is out of the picture, but he left something behind. In time, Henry, and only Henry, can control it.

Use it wisely.

This is your only warning. Fair is fair. And "we" bring light to bear.

Someone is coming amidst the turmoil. He will try to take what is "ours."

That must not happen.

Fail, and you belong to "us."

Luci ~ Fermina.

"Very interesting," said Armand Moreland.

"What does it mean?" asked Mercy.

"If it means what I think it does, I must remain silent. I am here to protect you. And I will do that full stop. This is something to be worked out by mortals... and non-mortals. I am neither. I am undead. But I think the minds in this room will *divine* the meaning rather quickly." Moreland's eyes glittered with mischief.

"Henry? They mentioned you by name. Any ideas?" asked Wanda.

He held out his hand. "Can I take a look at that Mercy?"

Mercy handed the note over.

Henry read each section aloud, raising his head for comment at the end of each passage, and receiving none until he finished.

"Well," said Wanda. "They clearly want us to know "they" are two halves of one entity. Each time there is a reference to "us" or "we" or "our," they've got it wrapped in quotes."

"They said Jagger was a pawn," Jo added, "meaning they manipulated him. Pawns are also used in chess to capture another player's piece. Jagger believed he was the one in control from the start. What better pawn could there be than one who doesn't know he's a pawn?"

"There's a simple answer to that," said Jazz. "Two pawns. Don't forget, the Red Witch was the one pulling Jagger's strings to get this whole thing started. Luci and Fermina were playing *both* of them."

"Okay," said Henry. "But how could they know what Jagger and Mondra were up to in the first place? And how could they know things would turn out the way they did?"

"It's in the letter," said Byron. "They, meaning Luci and Fermina, were answering a call from the darkness. The last line in that part says it all. *And when you use it to take what you want, you are taken.* Jagger and the Red Psycho practically opened the door for them. It's not a stretch to say once they were in, the twins nudged them in the direction they wanted. They took those two fools where they wanted them to go."

"Which was?" asked Wanda.

"To me," said Henry. "Think about it. For Jagger, it was all about envy. He wanted the life I have. And, in a way, Mondra's whole deal from the start has been about her envy of Mercy's abilities and wanting to rival the power of Hecate."

"Holy shit!" said Raul. "Henry, can I see that letter?"

Surprised, Henry extended his hand, placing the letter in

Raul's. The Salem cop's hands were shaking uncontrollably. Mercy placed hers on his, then took the letter. She held it in front of him so he could read it. "Their names. The answer is in their names!"

"What the hell are you rambling about, Raul?" asked Byron.

"When Henry mentioned envy, it got me to thinking. Envy is as old, no... older than the Bible itself. It existed *before* creation. The Devil himself is the poster child for envy. *'Better to reign in hell than to serve in heaven,'* as the Milton quote goes. Whatever it is he wants from you, Henry, I wouldn't want to be in your shoes." Raul ended by lifting the gold crucifix one more time to his lips.

"Who are you talking about, sweetie?" asked Wanda.

"The light bearer line? You don't get that?" Silence was his answer. "Anyone have a pen?" asked Raul. "I'd rather show you than speak the name."

"Voldemort?" teased Jazz.

"I wish," countered Raul.

Wanda returned from the bar, where she kept the supplies for the safe room, and handed a pen to Raul.

He placed the letter in the middle of the pentacle, then smoothed it out with his hand. Raul put pen to paper, circling first Luci's name, and next the first three letters of Fermina's.

No questions remained.

"Lucifer. Gemini is Lucifer," whispered Jo.

"See? I knew you'd get it." said Armand Moreland.

CHAPTER 40
JAGGER SINGS

Hey! Henry here, checking back in.

So... the devil. Great. Just when I thought things couldn't get any more insane.

Salem never disappoints, I'll give it that.

I'm not sure what to make of the letter. Jo told me Luci and Fermina never gave any indication they were more than just confused girls in need of help. She met them at an Alcoholics Anonymous meeting. They were a bit vague about how they'd ended up there. Jo and her friends listened to each of their stories when they spoke at the podium. Watched them shed tears when they talked about their pasts. Befriended them. Took them in. Showed them love.

Funny thing is, now that some time has passed, none of them can recall what either girl said the podium at those meetings.

You know what scares me most about all of this? It's the lies. Well, it's more than that. It's how easily two, not-exactly teenage girls infiltrated the lives of two powerful witches and an insanely intuitive gypsy. But that's just the tip of the iceberg. They were part of Jo's and her friend's lives for a long time. They know things. They've *seen* shit. That can't be good for any of us.

Mercy told me about Luci and Fermina's conversation after they'd kidnapped Jo. She'd heard them say how they felt bad about what was going on. How Mercy and Jo had been good to them. In light of that letter, Mercy told me she thought it was all an act. Like they knew she was there, hiding behind that pickup truck. I think she's right. That scares me even more because *that shit* is next level.

Jesus. Listen to me. I keep speaking of them as *them*. That's how nuts all of this is. It's not an easy thing for any of us to wrap our heads around. I guess if I think of them in the same light as Jagger, it would be easier. Like they're two personalities trapped in the same body. Jo said Luci was the one who seemed to have more of a conscience. Fermina was more about getting shit done, consequences be damned. The light and the dark. Yin and yang. Good and evil.

I'm not a big Bible guy, but I seem to remember something about Lucifer being God's most beautiful angel at one point. Loved above all others. But he wanted to be top dog. God don't play that. Pride goeth before the fall. And fall, he dideth.

In the letter from Gemini—maybe I'll call them that, it's just easier—they said I would be the first to understand. They said Jagger left something behind, and I'm the only one who can control it.

First off, let me just state for the record; I DON'T WANT IT. Whatever the fuck IT is. But I suspect my wishes have already fallen on deaf ears. What's a boy to do?

I think it's starting to happen. I had a vision last night. You know that moment right before you fall asleep? It's the one where you're not *quite* there yet. You've got one foot in this world and your big toe testing the waters of the astral plane. Sometimes you snap awake right before that moment. It's a falling sensation; like you're just starting a nice bike ride and the damn thing tips over. It's happened to all of us. That happened to me last night. Only, I saw something—and I wish it *had* been a bike ride.

There was a man in the vision. The only thing I remember about him was his hair. It was Q-tip white. He might have had glasses on. Or maybe he had some seriously bushy eyebrows. Anyway, the guy was standing before a scale. It was a big scale. Like the one's you see in a vets office to weigh the bigger dogs, only longer and waayyy more high-tech. Big enough to weigh a human being on. Which is what this guy seemed to be doing. I got the sense whoever was laying on that scale was close to death. And Q-tip was happy about it. Excited. I wanted to punch him in the face.

Right before I "fell off the bike," I saw something wispy-white rise from the body of the man on the scale. Q-tip was so ecstatic I expected to see him pitch a tent in his pants. He never spoke, but he didn't have to. My main jam is traveling the astral plane. It's my witchy super power, I guess. Wanda calls it an "elemental part of my soul." I buy that. What else explains how I can hear the thoughts of others in that realm?

And I heard his.

'It's true! One three-thousandth.'

Okay. Whatever the hell that means.

I believe what I witnessed was a soul leaving a human body. Am I sure? No. Do I know what this guy was up to? Again, no. But you can bet your ass I'm gonna find out. Not that I want to. But seriously, when was the last time I really had a choice in the matter?

Gemini also said, in the letter, the world was about to change. I didn't have the first friggin' clue what "they" were talking about. None of us did. I still didn't, right up until I opened my laptop tonight.

I might be wrong on this. Scratch that; I'm *probably* wrong. Shit, I *hope* I'm wrong. But I'm not. I can't explain why I know I'm right about this. I just do. The headline I saw on Bing!, the Microsoft search engine—the one they insist you use as a default, but we all switch it to Google Chrome every time—read as follows:

"Chinese government denies outbreak of mysterious pneumonia-like virus."

I'm not gonna name the three-letter news source. It's not important. As Han Solo, Captain of the Millennium Falcon once said—and apparently, Byron, a few nights ago, echoed his words—"I got a bad feeling about this."

If it's what I think it is, we're screwed. *The world is about to change*, and not for the better. Again, I can't tell you why or how I know this is going to be a big thing... but Gemini hinted I had a little something left over from Jagger.

Scapulimancy. The word keeps poking its way into my thoughts. I'll have to look it up, see if maybe it relates to what that psycho left me with. But not tonight.

I'm tired. I was almost asleep before I decided to write all this down. I figured I better get it all out now, while it's still fresh in my mind. Sometimes, when I put down my thoughts for you, I'll do it from the comfort of my couch, hunched over my laptop. That's where I'm sitting right now.

My eyes are heavy. I'm close to sleep. I've got a YouTube

music mix going and my Bluetooth headphones on. Jo and DeeDee are snoozing already.

I'm almost asleep when the song starts playing. It begins with bongos. Then, Mick Jagger screams "Yow!" I've heard it a million times. After a couple more "Yows!" the first piano chord rings out in time with the first line of the song, "Please allow me to introduce myself..."

It's "Sympathy for the Devil," by The Rolling Stones.

Sung by a guy named Jagger.

I swear to God I can't catch a break.

FROM THE AUTHOR

Hey! It's me again. *Black Magic & Envy* was probably the most fun I've had so far writing these books. *In Your Dreams* will always be my favorite of all my book children. It was the first, and it was, by far, the most emotional I've gotten during this whole writing adventure. But BM&E was such a blast!

When I call it an adventure, I sincerely mean it. Nothing has introduced me to my own mind like writing has, and I realized I really like what I've found traveling to parts of it heretofore undiscovered.

During all the years I thought about writing a book, I probably had a million different story ideas. I once heard a very famous author (he might be from Maine, I think) say there are two things required if you want to become a writer. He's not the first to say them, at least, I don't think he is, but he's the first one *I* ever heard say them. That advice is to read a lot, and write a lot. You can't really do one without the other, I've come to find out. I was always great with the first part of that; I devour books by authors I love. The second part, much to my chagrin, I put off for the majority of my adult life. But not anymore. You can't go back, but you can sure as hell choose your path forward.

I love doing this. I love when the idea for a story hits me and I start to flesh it out. There's nothing cooler in the world when it all starts to come together, and you start thinking about how your readers will react to it.

My wife is always my first reader. I've heard you should write the first draft completely before you show it to anyone. It's not a bad idea, and people way smarter than me have recommended doing just that. But alas, I disagree. My wife wants to read what I've written hot off the press. If I write a chapter at night, she'll tell me to leave it up on the screen so she can keep up. And, truth be told, I wanna hear what she thinks. I get a kick out of it, and her thoughts about what I'm writing usually turns over some rock I hadn't looked under.

In my last book, *Blood, Magic & Mercy*, I had trouble coming up with a cool name for one of the vampires. I had the first name, Xavier, but I couldn't come up with a surname that sounded cool when paired with Xavier. I forget the exact way we came up with it, but I remember her mentioning how vampires are soulless. Thus, Xavier Saulis was born. True, he didn't stick around for too long, but still!

My sister Susan is always my second reader, but the first to read the thing from start to finish as a whole. And she reads insanely fast, so I get super valuable feedback right away. It doesn't hurt that she's an avid reader in the urban fantasy, supernatural suspense genre, either. I've always told her to let me know if she thinks the book sucks, and trust me when I tell you, she will. So far, I've been lucky.

I plan to do this for as long as I can. There isn't a day that goes by that I'm not either thinking about my current story, or thinking something like, "Hey, that would make a cool story!" It can happen at anytime, and just about any place. And usually does. Thank God for cell phones and voice-to-text programs. A lot of great story ideas might have gotten lost in the ether without them.

I hope you enjoyed *Black Magick & Envy*, and thanks for coming along with me on this journey!

Here's to many more!

NEXT IN THE LEAGUE OF THE MOON SERIES

vinci-books.com/soulwitch

There's a new evil coursing through Salem, but something about it feels eerily familiar.

ABOUT THE AUTHOR

Robert Sanborn lives in north central Massachusetts with his wife, Diana, their sweet-natured dog, Coco, the Brussels Griffon, their psychotic black cat Luna, the Devon Rex, Jason, the extremely talkative African-Grey Parrot, Angus, the cranky Quaker Parrot, Artemis, the cute-as-hell Java Finch, and two parakeets named Sweetie and Sunny. (Correction: Sunny bit the big one! Luna figured out how to open his cage and it didn't go well, so now we have Snowball, and a new cage.)

He spends a lot on pet food.

Oh, yeah. And a Crested Gecko lizard named Gretel. Sheesh!

He is a survivor of Hodgkin's Lymphoma, diagnosed in 1993.

He has been clean and sober since September 24, 1991.

His first book, *In Your Dreams*, was written over the course of eighteen months and published in July, 2020, during the event which shall not be named, and between making deliveries to health care facilities as part of his day job. Not nerve-racking at all.